FIRST LIGHT

First Light

A POWs Rescue Mission That Can Never Be
Acknowledged

CHUCK GROSS

Hickory Hill Press
Nashville, Tennessee

Printed in the United States of America.

Permissions:
hickoryhillpress@gmail.com

ISBN-10: 0983915806 (paperback)
ISBN-13: 978-0-9839158-0-5 (paperback)
ISBN-10: 0983915830 (e-book)
ISBN-13: 978-0-9839158-36 (e-book)

Front cover design courtesy of Kevin Sparkman

First Light is dedicated to all the POWs and MIAs that were left behind in Southeast Asia.

Preface

The world of Special Ops is a world of its own. The most unsuspecting individuals complete missions under fictitious identities into secret locations. Since 9/11 special operations have become the spear point of our military engagements as we have operated into Afghanistan and Iraq, but these missions are not new to our soldiers. Our government has been asking our men for years to do things that any rational man would refuse to do, yet as a soldier or sometimes a civilian, we do them.

First Light is a historical fiction written about a secret mission to rescue American POWs from Southeast Asia. There are several statistics stated in the book concerning the war in Cambodia and Vietnam. These statistics are factual and accurate.

I hope that by reading *First Light*, the reader gets a better understanding of how the wars our government asks our young soldiers to fight can emotionally damage and affect them for years, if not for the rest of their lives. Everyone who has read the manuscript has asked, "Is the Ajax Cleanup mission based on actual events?" My answer is to let the reader decide.

Chapter 1

These Men's Lives Are At Stake

I'm truly amazed at how one unexpected phone call would put my life in a tailspin from which it would take a lifetime to recover.

It was the end of October 1984. The multicolored leaves had fallen, signaling the end of what had been a beautiful Minnesota autumn. I had just finished raking the front lawn when Paula, my wife of nine years, called out, "Curt, you have a phone call."

"I'll be right there. Who is it?"

"He didn't say."

Setting down the rake, I ran across the front lawn and up the back steps, which led into the kitchen. Picking up the phone from the counter, I said, "Hello."

The man on the other end introduced himself as Mr. Blackwell. He went on to explain that he was a photojournalist in charge of doing a PBS documentary on Vietnam helicopter pilots. Mr. Blackwell indicated that since I had flown helicopters for the United States Army in the late sixties and early seventies, he would be interested in interviewing me for a possible spot in his Vietnam film. A feeling of hesitancy immediately crossed my mind at the thought of doing an interview about Vietnam. I wasn't sure if I was psychologically ready to go there, to open up my thoughts and feelings to a complete stranger about my experiences during the Vietnam War, and especially to do it on film.

After several minutes of friendly chatter, I decided that it couldn't hurt to meet with Mr. Blackwell. I was intrigued with what he had told me he was trying to accomplish with his documentary. He suggested that we meet for lunch at Embers Restaurant. Embers was located on the southwest corner of the Crystal Airport in a northwest suburb of Minneapolis. After setting up a date and time, our conversation ended.

That evening I went to bed thinking obsessively about the war and the many memories that I had buried deep in the caverns of my mind. Vietnam hadn't been a popular war in the States. The war's unpopularity hadn't made for a good welcome upon returning home and gave me all the more reason to keep my memories hidden. After a few hours, I fell asleep. It was a long restless night, not unlike many nights since my return from Vietnam.

Backing my car out of the driveway, I realized that by agreeing to meet with Mr. Blackwell I was taking the first step towards coming to terms with my tour in Vietnam. I had returned from the war in the late spring of seventy-one at the tender age of twenty. During my tour, I had acquired over 1200 hours of combat flying and had experienced events beyond my belief.

The clock on the dash read a few minutes before twelve as I pulled into the Embers parking lot. Hopping out of my car, I walked into Embers not knowing what to expect from our meeting. A young hostess greeted me at the entrance and asked, "How many will be in your party?"

"I'm here to meet a Mr. Blackwell. Do you know if he's here yet?"

"He sure is. Please follow me."

As I followed her over to a corner booth, I caught my first glimpse of Mr. Blackwell. He was definitely not what I had expected. From our phone conversation, I pictured a tall, slim man, most likely in his late thirties or early forties with longer hair, maybe even a ponytail with John Lennon type glasses. To my surprise, sitting in the booth was a husky man with strong looking biceps, large forearms, and huge hands. His hair was cut close to his scalp. I instantly thought to myself, "Ranger type, or maybe even Special Forces." When Mr. Blackwell saw me approaching the booth, he stood up and greeted me extending his hand. As we shook hands, I could feel the power and confidence in his handshake.

Mr. Blackwell spent the first few minutes of our conversation talking about his love for flying, especially helicopters. Having continued to fly after the war, I had the same love. This mutual love for flying instantly gave us something in common to talk about. I told Mr. Blackwell that I had been flying a corporate aircraft for a firm based in Eden Prairie, Minnesota called APT. Unfortunately, in early June, the board of directors voted to close down the flight department and sell the planes. Of course with the closure of the flight department, I lost my job. My main focus since being let go from APT, was to try to get hired by a major airline. American Airlines had already interviewed me twice, and I was waiting for the third and final interview.

Once our lunch was served, our conversation turned to Mr. Blackwell questioning me about my tour in Vietnam. As we spoke about Vietnam, I started to notice a pattern to his questions. I began to feel that he seemed more concerned about my current feelings about the war and especially about the prisoners of war (POWs) and the missing in action (MIAs), than the missions I had flown or my experiences in Nam.

As we sat there eating lunch and talking about the war,

I found myself thinking less about his film and more about how to answer the tough questions he was asking. Shortly after the waitress brought the check and we were about to leave, he turned to me and asked, "Curt, do you think there are any American POWs still alive in Southeast Asia?"

I immediately answered, "No, not after this long."

He grabbed the check and said, "Let's go, I have something I want to show you." We got up from the booth and headed towards the cashier. Concerned about where he wanted to take me, I asked, "Where do we have to go?"

"Just over to one of the hangers on the south side of the airport. I'll drive," he answered.

My mind was racing with excitement as I climbed into his car wondering what Mr. Blackwell wanted to show me. The airport was just across the street from the Embers parking lot, so it was a short ride. As soon as we crossed the street, he turned right onto a gravel road which snaked its way around a fixed base operation back behind several rows of hangers. He turned left onto a small taxiway that led up to a long row of silver metal hangers then pulled the car up and parked in front of a door leading into a small hanger.

Not one word had been spoken as we rode over to the hanger. I thought to myself, "What is he up to?" We got out of the car, and I followed Mr. Blackwell as he walked over to the hanger door. He unlocked the large Masterlock padlock and opened the door. As he switched on the lights, he said, "Please step inside."

Entering the hanger, my eyes quickly scanned back and forth observing that it was empty except for a table, two chairs, and an easel with its back towards us. As I slowly approached the front of the easel, I could make out six, 8" by 10" photos of soldiers with captions below each photo. The captions contained each soldiers name, rank, serial number, and a date of capture or when reported missing in action.

Mr. Blackwell walked directly over to the easel and started reading out loud, "Major Paul Flanagan U.S. Air Force, MIA shot down over the Republic of North Vietnam April 8, 1969. Captain John Southerly U.S. Army, POW captured October 16, 1970." He continued until he had read all six of the soldier's descriptions, then walked over to one of the chairs and sat down. I moved closer to the board so I could get a better look at their photos. As I carefully studied their faces, it occurred to me how young they looked. I was startled from my deep thoughts by Mr. Blackwell's voice when he said, "Curt, I'm Colonel Mike Anderson with military intelligence. I'm here to request your return to duty to help these lost men and our country. I'm sorry for the deception, but this is a highly classified matter." As he spoke, I instantly felt my stomach tense and turn sour. My heartbeat was accelerating, as if it were a machine gun pumping out continuous fire.

I thought to myself, "This must be a practical joke or maybe even a dream. How could I be of help to the military intelligence? I'm just one of thousands who fought in the Vietnam War."

Colonel Anderson continued speaking, "You have been specifically chosen for this mission because of a contact you made during your tour in Vietnam." Then he asked, "Do you remember a young girl by the name of Lee Thi Com?"

"Of course I do, but what does she have to do with locating POWs?"

"She is currently the head secretary for General Hung Samrin who is one of the top commanders of the occupying Vietnamese forces in Cambodia. It has come down through intelligence channels that General Samrin's office has knowledge of the whereabouts of these six POWs." As he spoke, he pulled out a photo of General Samrin and slid it across the table. "We need you to make contact with Ms.

Lee, and then try to persuade her to give you the exact location of these men. If you can do that, we stand a good chance of rescuing them and returning them home. We owe it to them, their families and our country."

Up to this point, I still had thoughts of this being a practical joke, but now I realized this was a serious matter. It could mean either life or death, both to the men being held captive and possibly me. I knew I had an important decision to make and it wasn't going to be an easy one.

My mind drifted back to when I had first met Com. While flying helicopters in Vietnam, I was shot down and injured in the crash. Unable to escape and evade, my crew was forced to leave me behind while they went for help. Fortunately for me, Ms. Lee found me lying in the jungle. Instead of turning me over to the Viet Cong, she and her younger brother hid me out while nursing me back to health. During our time together, we spent a lot of time talking about our lives, both realizing how different our lifestyles were from each other. She was really interested in America, so I spent a lot of time answering her questions and telling her about life back in the States. She in return helped me learn Vietnamese. Even though I had only known her for eight days, our time together had been extremely intense and we developed a close and loving friendship. Unfortunately after my rescue, I was shipped home three weeks early and never saw her again. I would not be alive today if it had not been for her help.

I had written Com a few times after arriving back in the States. She once had an American soldier write a return letter for her, but since she was unable to write English, herself, we lost contact. Then a few years later, Vietnam fell. I thought of Com and her brother often and still wore a gold double heart necklace around my neck that she had given me.

Colonel Anderson continued to brief me on the mission.

"The code name of your mission is Ajax Cleanup. Due to the nature of this mission, it needs to be carried out in complete secrecy. There will be only four people, other than you, who will know the complete details of this mission. They are myself, General Mackie, who is responsible for organizing this mission, Colonel Sizemore, who will be responsible for doing your debrief, and the President."

He went on to explain that other missions had been sent to return POWs, but they had all failed due to security breaches. This time, he would personally make sure that there would be no leaks, period. Colonel Anderson said that my secret security clearance that I had received while on active duty had been upgraded to the top clearance available. This was required to allow General Mackie to be able to brief me on certain high-level national security items that I would need to know to accomplish my mission.

Colonel Anderson told me, "When General Mackie initially briefed the President about Ajax Cleanup, the President was very concerned. He was worried about sending a civilian on an espionage mission into a Communist controlled country, especially with no experience and with so little time to train. To address this concern, General Mackie told the President about your experience flying for the MACVSOG in Vietnam and said that if you accepted the mission, he felt confident that you would do just fine."

As I sat there listening to all this information, I felt as if the decision to accept this mission had already been made but without my consent. A degree of seriousness came over Colonel Anderson's voice when he said, "I cannot overemphasize the importance of you keeping this meeting to yourself. You cannot tell anyone about this mission or this briefing including your wife." Then the kicker statement came, "You must also understand, if for some reason the mission is compromised and you're taken prisoner or executed, we will not be able to come forward and acknowledge your existence. You'll be on your own. Do you understand?"

"I can't just disappear," I snapped, surprised at the tone of my own voice. "I have a pregnant wife, and a daughter to take care of; if I'm caught, what will happen to them? What will you tell them?"

"If you're killed, your family will be told that you died in an automobile accident. I'll personally take charge of all the funeral arrangements. We'll have a closed casket ceremony, and I'll also make sure that your wife receives a life insurance payout and a military pension." The question about being captured was left unanswered. But as I listened to Colonel Anderson, I realized that what he was saying was if I were captured, I would most likely be executed as a spy.

For the next twenty minutes, we talked over several aspects of the mission. When I was done with my questions, Colonel Anderson said, "Curt, we really need you to do this for these men. I realize that we're asking you to do something that you haven't been trained for, and that you'll need time to think it over before giving us your answer."

I was still in shock, trying to grasp the reality of what I had just been asked to do. I told Colonel Anderson, "I need time. I need to sleep on this before I can give you my answer."

"I understand, but remember, time is of critical importance to the completion of this mission. I'll contact you in 48 hours. Again, do not mention this to anyone. These men's lives are at stake!"

He took down the photos and secured them in his briefcase. I helped fold up the table and chairs then placed them against the wall of the hanger. He folded up the easel and put it in the trunk of his car, and then we drove back over to Embers, where my car was parked.

As I was about to get out of his car, Colonel Anderson turned towards me and said, "Curt, remember what I told you."

"Yes sir, I will." I answered, as we shook hands.

Driving home, Colonel Anderson's phrase kept repeating in my brain, *"These men's lives are at stake, these men's lives are at stake!"*

Chapter 2

Lies and Deception

I spent the better part of that night thrashing over in my mind what Colonel Anderson had told me, "These men's lives are at stake." When I awoke the following morning it was clear what my decision would be. It was a simple decision. Just say yes. In my inner most being, I understood that I had no other choice. To refuse to try to help rescue American POWs would be unconscionable. I knew and understood that what kept these prisoners alive from one day to the next was their hope that sooner or later, no matter how long it would take, America would not forget them and would bring them home. That was the American way!

The next 48 hours were spent discretely getting my personal affairs in order. I knew I needed to be prepared for the worst, for war was not new to me and I understood all too well the consequences. It would be interesting to hear what kind of cover story Colonel Anderson would come up with, which would allow me to slip away from my family and friends for several days without them suspecting that something was amiss. I wondered what kind of lies and deception I would have to tell my wife and family.

Once my decision to accept the mission was made, I

was anxious to get started and wished I had arranged a way of contacting Colonel Anderson to give him my answer.

Thursday morning his call came. I was out changing oil on our 1982 Honda Civic when Paula yelled from the back door, "Curt, Mr. Blackwell's on the phone."

"Tell him I'll be right there," I shouted, as I set down the quart of oil that I was pouring into the crankcase. Excitedly, I ran into the house and picked up the receiver, "Hello."

On the other end, I heard Colonel Anderson's voice, "Hello Curt, how are you this morning?"

"I'm doing great. How are you?"

"I'm fine. Look, I'm going to be in your neck of the woods, and was wondering if it would be okay if I stopped by and chatted about the film, plus, it will give me a chance to meet Paula."

"That sounds good, what time can I expect you?" I asked.

"Give me about thirty minutes."

"Okay, I'll see you then."

Hanging up the phone, I turned to Paula and said, "Mr. Blackwell's coming over in a few minutes to discuss his film. He said he wants to meet the family." Since we had talked earlier about Mr. Blackwell and his documentary, it seemed logical to Paula that he would want to come over to the house to discuss it. I told Paula that I was going back out to the garage to finish the oil change, but in reality, I wanted to make sure that I was outside when he arrived. This way, I would be sure that I could speak to him in private and give him my decision.

I poured the last two quarts of oil into the crankcase then popped the oil cap back on. After starting the car, I got down on one knee and checked to make sure that my oil filter wasn't leaking. Everything looked good, so I closed the hood and started cleaning up. Within a few minutes, Colonel Anderson pulled into the driveway. I walked over and greeted him as he opened his car door. "Hello, Mr. Blackwell."

Instead of returning my greeting, he came right to the point, "Well Curt, are we a team?"

"Yes sir, we are," I answered, as I wondered what I was getting myself into.

"Great, I knew you wouldn't let us down. First, I would like to meet your wife and daughter, and then we'll get to work."

"Come on into the house, and I'll introduce you to Paula and Janelle," I responded as we turned and headed towards the house.

Paula greeted Mr. Blackwell at the door, escorted him into our great room and then went to the kitchen for a few minutes returning with coffee and a plate of cookies. We sat there visiting for about 20 minutes. Then it was time to get to work. "Paula I'm going to take Mr. Blackwell outside to show him our yard."

As we walked down the hill towards the pond in back, Colonel Anderson told me that he had been working nonstop since our meeting on Monday. He explained that he had come up with a scenario that would allow me to get away from my family for twelve days without anyone getting suspicious. His plan would allow us three days for training and nine days for traveling and to accomplish the mission. He mentioned again, as he had indicated earlier, time was critical and the sooner they got me to Cambodia the greater chance we had for success.

Colonel Anderson went on to explain that he had brought with him a letter, supposedly from American Airlines, indicating that I had been accepted for employment. Included in this letter were instructions for me to call the personnel office as soon as possible to schedule a class date. The phone number in the letter went directly to his personal secretary. He said he would make sure the letter arrived in my mailbox today. He instructed me to let Paula go and get the mail. He was confident that when she saw the envelope with the American Airlines letterhead, she would get excited and rush back into the house anxious for me to open it. He told me to make sure that when I opened the letter, I acted as if I had really been hired. Once I got done hugging Paula, I was to go and call the number in the letter to set up my class date. His secretary would schedule a false class date three weeks from today. He explained that the letter and phone call would make everything appear realistic to Paula and family. The only problem was we didn't have three weeks to accomplish the mission, but he had that detail covered also.

The Colonel continued, "I want you to make sure that you're out of the house tomorrow morning between nine and ten and be sure that Paula is home to answer the phone. I've instructed my secretary to call and identify herself as Judy Tarver from American Airlines. She'll tell Paula that one of the other pilot applicants has decided to take an offer with Northwest Airlines instead of American. She'll explain that his departure has left a class opening with a starting date for this upcoming Sunday at noon. I told her to make sure that Paula understands that by you agreeing to go three weeks early, you'll gain approximately sixty seniority numbers versus if you stay with your scheduled starting date."

As I listened to Colonel Anderson explain the details of my cover story, I thought to myself, "This man is brilliant." All pilots and their families know that seniority is everything in the airline business, because all flying is bid by seniority and sixty numbers could make the difference between working holidays and birthdays or getting them off. This was an offer that no pilot would be able to refuse.

Colonel Anderson went on to explain that he had several contingencies worked out that would complete my cover story and allow me to return to a normal life, but which one he chose would depend on the outcome of the mission. He said he had already scheduled an Air Force jet to leave at 7:00 am Sunday from the Minneapolis/St. Paul International Airport to take us to Washington. The jet would be parked on the north side of the field at the Air Force Reserve ramp. I would have Paula drive me out to the airport then drop me off at the upper level in front of the American Airlines ticket counter. We would say our good-byes, making sure that Paula didn't come into the terminal. As soon as I was sure that Paula had left, I would walk down to the lower level where there would be a military vehicle waiting. This vehicle would take me to the north side of the field to meet my jet. We would fly to Washington where I would receive my formal briefing and start my training. He would have all the appropriate papers ready for me to sign, including my orders cut for fifteen days of active duty. Even though we were hoping to accomplish the mission in twelve days, he added three extra days for unforeseen circumstances.

I would be allowed to call Paula only once before leaving the country. That call would take place on Tuesday evening after completion of my training. It was very important that I made sure Paula would be home to accept the call. That would be the last verbal contact I would have with her until I completed the mission.

Colonel Anderson handed me a list of things to pack and said, "Curt, I want you to take tomorrow and Saturday and spend them with your family. Don't worry about your training or the mission. We'll cover everything that you'll need to know in your training. I want you to act like you've gotten a real airline job, and be sure to take your wife out to celebrate." He handed me a hundred dollar bill and asked, "Do you have any questions?"

"Yes, if I need to contact you for any reason, how do I

15

do it?"

"Just call the number in the letter, and tell the person that answers the phone that you need to talk to Mr. Blackwell, and I'll get back to you as soon as possible."

I thanked Colonel Anderson for the money then took the hundred-dollar bill along with his list, folded them and stuffed them into my pocket. We walked back up the hill, towards the house, making small talk as we went. I found myself starting to like Mr. Blackwell / Colonel Anderson. He was quick-witted, articulate and had a good sense of humor, a real man's man. We walked back over to his car and said our goodbyes. I stood there and watched as he backed out of our driveway and drove off, noticing that he didn't stop by our mailbox.

I walked back in the house and went directly into the bathroom and closed the door. I reached into my pocket and pulled out the list anxious to see what was on it. The detail of Colonel Anderson's list was amazing. It instructed me to bring one coat and tie, three casual slacks and three polo/sport shirts, underwear, socks, a pair of dress shoes, one pair of tennis shoes, a manual shaver, shaving cream, one toothbrush, aspirin, deodorant, and one empty wallet. It also instructed me to bring the photo that I had of Com from the war. Below the list of what to bring, was a list of what not to bring. It stated: no rings, no types of identification, drivers license, or pilot license, not even my passport. No photos of my family, no credit cards, no phone cards, no checks, no letters, and nothing with my name engraved on it. As I read the list, I realized that Colonel Anderson was no amateur at what he did. But exactly what he did, I was still not sure.

When I got done reading the list, I tucked it back into my pocket and went into the kitchen to talk with Paula about Mr. Blackwell and get her thoughts. I wanted to make sure that she believed and accepted his story about being a documentary filmmaker. She told me she thought it was exciting that I had a chance to be in a documentary and as we talked, I could tell that she believed him. However, her belief did not come without the cost of guilt on my part.

Everything went as Colonel Anderson had planned. Paula went out to get the mail and sure enough, there was a letter with American Airlines logo and return address on the envelope. She came back into the house yelling, "Curt, you have a letter from American Airlines."

I rushed over, opened it, and acted surprised. I showed the letter to Paula and said, "This must be my lucky day." I went over to the phone and placed my call as instructed. Colonel Anderson's secretary answered the phone playing her part. She asked me to confirm my address and social security number then assigned me a class date of November 14, 1984. If I hadn't known ahead of time that it wasn't American Airlines, I would have believed that I was actually getting a real class date. When I hung up the phone, Paula ran over and gave me a big congratulatory hug and kiss. I lifted her up and spun her around the kitchen telling her that we needed to celebrate. Paula went over and marked the calendar with a big red circle around the date. We were both excited, but not for the same reasons.

Friday morning I got up as usual and ate breakfast with the family. I told Paula that I had to run down to the hardware store and planned my trip so that I would get back shortly after ten. This way I was sure Paula would be home alone to answer the phone. Upon my return, Paula met me in the driveway, "You're not going to believe who called?"

"I don't know, tell me," I replied.

"Judy Tarver from the American Airlines training department."

Paula then went on to explain her phone conversation

with Judy.

When she finished, I said, "What do you think? Sixty numbers is a lot of seniority numbers. It could mean the difference between having to work Christmas and having it off."

"I think you should take it, we'll be all right," Paula replied,

"Are you sure?"

"Yes, I would rather have you go now than being stuck working holidays."

I walked over to the phone, returned the call and accepted the new class date.

That evening I took my family out for dinner to celebrate my new airline job. Paula and I spent Saturday together packing and talking about my new career. My conscience was bothering me, and I wanted to tell Paula so bad that it was a lie, but I knew better.

We went to bed early Saturday night so that I would be fresh for my first day of training at American Airlines. As we hugged each other good night, I couldn't help but wonder what price my deception would cost our relationship.

The next morning Paula dropped me off on the upper level of the terminal in front of the American Airlines ticket counter. After taking my suitcase out of the trunk and setting it on the curb, it was time to say our goodbyes. Our daughter Janelle ran over and gave me a big hug and said, "Goodbye daddy."

I hugged her back, lifting her into the air and told her, "You be sure to take care of mommy." I hugged Paula and gave her a kiss. I told her, "I'll call you Tuesday night."

Since I had been flying corporate, we had gotten in the habit of calling every third night to keep our long distance phone bill down.

Paula and Janelle climbed back into the car as I picked up my suitcase and headed for the terminal. Before entering the terminal, I turned and waved as they drove off, wondering if this would be the last time I would ever see them. Once I was sure they were gone, I entered the terminal and took the escalator down to the lower level and went back outside through the double glass sliding doors. Scanning the drop off area, down to my left, I noticed a military automobile parked along the curb. I walked over to the vehicle and greeted the driver, "Hello, may I ask who you're waiting for?"

"Are you Mr. Gray?" the driver asked.

"Yep, I sure am."

He got out of his seat and grabbed my suitcase then put it in the trunk. I got into the vehicle and fastened my seatbelt as he drove off. We left the passenger terminal and went north around the east side of the field, then got back on the service road that took us into the Air Force Reserve base. The ride took less than five minutes.

Pulling onto the ramp area, I could see a military Sabreliner jet parked on the ramp. As our vehicle approached the jet, Colonel Anderson exited the jet and walked over to greet me. We shook hands and chatted as the driver stowed my suitcase on the plane then climbed back into the car and drove off. I took one final look at my surroundings, not knowing for sure if I would ever return, then boarded the plane.

Being a pilot, it felt strange to be sitting in the back of an aircraft as a passenger rather than in the cockpit. We spoke to the pilots for a few minutes then watched as they performed what is called the "before starting" checklist. Once the engines were running, Colonel Anderson and I sat in back and strapped in. Within minutes, we were taking the runway for departure. As the Sabreliner accelerated down the runway and lifted off from the Minneapolis/Saint Paul International Airport, my thoughts were much the same as the day I departed McCord Air Force Base enroute to Vietnam. The excitement and uncertainty of what lay ahead danced around and tugged at my mind.

Chapter 3

Sworn to Silence

Vietnam had been so long ago but my memories were as if it were yesterday. I knew that it was time to focus on the matter at hand. Once our aircraft was airborne and clear of the terminal control area, Colonel Anderson turned to me and said, "Curt, we should try to make good use of our limited time and accomplish as much as possible while enroute."

He flipped open his briefcase and pulled out several documents. Opening a manila envelope, he pulled out a contract, handed it to me to and told me to read then sign. It was the terms of my mission. It basically said that, I, Curt Gray, on my own accord, agreed to accept this mission. I understood that I was accepting active duty orders for fifteen days, and agreed not to disclose any information or knowledge of this mission to anyone, including my wife. If I did, the violation was punishable under military law with a penalty of up to ten years imprisonment and/or a one hundred thousand dollar fine. The contract also stated that if I was captured, I would not be recognized as an American soldier by the United States Government but would be acknowledged as a civilian operating on my own accord. I expected something of this nature, but as I sat there reading the document shivers ran down my spine.

I dated and signed the document then handed it back to Colonel Anderson who dated and signed it as a witness. He placed the contract back in the manila envelope and sealed it, then filed it in his briefcase. There was no turning back. He handed me a copy of my active orders and told me to read them. After I finished reading them, he took them back. I knew that I wouldn't want to be caught carrying any documents, especially orders that could link me to any government mission. If caught, I didn't want to be executed as a spy.

Colonel Anderson handed me a paper that contained common expressions translated into Vietnamese and told me to review and try to familiarize myself with as many as possible. He told me to keep it with me as it might come in handy, plus it would be expected that a foreigner would carry such a paper to be able to communicate in a foreign country. We talked about our expectations of the mission and the hopeful outcome. The flight went by quickly and before we knew it, we were landing at Andrews Air Force Base, Washington D. C.

As the aircraft pulled onto the ramp, I watched as a military vehicle pulled up and parked alongside our aircraft. The pilots completed their checklists then the copilot unbuckled from his seat and opened the door. Colonel Anderson and I deplaned. The driver saluted Colonel Anderson, picked up our luggage and loaded it into a helicopter that was standing by. I thought to myself, "It sure must be nice to receive executive treatment all the time." When I had been flying corporate, I was the one who was always taking the suitcases from our clients and loading them into the plane. For once, it was nice to be on the receiving end.

From Andrews Air Force Base, we boarded the helicopter for a quick flight to the Pentagon. Having never been to the Pentagon, I was anxious to see its interior. I had flown by it several times on the approach to Washington National but never thought that I would have an opportunity to go inside. Upon arrival, Colonel Anderson led me into what appeared to be a briefing room. "Curt, take the seat at the end of the table. Relax and make yourself at home. I'll be right back," and closed the door behind him as he left.

As I sat there looking around the room, the first thing I noticed was there were no windows. I was seated at a large rectangular table that was at least fourteen feet long. It was made of dark maple and had ten chairs placed around it. Behind the left side of the table was a chalkboard with a projector screen hanging above the center of it. The walls were painted a dark green with decorative cherry wood-work. The room projected a feeling of richness and warmth and made me feel special being there.

I was still studying the room when the door opened. In walked General Mackie followed by Colonel Anderson, a major, and two captains. Seeing that it was General Mackie, I immediately stood up and saluted him. He returned my salute then walked directly over to me, welcoming me as he shook my hand. It was one of those good solid handshakes. The type you would expect from a leader of men. He asked me to please be seated. As I sat back down, the general and the colonel sat on my right and the major and the two captains sat on my left with the chalkboard behind them.

General Mackie began by thanking me for accepting the mission and apologized for giving me such short notice. He introduced Major Stevenson, explaining that he was a specialist in Vietnamese and Cambodian language and customs. It would be Major Stevenson's duty to work with me in refreshing my limited knowledge of the Vietnamese language. He would also be introducing me to and explaining the differences between Vietnamese and Cambodian customs.

The general then introduced the captain sitting on the major's right as Captain Donaldson, an espionage expert. He would be responsible for instructing me on the emotional and physical aspects of the art of manipulation. He would be teaching me how to manipulate Ms. Lee so that I could get her to do what needed to be done. It was also his job to fabricate and establish the cover story that I would be using while in Cambodia then mold me into fitting it. He would also be teaching me what he called, "Canned answers." These were answers that I would memorize and use to explain to Com what I was doing in Cambodia and what I had been doing since I had left Vietnam fourteen years earlier.

Last but not least was Captain Edwards. Captain Edwards's expertise was in firearms and hand-to-hand combat. He would be instructing me in the use of any firearms that I would possibly have to use and any other equipment, including the survival radio, map reading, etc. Having started martial arts training in the fall of 1971, shortly after returning from Vietnam, I was anxious to see what type of hand-to-hand techniques Captain Edwards would be teaching.

After their introductions were completed, they were excused. They got up, saluted General Mackie and left, leaving behind General Mackie, Colonel Anderson and me. Once the door was closed, General Mackie started the formal briefing. He asked Colonel Anderson to dim the lights and turn the slide projector on. He began the briefing by showing slides of photos of each one of the allegedly held POWs. As he read off their names, he gave a brief history of how they were captured. I was a bit surprised when he said. "When the intelligence information first came in, I was surprised, and to be truthful, I found it hard to believe that any of the Vietnam era POWs are still alive. With the known brutality of the North Vietnamese and the historical treatment of their prisoners, then you add in the lack of good diet and disease, I really have to question how they could survive this long? But even though I personally feel this way, the information we received is from a source that has been known to be accurate in the past; therefore, I cannot afford to ignore it. Mr. Gray, if you can return one live POW, I will consider the mission a success." As I sat there listing to General Mackie, I could feel my emotional psyche changing from a civilian back into a hardened war veteran.

General Mackie said that the information he was about to brief me on was highly classified material and that I owed it to my country to never repeat it. He then went on to explain how they had become aware of the information they had received and why they believed it to be accurate. He explained how they accidentally discovered that Lee Thi Com had been a hootch maid in Da Nang and how they connected her to me through a letter I had written. As I sat there listening to his briefing, I found it hard to believe how much knowledge our government had concerning Com's movements and activities, especially since she was living in a third world communist country half way around the world. I thought to myself, "If I hadn't written her after the war, I wouldn't be sitting here now." Little did I know at the time, that the couple of letters that I sent Com would volunteer me for a mission fourteen years later!

General Mackie continued to explain in detail what they expected me to do. I would be flown into Phnom Penh on a Red Cross plane. There I would be expected to make contact with Ms. Lee. After making contact with her, I was to use my old relationship that I had established with her from Vietnam to try to rekindle any old feelings that she might still have for me. General Mackie said that to accomplish my mission, it would be imperative that I get her emotionally involved, because without her emotional involvement, she would never betray her country. When I thought the time was right, I would persuade Ms. Lee to help me obtain the location of the alleged POWs.

General Mackie stated that since she was General Samrin's head secretary, he believed she would have free access to his headquarters and documents if she didn't already know their location. Upon accomplishing my task, I would be extracted at a specific time from a predetermined location. He would have a special operations team on standby, ready to launch a rescue within hours after my extraction.

As I sat there listening to General Mackie explaining the details of the mission, I could tell that it was well thought out and planned. It sounded like it would be easy to accomplish. But I also realized there was one problem or weakness in his plan, and that weakness was me. As the famous General Dwight Eisenhower once said, "That in war, before the battle is joined, plans are everything, but once the shooting begins, plans are worthless."

This whole mission centered on me making contact with a girl that I hadn't seen in fourteen years. Once I found her, I would have to convince her that I was not who I really was. I would have to seduce her and get her emotionally involved in a short period of time. Then on top of that, I would have to convince her to betray the people that she worked for. I had never been good at lying or deception and now our men's lives depended on it.

The next couple of days went by like a Kansas tornado skipping and jumping across the countryside. Up and down it went, touching this point then skipping over to that point. My mind was like a whirlwind trying to absorb this and memorize that. I had a good class on escape and evade (E & E) techniques by Captain Edwards. He discussed the best way to travel by land and when I should travel by night versus day. We reviewed radio phraseology and how to use a survival radio. In one class, Captain Edwards brought in a M16, an AK47 and a 9mm pistol. He demonstrated how to load and operate each weapon, and then taught me how to disassemble, clean, and then reassemble them. We went to an indoor range where I qualified with the weapons. I hadn't shot a weapon since leaving Vietnam, and it felt strange at first to be doing so. My skills came back fairly quickly; within a few minutes, I was hitting the targets in the bull's-eye. Even though I had been in Vietnam, I had never had the opportunity to shoot an AK47 and found shooting it fun. I found shooting the 9mm to be a lot more accurate than the old military forty-five that we were issued in the Army.

While we were at the shooting range, I asked Captain Edwards, "Sir, my commanding officer in Vietnam was Major John Edwards. By any chance, are you related?"

"Yes, John is my uncle on my father's side of the family."

"He was a great CO. I really enjoyed serving under him. The next time you see him, will you say "hi" to him for me?"

Captain Edwards smiled with this big grin and said, "Sorry, I don't think I can do that."

I thought for a moment then realized why he couldn't and replied, "Yes sir, I understand."

Captain Edwards started our hand-to-hand training by explaining, "Curt, there are two basic reactions that humans have when confronted with fear. One is to stay and fight. The other is to flee. It is very important that you understand that these are natural instincts. If you experience the urge to flee, it doesn't mean that you're a coward. Your mind is just reacting to your psychological makeup. Understanding that these feelings are natural will also help you to understand how the person you are having the conflict with will tend to react."

When we finished the psychological aspects of confrontations, we started the hand-to-hand techniques. This is the training, which I really enjoyed. Captain Edwards showed me a move that I had never seen before. It was a technique on how to quickly snap an enemy's neck from behind. It was so simple, I was amazed that I hadn't seen it or thought of it. We spent a good hour and a half practicing techniques. When we were done with his lesson he asked, "Curt, when did you first get interested in the martial arts?"

"While I was in Vietnam, I saw some South Vietnamese Special Forces working out. This sparked my interest and upon returning from Vietnam, I started studying and have been doing so ever since."

"What style of martial arts have you studied?"

"I practice a soft style kung fu called Kwong Sai Jook Lum Tong Long Pai."

"Wow, that's a mouth full."

"Yes sir, I know. We normally just call it Jook Lum or Southern Praying Mantis."

"I've never studied a soft style. Would you mind showing me some of your moves?"

"Sir, I would be glad to."

"Let me first explain the difference between a hard style and a soft style. In a hard style martial art you meet force with force and because of this; if you have two practitioners of the same skill level, the stronger one will win. This is not necessarily the case in a soft style. In a soft style, you learn to fight relaxed. You rely on feeling and muscle memory versus strength and eye to hand coordination. In our style, we practice what we call sticky hands where you learn to feel your opponent's arms and train your hands to find and create openings for attacks. A Jook Lum practitioner will take an attacker's punch and redirect it until it's fully extended, instantaneously striking back before the attacker has a chance to withdraw his attack."

I showed him my favorite move, which can be used when someone attacks you from the front with both hands. You place your two arms so that your right arm is between his arms and your left is on the outside of his right arm. You deflect his arms to your right then rapidly strike with your right hand into the left side of his neck into the acupuncture point called the stomach nine. A direct strike to the stomach nine, when done properly, will cause an instant knockout. You immediately follow up with a palm strike with the left hand to the enemy's chin, followed by another strike with the right to the stomach five point on the enemy's left jaw. The palm strike to the enemy's chin kinks the back of the spine causing a knockout, and the third strike to the opponent's jaw, when done properly, also causes a knockout. I explained to Captain Edwards, "The reason I like this move so much is it's so quick that the opponent doesn't have time to block your first strike, plus you're hitting him in three different knockout points in rapid succession. Because the three strikes come so quickly, the chance of hitting one of them is pretty good."

I told him that I had put this combination together myself. Explaining that during my training, I was always trying to figure out the most expedient way to end a fight in the least violent way possible.

This technique captured Captain Edwards's interest. He asked me to explain more about Jook Lum. I decided to show him a one-man form from our style that trains one to do short power punches. It is called Sam Bow Gin, which translates to Three Step Arrow or Three Steps Forward. When done properly, it trains the practitioner in proper breathing and short power strikes.

When I completed the form, Captain Edwards said, "The form looks interesting, but I can't see how you could make it work in a real combat situation. Even if you could, how could you hurt your attacker when striking from such a short distance?"

I wasn't surprised by his response. Through the years, I had learned that a hard style practitioner found it very difficult to understand how you could hurt someone with a three inch punch. I asked, "Captain Edwards, is there any way you can get a volunteer to come in so I can demonstrate."

"I wish I could, but that's not possible due to the classification of your mission."

I thought for a moment then asked, "Is it possible to go to the rest room? There, I can demonstrate a short power punch to you using a mirror. This will allow you to feel the effects of the punch and observe the move as I do it."

"I think that will be acceptable."

We exited the room and walked down to the john. Once there, I explained to Captain Edwards that I was going to hit him from behind in the gallbladder twenty point from three inches away. The point is located on the backside of the neck slightly above the hairline. I carefully placed Captain Edwards where he could watch in the mirror to make sure that I didn't cock back my hand before striking him. Once we got in the correct position where he could observe the punch, I told him, "Relax," then quickly struck him in the point with an open ridge hand. I used the bone from the first joint on the thumb to hit the point. Within seconds after striking him, I watched as his right leg buckled and he started to collapse. Grabbing him, I quickly massaged the antidote point to bring him back. By the expression on his face, I could tell that he was dumbfounded and in awe. He said, "That's amazing. If I hadn't seen it with my own eyes, I wouldn't believe it. That strike really rocks you."

I replied, "Yes sir, the first time I saw it demonstrated, I thought it was a setup. I couldn't believe such a short punch could have such a devastating effect on someone. So after class, I went to the instructor and asked him to strike me so I could feel it. He was more than happy to oblige, and I quickly became a believer. I was truly amazed by its effect to the body and realized that I had to rethink and change my philosophy on striking and attacking."

Walking back to our training room Captain Edwards said, "I'm going to have to do some research on pressure point strikes and see what I can learn about them."

"If you're ever in Minneapolis you should look me up, and I can give you some private lessons." As I extended my invitation, I realized that it would never happen.

The class that I enjoyed the most was given by Major Stevenson who was a language and customs expert. He started our class by bringing me up to date on what had been happening both politically and militarily in Vietnam and Cambodia since I left in 1971. Major Stevenson gave me a very brief history lesson, which I found very interesting. He explained that one of Ho Chi Minh's dreams was to reunite all of Vietnam under the authority of Hanoi. Once that was accomplished, he wanted to form a Federation of Socialist States of Indochina, under Vietnamese domination. But after Saigon's takeover by the North Vietnamese and the takeover of Phnom Penh by the Khmer communists, the circumstances changed dramatically. Pol Pot, the leader of the Khmer Rouge didn't want to pay allegiance to the Hanoi government. Hanoi had misread Pol Pot's intentions and considered him a traitor to a united Indochina Communist Party, and so began the conflict.

When Pol Pot and the Khmer Rouge defeated the Lon Nol regime on April 17, 1975, they started assigning the majority of the cities dwellers to the country to do agricultural labor. They renamed the country the Democratic Kampuchea and terrorized their citizens. He went on to explain about the mass atrocities that the Khmer Rouge committed under Pol Pot's direction. He said that close to

1.7 million Cambodians were killed, starved, or worked to death. I was amazed that living back in the States, we were not aware of how bad the Pol Pot regime was or the number of Cambodians that the Khmer Rouge had massacred. I found all this death and inhumanity shocking! I could not believe that we as a nation ignored these atrocities and executions that took place and allowed this to go on. I had heard, growing up, how bad the Nazis had treated the Jews; I thought that we, as a nation, would never allow this to happen again. I guess I was wrong.

Major Stevenson went on to explain that the Khmer Rouge was being backed by China, and Hanoi was backed by the Soviet Union. Hanoi spent the mid seventies trying politically to get Pol Pot out of power and the Khmer Rouge back in line. Once Hanoi realized that this would not work, they chose General Heng Samrin to lead this new organization called the United Front for National Salvation of Kampuchea (UFNSK) and its military force would be called the Kampuchean Revolutionary Armed Forces. Heng Samrin had been a political commissar and commander of a division of the army of the Khmer Rouge, but had defected to Vietnam in May of 1978. The goal of this new Vietnamese backed organization was to overthrow the Chinese backed Pol Pot regime. Hanoi also formed the People's Revolutionary Party in which they put longtime Khmer residents of Vietnam, who the Hanoi government trusted, in leadership positions. They appointed Pen Sovan head of the Party Construction Commission. On January 7, 1979 the Kampuchean Revolutionary Armed Forces captured Phnom Penh and General Heng Samrin became the Head of State. Major Stevenson explained that even though technically the new leaders were Cambodian they were actually leading a Vietnamese occupation.

When we finished the history portion, Major Stevenson instructed me in the cultural differences between the

Vietnamese and Cambodian. In my mind, I had always grouped the two together like two different states in our union, never thinking or realizing that they were two separate countries with different languages and customs. After a long discussion with Major Stevenson, he decided that it would be best for me to concentrate mainly on the Vietnamese that I knew and learn just a few key phrases in Khmer, which was the language that most of the Cambodians spoke. They knew that Com spoke English, but they weren't sure how fluent she would be in it or how long it had been since she had last spoken it.

The major reached over and grabbed his briefcase. He opened it and took out detailed maps and satellite photos of Phnom Penh and an abandoned village outside of the city. He explained, "Mr. Gray, this abandoned village will be your extraction point. I want you to memorize the layout of the village and its location, plus the roads, which you will need to travel from Phnom Penh." He emphasized, "Your life will depend on it." I was given one hour to study and memorize the photos. When the hour was up, Major Stevenson gathered up the maps and photos. He wished me luck then got up and left.

My classes with Captain Donaldson were just the opposite from Major Stevenson. Instead of being interesting, I found them hard and not very enjoyable. Captain Donaldson was an espionage expert and had the responsibility of teaching me a six week course in less than two and a-half days. The first words out of his mouth, after our short greeting were, "Mr. Gray, do not trust anyone!" These words would be repeated over and over throughout my lessons. Captain Donaldson then requested, "Mr. Gray, I want you to take your time and tell me everything about your tour in Vietnam. This will help me in accessing your emotional character and building a psychological profile."

Chapter 4

Signing Up

It started in June of 1968, when I graduated from Golden Valley High School. I wasn't emotionally ready to follow in my brothers' footsteps and go off to college. With my high school grades, I knew I wasn't going to win any scholarships. Besides, I figured that college would be as boring as high school had been. Watching the Vietnam War on the nightly news had become a common occurrence during the sixties. I felt intrigued when I watched the film clips of the Huey helicopters landing in the rice paddies, dropping off their troops and watching as the troops ran off into combat. Watching those film clips, I could visualize myself piloting one of those army choppers, thinking that flying choppers would be the proverbial "cat's pajamas".

When you're eighteen years old, you don't always think objectively about the decisions you make. You don't weigh the good against the bad. You tend to make your judgments on emotion, and my emotions were telling me that flying helicopters would be exciting. One morning, I was driving down to Jensen's Super Value, a grocery store, where I had been working part time as a carry out boy for the last couple of years. As I was driving, I suddenly got the idea that after work I would go down to the Army recruiter and see what it took to become a pilot.

As I walked through the recruiter's door, I saw a sergeant get up from behind his desk and walk over to greet me. He was in his mid twenties and looked real macho in his army uniform. His hair was tightly cropped, and he had several ribbons pinned on his chest. What I didn't understand at the time was this sergeant viewed himself as a tiger and I was fresh meat, free for the taking. As we shook hands, he introduced himself as Sergeant Fuller and asked, "What can I help you with?"

"I'm thinking about joining the army. I would like to be a pilot."

"Well, the first thing you need to do is take a battery of tests to see if you qualify to take the entrance exam for flight school. Do you have a minute?"

When I replied yes, he immediately ushered me into a smaller room in back where he handed me a pencil and a pile of tests. Grabbing one of the chairs at the table, I sat down and began to take the tests. I was surprised when it took over two hours to complete all of them. When finished, I turned them back into the sergeant for grading. After the sergeant finished scoring my tests, he lifted his head with a big smile and said. "Mr. Gray, you qualified to take the entrance tests for the Warrant Officer Rotary Wing Aviation Course (WORWAC)."

He scheduled me the following Thursday to return to take the WORWAC test. I had never been in an airplane much less a helicopter so upon leaving the recruiter's office, I headed straight for the library to do some research on flying. I couldn't find any books on helicopter flying, but I found two books on how to fly airplanes. I grabbed them and headed for the checkout desk.

The next five days were spent studying the flying books. By the time Thursday rolled around, I think I could have copied them from memory if the recruiter had asked me to do so. I went down to the recruiter's office and took the WORWOC test. After Sergeant Fuller finished grading the test, he called me into his office and congratulated me on passing. He explained that the next step in the process of being accepted to flight school was appearing before a board of officers. All candidates were required to go in front of a board of officers for an interview and if I passed, I would be offered a flight school slot. Sergeant Fuller set up an appointment for the review board and told me to make sure I wore a coat and tie. I thanked him and left. As I walked down the hallway, I felt excited and could already see myself in the cockpit of a helicopter, hands on the controls, soaring over the treetops...

I wanted to surprise my mom and brothers. My father had passed away when I was eight years old. I decided that I wouldn't say anything to my family until I passed the board and was officially accepted for flight school.

The night before the board, I snuck my coat and tie out to my car because I didn't want to have to explain to my mom why I was all dressed up. For me to come walking downstairs all dressed up on a weekday morning would definitely get my mom's attention, and I didn't want to ruin my surprise.

Feeling excited, I straightened my tie and buttoned my coat then pulled open the door leading into the room where the board was assembled. There were several Army officers seated behind a long table. In front of the table was a single chair. I walked up in front of the chair and introduced myself to the board. A major in charge said, "Hello Mr. Gray, please be seated." Once seated, he proceeded to introduce each one of the board members. After the introductions were complete, the major said, "Mr. Gray, do you realize that by signing up for flight school you are volunteering to go to Vietnam?"

I had not actually thought much about Vietnam, or the

war, but quickly answered, "Yes sir."

The interview lasted twelve minutes, and before I knew it I was signing papers that were going to drastically change my life forever. This one stroke of the pen would affect my life in ways that were unimaginable to an eighteen year old. That I did it with such little thought to the consequences still amazes me to this day.

Bubbling over with excitement, I walked back to my car. I couldn't believe it. I, Curtis Gray, was going to be an Army helicopter pilot! I couldn't wait to get home and tell my family and friends. That night at the dinner table, I anxiously announced to my mom and brothers that I had been accepted to go to military flight school. My four brothers thought it sounded cool and were excited, but my mom looked shocked. All she could say was, "You didn't."

"Yes mom, I did," I said, as I pulled out the papers to show her. "They will be mailing me my orders with my report date within a few days."

"What about the war?" she cried.

"Mom, don't worry, basic training takes eight weeks then flight school takes another nine months. The war will be over before I ever graduate from flight school."

Chapter 5

Vietnam Bound

I thought about that last statement as I listened to the whining of the landing gear of the 707 as it extended to its "down and locked" position. We were on final approach to the Air Force base at Cam Ranh Bay, South Vietnam. My training had gone by quicker than I had anticipated and the war had not. As I walked down the stairway of the 707 leading to the tarmac, I found it hard to realize that I was actually in Vietnam.

My first five days were spent in an indoctrination center learning about the Vietnam conflict and how the US ran its operations. We learned about the Vietnamese culture and its customs. One class that I found interesting was on the different venereal diseases that the soldiers were contacting. They had enlarged photos to show us the consequences of the diseases. We were told that with all the soldiers and whores in Vietnam, sexually communicated diseases were rampant and if you choose to partake, you were guaranteed to receive. That didn't sound like a good guarantee to me!

Upon completion of the indoctrination training, I was flown by an air force C-130 to Duc Phu which was a US base located in the southern part of I Corp, south of Quang Ngai. I was assigned to the 91st Assault Helicopter Company (AHC), 14th Combat Aviation Battalion (CAB), 23rd Infantry Division.

The 91st AHC had twenty seven Hueys. They were divided between two slick "lift" platoons and one gunship platoon. The "slicks" were the nickname for the troop-carrying Hueys. The slicks were responsible for flying combat assaults, resupply (referred to as ash and trash), observation flights, flares, electronic surveillance, and special operations.

The Huey was the nickname of the Bell UH I Iroquois helicopter. The nickname came from the pronunciation of the original U.S. Army UH-1 designation. The Huey had been in combat in Vietnam since 1962. It became synonymous with the Vietnam War and was well on the way to becoming the greatest military helicopter of all time. The 91st had D and H models, which were the second generation of the Huey.

Vietnam was the first time that the helicopter was used in combat assaults, and several of the tactics used in Vietnam centered on the use of the Huey. The mobility of the helicopter allowed the ground commanders the ability to rapidly deploy troops from one locale to another. They could resupply their ground units with ammunition and C-rations allowing them to remain out on their search and destroy missions for longer periods of time. The helicopter was used for aerial reconnaissance and bomb damage assessment. It was also used as a medevac to transport wounded soldiers out of combat. Helicopters that were assigned specifically to air ambulance units used the call sign Dustoff. At the peak of Vietnam, there were over one hundred and ten Dustoff choppers. Due to this ability to remove the wounded from the battlefield quickly, the death rate in Vietnam was substantially lower than it would have been if they hadn't had helicopters.

Another job that the helicopter was used for was to insert Special Forces or long-range reconnaissance teams into remote areas. This was dangerous flying and I would get to experience firsthand how dangerous it really was. Helicopters were also used for scouting. The scout teams normally used an OH-58 and sometimes an OH-6 teamed with two gunships. The OH stood for "observation helicopter." The gunships used on these scout teams were either the Huey UH-1C model or the AH-1G Cobra gunship. The OH-58 would snoop around suspected areas of enemy resistance flying low and slow trying to draw fire from Charlie. If Charlie was dumb enough to take the bait and fire on the OH-58, the crew would mark the spot with a smoke then get out of there as fast as possible. Once he was clear of the area, the gunships would go to work blowing the hell out of the area. Flying a light observation helicopter in Vietnam was dangerous work.

Contrary to what most people thought, the Huey didn't have armor plating. Due to the weight of armor plating, it would be impractical. What the Huey did have for protection was two armor seats for the pilots. This seat only protected the pilot from a shot from the rear or directly under him. The seats had a sliding piece of armor attached on the outboard side that would slide forward once the pilot was in the seat. This gave the pilot a little protection from taking a hit on his one side. The only protection the rest of the crew had were chicken boards. This was a piece of armor that crewmembers could wear strapped to their chests much like a flak jacket is worn today. It was an inch and a half thick and weighed close to fifteen pounds. Due to its weight, I ended up taking the chicken board out of the vest and only used it when I was flying into hot landing zones (LZ). When needed, I would tuck the chicken board behind my shoulder harness straps in front of my chest to hold it in place.

Upon arriving at my new duty station, I went to headquarters and reported to the commanding officer (CO) Major John Edwards. Major Edwards welcomed me to the 91st AHC and proceeded to give me a short briefing on the company's operations. My first impression of Major Edwards was that he appeared to be a take charge CO and seemed like he had, as we said in the service, his "Shit in order." I looked forward to serving under him. He informed me that I would be assigned to one of the slick platoons. He called in Lieutenant (Lt.) James and introduced him to me. He ordered Lt. James to take me to my living quarters and show me around the company area.

Lt. James was one of the aircraft commanders (ACs) for the second platoon, which I was assigned to. He explained that he had been in Vietnam for eight months and as he talked, I got the feeling that Lt. James was not the typical Army aviator. He was very articulate in his speech, and I could tell he was a well-educated man. He told me that after graduating from Princeton in 1965, he decided that he wanted to see firsthand what the war in Vietnam was about. When I questioned him as to why he had chosen the Army instead of the Air Force or Navy, he explained, "My family has a long history of being in the Army. My father, grandfather and great-grandfather were all in the Army dating back to the mid 1800's."

He went on to explain that his great-grandfather had ridden with General Custer during the 1876 Centennial Indian Campaign. Luckily for his great grandfather, he was assigned to one of the companies that remained with Major Reno during the Battle of the Little Big Horn and had lived to tell about it.

Lt. James gave me a tour of the company area. I was assigned to one of the 2nd platoon hootches. Hootch was the name used to describe a small hut or home in Vietnam. They were built about a foot above the ground and had plywood floors. The bottom portion of the walls were made of plywood, which had screening attached from the knee wall up to the roof, which was built of tin. My hootch had plywood partitions to help separate the living areas. There were eight pilots assigned to each hootch. As we entered the hootch, Lt. James instructed me to take the second area on the left. Each area contained a cot and a footlocker. That was the extent of the furnishing of my new home. I noticed that most of the other pilots had fans set up in their areas, so I mentally added that to my list of things to get. It was already the hot season and a fan would make it more comfortable for sleeping.

The time was approaching 1800 hrs, so Lt. James suggested we head for the mess hall. During dinner, I met several of the pilots from the unit. Most of them were the same rank as I, warrant officers (WO). I liked being a warrant. The warrant officer was a rank above the non-commissioned officer but below the commissioned officer. The rank of the warrant officer commanded a salute and was called mister rather than sir. Warrants were specialists in their field of expertise, ours being the operation of helicopters.

After dinner, most of the pilots headed over to a larger hootch set up as an officer's club. In the officer's club, they had a bar set up along the back wall with several tables in front to sit and socialize. At the entrance to the club, they had stuck two rotor blades into the ground at angles so that they crossed at the top end of the blades. It made for a pretty cool looking entrance. The officer's club was the center point of the pilot's company area and most of them spent their nights there. It had been a long day and I felt tired, so I went back to my hootch to get some rest. I had orders to report to the flight line at 0530 hrs the next morning for my first flight.

Chapter 6

Combat

It was still dark when I stepped into flight ops. I checked the schedule board and saw that I was scheduled to fly with Lt. James. Having enjoyed my company tour with Lt. James, I felt honored to be flying my first flight in Vietnam with him. I went out to the bird and started the preflight check. A few minutes later, the gunner and crew chief arrived. We introduced ourselves then I went back to checking the aircraft. The preflight check consisted of checking all the fluid levels, opening the cowlings and looking for leaks and any unusual wear and tear. I was on top of the helicopter checking the rotor head when I heard, "Good morning Curt. Isn't it a beautiful morning?"

Still half asleep I turned to Lt. James and said, "Yes it is, good morning."

A Huey's crew consisted of four crewmembers: the AC, copilot, crew chief and gunner. The crew chief sat in the gunners well on the left side of the bird behind the AC and operated one of the M60 machine guns. The gunner sat on the right side of the bird behind the copilot and fired the other M60. The crew chief was responsible for inspecting and helping maintain the bird while the gunner was responsible for getting the ammo, cleaning and maintaining the guns. I would learn in Vietnam that you would get very close to your crew and would think of them as an extended family.

The sun was breaking over the horizon as Lt. James lifted our bird to a hover and departed northbound. We were headed to LZ Baldy, one of the many landing zones (LZs) situated throughout our area of operations (AO). As we flew, Lt. James explained that LZ Baldy was actually a fire support base (FSB). The FSBs always had a helicopter pad to shuttle troops and supplies in and out. He went on to explain that FSBs were built on high ground and each contained several pieces of artillery, which were used to provide support for the ground troops as they did their search and destroy missions. The ground troops would do the searching and when they discovered the enemy they would use the artillery, along with air support, to do the destroying. He said that was a simplified explanation of the nature of combat in our AO.

If the ground troops were lucky enough to locate a large enemy unit in the open, they would call for a combat assault (CA). When it was time for a CA, our battalion would order all the available slicks to report to a pickup zone (PZ) to transport the troops into battle. I equated a combat assault to being in a cavalry charge during the Indian wars except now instead of using a horse we were using the helicopter.

Lt. James went on to explain, "Curt, our mission today is to fly resupply for the infantry company that we are supporting. Our job is to carry ammunition and C-rations out to the different platoons in the field. I believe that flying resupply is one of the most dangerous missions that we fly, because we fly it single-ship. When we fly combat assaults, we always have a high ship flying overhead. His mission is to come down and rescue us if we're shot down. That's not the case when flying resupply. If we get shot down today, we'll be on our own to get to the safety of our troops."

As Lt. James spoke, I listened attentively hoping to learn as much as I could about combat flying. I knew that the more I learned the greater chance I had of surviving my tour.

We landed at LZ Baldy and shut the bird down. The crew stayed with the bird while Lt. James went over and talked with the infantry commander. During his briefing, Lt. James marked the coordinates on his map of the different units' locations. He numbered them in the order that we would be resupplying them. As the briefing was taking place, the ground troops helped our crew load supplies into the chopper.

One of the responsibilities of the crew chief was to supervise the loading of the aircraft. He was to make sure the supplies were placed in the right location to keep the helicopter in its center of gravity (CG). The CG works like a teeter-totter. If the weight is placed too far forward or aft, the CG moves outside of its normal operating envelope and affects the flight characteristics of the aircraft. If the weight is too far forward, you can end up running out of aft cyclic and not be able to bring the nose up when needed. This would cause a very dangerous situation; therefore it was very important to load the aircraft properly.

When Lt. James finished his briefing, he came back to the bird and said, "Curt, are you ready to do some combat flying?"

"Yes sir."

"Well, climb in and we'll get started."

I climbed into the right seat and strapped in. We cranked up the rotors and Lt. James lifted off. He explained that he would fly the first sortie (sortie was one takeoff and landing) and I would fly the second. He explained that he would talk his way through the procedures as he did them. We flew out to the first location, which was grease marked on his map. When approaching the vicinity of his marking, he radioed the unit on the ground. "Charlie Platoon, this is Cobra 4 over."

"Roger Cobra 4, this is Charlie Platoon, go ahead."

"We're inbound with supplies, pop smoke."

Charlie Company responded, "Smokes out."

Whenever you flew into a unit's position you always had them pop smoke. This was done for two reasons: first, you wanted to make sure that you had the correct position and second, so that you could determine the direction of the wind. It was very important when flying a helicopter, especially if it was heavy, that you land into the wind.

When the ground unit popped smoke, they wouldn't tell you what color smoke they popped. You would look down, locate the smoke then call the color. They would come back and confirm that you had the correct color. This way you were sure you had the right location. If the ground unit compromised the color of smoke by announcing its color, and Charlie (a nickname used for the enemy) was monitoring the frequency he would throw out the same color smoke and you could end up flying into an ambush. During my tour, I saw this happen several times when the ground unit would screw up and call out the color of the smoke that he was popping. We would look down and see two or three of the same color smoke.

Looking down at the ground, we could see red smoke. "Charlie Platoon we have red smoke over."

"Roger Cobra 4, we confirm red smoke."

Lt. James flew our bird directly over the unit's position and executed what was called a high overhead approach. This maneuver was a descending circular approach. By doing an overhead approach, if you were shot down while executing the approach, you could autorotate down and land within the safety of the troops.

An autorotation is a maneuver that allows the pilot to

safely land his helicopter if his engine fails. The transmission is designed using a clutch, which allows the rotor to disengage from the drive train and free wheel. The pilot, by lowering the collective pitch lever, is able to maintain his rotor RPM by utilizing the air passing from under the rotor through the rotor to keep the rotor turning. Even though his descent angle is steep, it allows the pilot to maneuver the bird towards the ground. At approximately fifty feet above the surface, the pilot pulls back on the cyclic stick, which reduces his forward airspeed and slows his rate of descent. When his forward airspeed is reduced to the desired groundspeed, the pilot pushes the cyclic stick forward to level the aircraft for landing. Once the helicopter is level, the pilot pulls the collective pitch lever up to help slow the rate of descent and cushion the landing.

Within seconds after Lt. James entered his high overhead approach, we were on the ground. The soldiers quickly unloaded their supplies. As soon as their supplies were off the bird, we were pulling pitch, headed back airborne, climbing to the safety of altitude. Lt. James told me, "Most of the hits that our helicopters take in our AO are from small arms fire. Our enemy is mainly the Viet Cong not the NVA (North Vietnamese Army) and their main weapon is the AK-47."

When we were safely at an altitude of 1500 feet, Lt. James keyed the intercom and said, "You got the aircraft."

I got on the controls and keyed my mike saying, "I got the aircraft" and so began my combat flying. I had never flown a helicopter with heavy loads and it would take a few days to get use to it. We spent the rest of the day flying resupply and by the time we landed back at Duc Phu, I had shot seven approaches. I survived my first day of combat flying without being fired upon. As I walked back to my hootch, I realized that I had a lot of learning and work ahead of me.

CHUCK GROSS

On my second day of flying, I was assigned to fly with WO Jim Phillips. In the military it was a custom to call people by their last name. Phillips had been in Nam for six months. He was exactly half way through his tour and starting on the downhill slide. In Vietnam, unlike previous wars, you knew when you would be returning home, for your tour was exactly one year.

That afternoon we were out flying ash and trash when we received a radio call to report to Hawk Hill to refuel. After refueling, we would be doing a combat assault. One of the ground units had come in contact with a sizeable force and needed reinforcements. Descending into Hawk Hill, I counted eighteen slicks already lined up for the combat assault. We flew over to the POL (petroleum, oil, and lubricants), refueled then hovered over and joined the line of slicks.

Phillips climbed out of his seat and walked over and joined the other ACs for the briefing. Normally, only the ACs attended the main briefing, and when finished would return and brief their crews. Not knowing what to expect, I was excited. I had seen war portrayed in the movies, but when I realized that I was going to be participating in it for real, my emotions were different from what I had expected. It was not until my first combat assault that I realized I could actually be hurt or even worse, lose my life. Reality was setting in.

I was jolted from my deep thoughts when Phillips yelled, "Listen up. We'll be inserting over two hundred troops into a hot LZ. The LZ is tight and can only handle three Hueys at a time. We have twenty-one slicks, which have been divided into seven flights of three ships each. The flights will be flying at one-minute intervals. We'll be chalk three in the first flight and we'll be making two sorties. Since the LZ is hot and we already have some of our men on the ground, we'll not be able to use our gunships for support. Guys, as we get closer to the LZ, I want you to make sure that you don't shoot our own men. Any questions?"

We climbed into our choppers and cranked up. Lt. James was our flight lead. WO Bob Kelly was Chalk Two and we were Chalk Three. Phillips had just brought our bird to an idle when the radio cracked. I could hear Lt. James voice, "Chalk One's up."

Then I heard Kelly's voice, "Chalk Two's up."

Phillips keyed the mike and said, "Chalk Three's up."

Within seconds our small flight was lifting off. We picked up a heading of 255° flying west in a tight formation. Exactly one minute later, I heard the second flight lift off. During our flight, Phillips explained that since there were already friendly troops in the LZ, it would not be possible to prep it before our landing. He went on to emphasize that it was very important that you never fly into an empty LZ without prepping it first. The helicopter on short final, due to its slow speed, was very vulnerable. Charlie could be hiding in the LZ and waiting till you were on a short final approach then blow the hell out of you.

It was an eight-minute flight from Hawk Hill to the LZ. As we got closer, I could see a lot of action taking place around the perimeter. Our C&C (Command and Control) ship had already done a recon of the area and was directing us in. As we began our descent, James told our flight, "Go hot."

When Phillips ordered our gunners to go hot, the whole aircraft seemed to come alive. It felt and sounded like the helicopter was going to shake apart. I was surprised at how loud the M60s were. At about eight hundred feet, I could see tracers coming up at us. They looked as if they were flying between my legs. We were in our flare when I saw Chalk One suddenly veer left towards the trees. He chopped several branches and spun back to the right then exited the

LZ without dropping off his troops. As this was happening, I heard Lt. James, "We've taking hits, Oh shit, I'm out of here."

Chalk Two came to a hover and dropped off his troops. We were right on his tail. Within seconds, our troops were off and Phillips was pulling pitch. I could see tracers flying everywhere. I felt and heard some loud popping sounds as we lifted over the trees. Our crew chief yelled, "We're taking hits from ten o'clock low." I turned and could see him returning fire.

I watched as Phillips kept flying. He remained calm and didn't appear excited. He keyed his mike and said, "Chalk Three's taking fire at ten o'clock along the tree line about two clicks to the left of our departure path."

The radio frequency buzzed with chatter. Thank goodness our hits had been superficial and caused no flight problems. James had been talking on the radio, but I was so busy that I hadn't paid attention to what he was saying. As we got to altitude, I could see what had happened. Lt. James' ship was down in the field about five clicks from the LZ. The high ship was already there hovering alongside his ship. There was no time to waste; we had to return to Hawk Hill for our next sortie.

When we arrived back at Hawk Hill, we hopped out and took a look at our helicopter. I could see three holes in the skin, but no serious damage. Phillips turned to me chuckling and said, "Curt, welcome to Vietnam."

The second flight by now had returned, so the fourth helicopter moved up to Chalk Three and we became Chalk Two for our second flight. We quickly loaded up more troops and departed. I was concerned about Lt. James, but would have to wait 'til after the combat assault was finished to find out the details. By the time we arrived back to the LZ, it was not as hot as it had previously been. The reinforcements had secured the perimeter of the LZ, and we got in and back out without taking any more hits.

Upon returning to Hawk Hill, I was shocked to find out that Lt. James's copilot was dead and James had taken a hit in his left thigh. He had already been medevaced to the hospital. This was his ticket home. Even though I had only known him for a few days, I would miss him. Lt. James reported that on short final they were taking a lot of fire from his left front. As he tried to bring his bird to a hover, his copilot took a hit to his neck killing him instantly. He thought he had also taken some hits in his hydraulics, but he couldn't be sure. He momentarily lost control of his bird as it swung towards the trees. He was able to get it back under control and depart the LZ, but as soon as he got up over the trees he took several more hits from the left. That was when he took the hit in his left thigh and one into the helicopter's turbine. He milked his bird up to about a thousand feet when he began to lose power and started to look for a place to put her down. He said he was fortunate that the engine didn't quit until he got his bird on the ground. Recalling yesterday's conversation, I thought to myself, "Lt. James had the same luck as his great-grandfather!"

When I arrived back at our company area, I was still replaying in my mind everything that had happened during the combat assault. What bothered me the most was I couldn't help but think: if this had been a day earlier, I would have been James' copilot.

Walking into my hootch, I heard someone shout, "Curt, what the hell are you doing here?" I had no trouble recognizing the voice. It was my good friend WO Ken Duncan. Ken and I had met while going through flight school and had become good friends. Ken said he had signed into the 91st a few hours ago and was assigned to the first platoon. I was excited. I couldn't believe the luck of having one of my best friends assigned to the same unit. This friendship definitely would make my first couple of weeks easier.

Ken and I had taken our primary training at Fort Walters, located in Mineral Wells, Texas. Mineral Wells was a little cowtown about an hour and half drive west of Fort Worth. After completing our five months of primary training at Fort Walters, we were sent to Hunter Army Airfield, Savannah, Georgia. At Hunter, we spent four months completing our instrument and tactical training.

During our last few weeks of flight school, we received E&E training. Our E&E training took place out at Fort Stewart, located on the outskirts of Savannah. Ken and I were assigned to the same team. Our team was comprised of four warrant officer candidates and four commissioned officers. In the late sixties, the army was training some of the helicopter pilots for the navy. These navy officers along with the army's commissioned officers would train alongside us. As we introduced ourselves to each other, I was impressed by two of the officer's qualifications. One was an Army captain from the Special Forces. He was a Green Beret and had already served a tour in Nam. Since he was a Vietnam Vet, Ken and I looked at him as a real soldier and not just another trainee. The other officer was a Navy Lt. JG who had been through SEALS training. Hearing these two officers' qualifications, we felt that we had our E&E exercise licked. How could we go wrong with such experts on our team?

It was late Friday afternoon when we received our final briefing for the tactical exercise, which would begin later that night. During the briefing, we were assigned an objective. Our mission was to navigate through the woods and swamps to locate the objective and get to it without being captured. Teams of LRRPs (long range reconnaissance patrols) were strategically placed between our objective and us. Their mission was simple: to capture us. These LRRPs were Vietnam Vets. To motivate them, they were given the incentive of receiving a weekend of leave for each pilot captured. The more pilots they captured, the more leave they received. This was a great motivator, because when you're a GI everyone wants leave. We also understood that being Vietnam Vets, they would be good at their mission.

We were told that to capture us, all the LRRPs needed to do was tag us. When tagged, we were required to give up. If we decided to get physical and tried fighting to escape, we would be punished severely. For those unfortunate enough to get captured, they would be taken to a POW camp for torturing. We were given strict orders not to disclose anything but our name, rank, and serial number. The enemy's objective was to extract information from us and get us to sign their document. We were told that if we signed this document, we would fail the exercise and wouldn't be allowed to graduate from flight school. Listening to the instructor, I decided that I definitely didn't want to get captured. This torturing didn't sound like fun. I would find out later they had several effective ways of torturing their captives. One of the last things the instructor said was, "Men, we have a few surprises in store for you this evening."

Our equipment for this exercise consisted of a compass, map, flashlight and canteen. We were issued goggles to protect our eyes from the branches and underbrush and a whistle to wear around our neck. If we got into serious trouble, we could blow the whistle for help. The sound would help them locate us. We hadn't been fed since the night before and were starting to get hungry. Each team was given two live rabbits and two chickens for cooking and stew. These were divided evenly between the officers and the candidates. We were then released to set up in a bivouac and to prepare our meal. During our briefing, we were told that sometime during the night the camp would be attacked. This attack would signal the beginning of the exercise.

When we got in camp, Ken and I decided that we didn't want to kill the cute bunny and let her go. Chicken stew would be good enough for us. We rung the chicken's neck, plucked her feathers and threw her in the pot. When our stew was ready, our team got together and ate as we discussed out tactics for the night. Captain Bruz, the Green Beret, told us, "Even though they taught us on the initial attack to stay put till the flares burn down, I want you men to be ready. On the first indication of an attack, we're going to make our move. We want to get out of camp as quick as possible. It's too dangerous to wait."

The attack came at 2050 hrs. We heard a lot of firing followed immediately by explosions as the flares lit up the dark night. Our team was ready. As the first flare went off, our team was up and moving. Captain Bruz led, followed by the Navy Seal and the rest of the team. We were in the woods within seconds. I found out later that over half of the pilots of other teams were captured without ever getting out of the camp. Thank goodness for us, we had Captain Bruz.

It was one of those dark, cool nights. The sky was clear and the temp was hovering around the low fifties. During the first few hours, we made good time. We felt confident that we knew our exact whereabouts and it appeared that we would make our objective by 0100 hrs. There would be no POW camp for our team. We had been in the field for almost two weeks and I was looking forward to a good shower and my clean bunk.

We were working our way through marshy woods when we came upon a dirt trail that we had to cross. The trail was elevated out of the marsh and had steep embankments of four to five feet on each side. We scouted the area and discovered that there were several LRRPs stationed along the trail. To our amazement, we discovered a big pile of dead snakes up on the trail. The LRRPs, while biding their time waiting for us to come along, had been killing them. Here, we had been walking knee deep in water for the last hour or so and I hadn't even thought about snakes. I never liked snakes and seeing this huge pile of dead ones gave me the willies and made me feel like scrambling out of the water as quickly as possible.

After rechecking our maps, we determined we had to cross over the trail to get to our objective. We moved to our left staying parallel to the trail searching for an opening from the LRRPs where it would be safe to cross. After covering about seventy yards, we located an opening. Captain Bruz decided that we should cross the trail single file at twenty-second intervals. We would rejoin on the other side at a point fifty yards into the woods. If we got separated, we would be on our own. I would be the sixth one to cross with Ken right behind me. The first four team members made it across without being seen. While the fifth man was making his dash, we spotted some enemy coming down the trail in our direction. Thank goodness they hadn't spotted us. A quick decision had to be made, either go now or risk getting separated from the rest of our team. I motioned to Ken and the other team member for us to cross together. We scrambled up the embankment and dashed across the trail. I was coming down the far side of the trail when I heard a bunch of yelling and screaming. I ran approximately a hundred yards then threw myself into some tall weeds. Breathing heavily, I was afraid that my breath would give my position away. I could hear voices whispering, but I couldn't make out any bodies through the tall grass. My adrenalin was pumping and for a moment I forgot it was a training exercise. Deciding that I didn't want to be captured, I closed my fists as the voices came closer. In a low whisper, I could hear, "Over here. He's over here."

Crouched down in the tall grass, I was ready to jump. I

was going to hit the closest soldier as hard as possible then turn and run. Being so dark, I figured they would never be able to identify who hit them. I waited. When the voices got within a foot, I sprung up to strike. As my eyes made contact with their faces, I was surprised to see it was Ken with four other team members.

We located our other two team members and were trying to get a fix on our current location when the LRRPs discovered our position. We had no choice but to run. Our team took off in a direction away from the LRRPs. Looking over my shoulder; I could see a large group of LRRPs closely on our tail. I understood now why we had goggles. We were running through the woods, smashing through the brush and branches as we went. The ground was getting mushier as we went and before we knew it, we found ourselves waist deep in frigid water. It quickly became apparent that the LRRPs didn't want to come into the cold water after us. I'm not sure if it was the snakes or just the cold water, but this gave us the chance we had been looking for. We decided to take advantage of this newly gained knowledge and put some distance between them and us. Our only problem was, we had been running for fifteen minutes and had no idea where we were, much less which direction our objective was.

Being inexperienced soldiers, we relied on our Green Beret and Navy Seal leaders to guide us out of our mess. After studying the map, they took a compass bearing, chose a heading then we headed out. We were strung out in single file at ten foot intervals to have a better chance of scattering if we came across another group of LRRPs. While working our way through a dense area of forest, we heard dogs barking in the distance. I thought to myself, "Oh great, how can we get away from hound dogs? This must be one of the surprises the instructor warned us about." As the sound of the dogs got closer, Ken and I closed our distance and stooped down. We could hear the dogs making a loud commotion when suddenly this large wild boar came running right at us. It ran so close that it almost knocked us over. Right on its tail were three dogs. This huge boar had to weigh close to four hundred pounds. Luckily for us, the bore was so intent on his own survival that he never saw us. What a relief. Ken and I broke out laughing. We thought the dogs were tracking us.

We spent the rest of the night and early morning slogging through the woods. We never did locate our objective. The exercise terminated at 0600 hrs for everyone but us. We were so disoriented that we didn't even remain in the boundaries of Fort Stewart much less the perimeter set up for the exercise. It was close to 1000 hrs when we finally got picked up. By the time Ken and I finally got back to the barracks, everyone else had already showered and were in bed sleeping. Feeling like losers, we showered then went to bed.

Later that evening, we heard the tortures in the camp were so realistic that everyone captured ended up signing the document. Yes, they all got to graduate. The government had spent too many dollars on each student to wash them out in their final days. Ken and I had not done well in our E&E exercise. I hoped that we would fare better in Vietnam.

Chapter 7

Huey Flying

My first few months in Vietnam went by quickly. I was busy learning the ropes, meeting all the guys and trying to adapt to the war and my new lifestyle. I learned very early in my tour that the tactics taught in flight school didn't always apply in Vietnam. This was due to the drastic differences in topography in Vietnam. Down in the delta, the land was mostly flat and contained numerous rice paddies. As you moved farther north and west, the terrain became more mountainous and dense. In our AO, the land was flat from the sea inward for about five miles. Then as you went west, the terrain quickly changed into dense mountainous jungle. Your flying tactics also depended on if you were fighting the Vietcong guerrillas versus the NVA.

In our AO, it was SOP (standard operating procedure) to fly at least fifteen hundred feet above the surface. This altitude would protect us from the small arms fire from the Vietcong. Anytime the clouds were lower than fifteen hundred feet, we would low-level. The objective of low-level flying was to get from point A to point B without getting shot. Due to the slow speed and size of a helicopter, it became an easy target to hit when flying low. I always equated shooting at a helicopter like shooting at a barn. Even a blind man couldn't miss. When flying low-level, we would try to maneuver the bird as close to the surface as possible. This would help minimize our exposure to the enemy. If Charlie was standing in the tree line, he could put a bead on you and with an AK47 automatic rifle get off several shots. To counter this, we would try to fly perpendicular to the tree lines rather than parallel to them and s-turn back and forth across the open fields.

I found low-level flying exhilarating and discovered that it gave me an emotional high. There was nothing greater than screaming over the tops of the trees at one hundred plus mph while weaving back and forth over the open areas. Vietnam, compared to the States had fewer power lines to worry about hitting. Still, we always kept our eyes peeled. A power line strike in a helicopter almost certainly meant death.

I quickly discovered that flying helicopters in Vietnam was hot and dirty work. When landing in the field, the rotor blade would kick up a lot of dirt and dust. This dirt would get all over everyone in the rotor wash area. The term we used to describe this was being "dusted off." We wore Nomex flight suits and gloves. Nomex was a fire resistant material. It was designed to protect us from fire. The Nomex material was fairly heavy and didn't breathe well. With the hot temperatures, wearing the Nomex caused us to sweat. It wasn't too bad when airborne, but when we were shut down or sitting at flight idle, I could usually feel the sweat running down my body. It always felt good, when possible, to take a shower after a day's flying even if it was a cold shower. After being in Vietnam for a few months, I swore if I ever made it home, I would take a shower every day for the rest of my life.

Each day brought with it a new experience and they were not necessarily good ones. I was seeing and experiencing things that would change my life forever. One day we were flying support for an infantry company when one of their platoons got ambushed. We had just finished resupplying the platoon minutes earlier and were headed towards their sister platoon when it happened. The troops were working their way down a trail when suddenly they were hit by a land mine. As the mine went off, Charlie opened fire. They couldn't tell if it had been a booby trap or if Charlie had set it off. An intense firefight followed lasting about five minutes before Charlie disappeared into the jungle. In those five minutes, the Americans ended up killing four VC. Unfortunately, two men of the platoon were killed and three were seriously injured.

Upon receiving word of the ambush, we radioed the ground unit and requested that they pop smoke. After identifying the smoke, we did a quick high recon of their location then executed a high overhead approach. As we set the Huey down, the wounded were loaded on board. One of the soldiers had taken a hit in his calf but it didn't appear to be life threatening. He was the lucky one. The other two were not that fortunate. One had a wound in his chest that was bleeding profusely and he would be lucky to survive the flight back to the hospital. The other had taken three hits. One hit appeared to be a superficial hit across his cheek but the other two were a lot worse. The second hit had entered below his armpit and exited through the top of the shoulder leaving a massive hole. The third hit was in the abdomen. As I looked in his eyes, I could see the terror and suffering that he was experiencing.

Once the wounded were on board, they carried the remains of the two dead soldiers over to the chopper and loaded them. They didn't have body bags so we could see their battered bodies. One soldier had both his legs blown off. All that was left was the top half of his body beginning about three inches below his waist. His torso had been badly mutilated from the blast of the mine. The other soldier must have been farther back on the trail. His right side was severely damaged but all his limbs were intact. We quickly lifted off and flew back to the hospital as fast as the Huey would take us.

Throughout my tour, I would end up flying several medical evacuations. I would drop these wounded soldiers off at the hospital pad, never knowing what would become of them. Even though it was hard to look at these guys, seeing their battered bodies and the suffering in their faces, it made me feel good to know we were helping our troops, often saving their lives.

When our crews were assigned the duty of transporting dead soldiers out of the field, we tried to bring gas masks. If the bodies had been out in the field for several days, the maggots and rigor mortis would have already set in. The stench was so bad that if our crew didn't have gas masks they would be vomiting all the way back to Graves Registration. Graves Registration was where we flew the bodies to be prepared for shipment back to the States. For me, it was harder to fly the dead guys than the wounded, because we knew that the wounded guy at least had a chance of survival.

After three months in country, I made AC. It came as a pleasant surprise. I hadn't been expecting it for another month or so. In the 91st, the ACs were chosen by votes from the other ACs. Making AC wasn't necessarily an indication of how good a pilot you were, but how well you got along with the other ACs or when your unit needed replacements. Making AC was a big event because now I would be in charge. I was assigned my own helicopter with crew, and was given the call sign Cobra Twenty-Seven.

My first few weeks of flying AC were non-eventful. I flew resupply in our AO and enjoyed being in command. It took a little adjustment to learn to fly the bird from the left seat versus the right. The Huey was designed, as most helicopters are, to be flown from the right seat by the AC. But in Nam, it was our company's policy for the AC to fly from the left seat due to tactical reasons.

One evening around 2300hrs, I was awakened by our platoon leader Captain Green. "Gray, wake up. We need you to fly."

Half asleep I blurted out, "Okay, I'll be right there. What's up?"

"Report to flight ops ASAP. We need to extract a team."

Our unit had received a call from the MACV-SOG unit that we had been supporting for the last few weeks. Their mission was to perform strategic reconnaissance and interdiction deep into the western borders of Vietnam, Laos and Cambodia. At the time, our government was claiming that such missions into Laos didn't exist. The missions were on a volunteer basis only. When our unit was first offered the missions, Ken Duncan and I talked it over and thought the missions sounded exciting and decided to volunteer.

The SOG missions were conducted by CCN, which stood for Command and Control North, and were flown separate from our ordinary missions. CCN soldiers stayed to themselves. We were required to sign a document stating that if we were shot down or captured, we would not be recognized as U.S. soldiers. It also contained a clause that read, "If you disclose any information about this mission, you can be sent to prison for up to ten years and receive up to a ten thousand dollar fine." In 1970, ten thousand dollars was a lot of money. It was scary to read that statement, but heck, by then I didn't think I would make it home from Vietnam anyway, so what did I have to lose? Ken and I both signed it.

My thoughts were suddenly jolted back to the reality of the Pentagon briefing room when Captain Donaldson asked,

"Mr. Gray, What were your feelings concerning working for Special Ops? Did you feel that your participation in these missions were honorable or did you feel they were deceitful due to their clandestine nature?"

I thought for a moment then answered, "At the time, both. I felt that what we were doing, even though it was very dangerous, was very important to our cause, therefore it was honorable, yet, I still felt that we were being a little deceitful, telling our citizens one thing and doing another."

"Did you have any trouble when you got home with wanting to tell your family and friends about these missions?"

"No sir, I did not," I firmly replied.

As I continued to listen and answer his questions, I realized how detailed and analytical Captain Donaldson was. When he finished acquiring the information he was searching for, he told me to continue.

We had been spending the last few weeks inserting special teams into Laos along the Ho Chi Minh Trail. The Ho Chi Minh Trail was a network of parallel and often intersecting trails that ran the length of South Vietnam from north to south. A good majority of these trails were in Laos and Cambodia. The more our troops could stop the flow of supplies moving down the trail, the better chance we had of winning the war. But we have to remember, the Vietnam War was run by politicians, rather than generals, so the war wasn't always fought the way it should have been.

As I pulled my boots on, I wondered how many ships we would be sending into Laos this late at night. Beside me, the only other pilot in my hootch that Captain Green woke was WO Fisher. As Fisher and I left our hootch, we ran into AC's WO Duncan and WO Snyder and copilots WO Arnold and Lt. Johns. When we arrived at operations we received a quick briefing. "Gentleman, we've been informed by CCN that a SOG team had been discovered. They've been in close contact with the enemy and have been on the move since 2000 hrs. The team feels they cannot survive until daylight and have requested an expedited extraction. We'll be sending three slicks to accomplish the mission. One ship will be used as a high ship. Duncan, you'll be flying the high ship. You'll be carrying Major Hibbler, the CCN commander. Snyder and Gray, you'll be doing the extraction. Fisher, you'll be flying with Gray, and Johns with Snyder. The team said they were doubtful if they could find an open area, so your birds are being outfitted with rappelling ladders as we speak."

The officer answered our questions then completed the briefing by wishing us good luck. We left operations and headed to our birds.

Shortly after midnight, our flight of three birds lifted off and headed west towards Laos. We would stop at Cam Duc, which was a staging area that our unit was using to fly support for the ARVN who were engaged in a search and destroy campaign. There we would refuel, then head into Laos to locate and hopefully extract the team. A high overcast ceiling blocked the rays from the moon forcing us to fly in darkness. Once we located the team's location, we would blackout. This meant that Snyder and I would turn off our outside lights and dim down our instruments light so that we could barely see them. This allowed our eyes to adjust better to the darkness, since we would be flying visually and needed to see as well as possible. It also gave us a better chance of not being spotted by the enemy. We knew that a helicopter sitting at a hover while lowering down a ladder was a sitting duck and could easily be shot down.

After refueling at Cam Duc, we cranked up and headed for Laos. We flew a loose trail formation with Duncan flying lead, Snyder second, and me following up in trail. We had been flying over Laos ten minutes when the CCN major keyed his mike trying to raise radio contact with his team. "Team Four, Team Four this is Waterman over."

The frequency had been quiet since we entered Laos and to hear the major's voice made us realize that the excitement was about to begin.

His team member answered in a low quivering voice, "Waterman, this is Team Four over."

"Roger Team Four, what's your status?"

"We're sure glad to hear you're on station. We've been in and out of contact with Charlie for the last few hours. We've been on the move all night."

"Roger Team Four, What's your location?"

The team leader radioed his location indicating that the jungle was too dense to find a LZ. I had been hoping they would be able to find an opening and we wouldn't have to use the ladders. It was bad enough having to do a night extraction, let alone trying to do it with ladders. This would be a first for us.

As we flew towards the coordinates, the team leader radioed that he could hear us coming. The team had a small hand-held strobe they would turn on and hopefully as we looked down through the jungle, we would be able to see it flashing. The team consisted of ten soldiers. I stayed higher so as to not have a mid air with Snyder since we were both blacked out. The ceiling was starting to breakup and the moon's rays were beginning to light up the sky. This allowed us to be able to see the tops of the trees better, but at the same time would help Charlie in seeing us. Snyder radioed, "We've picked up the strobe and we're starting our approach. It's mighty dark down here."

With the moon rays breaking through, I could barely make out Snyder hovering over the jungle with his ladder hanging below. I continued to circle as he hovered. He had been hovering about two minutes when the radioed cracked, "Cobra One-six is loaded, we're coming out. I think we have about half the team on the ladder, negative on fire."

I thought to myself, "Thank God." Two minutes can be a lifetime in a bad LZ.

As soon as Snyder was clear, I began my descent. I knew that the quicker I got down, the safer it would be. Receiving no fire on our descent, I brought the bird to a hover and called for my crew to lower the ladder. As each team member climbed on the ladder, I could feel his weight pulling the helicopter from side to side. I really had to work the controls to maintain a steady hover. Suddenly the darkness erupted with tracers. The fire was coming from the right side of our bird. I told my gunners, "Go hot." I felt the sudden urge to pull pitch and get the hell out of there, but I ignored it. The darkness disappeared as the tracers lit up the night. I radioed to Duncan, "Cobra Seven, we're taking fire at three o'clock."

Duncan quickly answered, "Roger Cobra 27, we're coming down to give you cover." By then the last team member climbed onto the ladder and my crew chief yelled, "Mr. Gray, the teams on. Let's get the hell out of here."

I pulled pitch and started our climb. As we started lifting forward, I heard a loud thud as a bullet hit the bulkhead right behind Fisher. I yelled, "Fisher, are you alright?"

"Yeah, but that was to damn close."

Duncan swung down to give us cover. Both his gunners were laying down heavy fire to our right in the direction of the tracers. Suddenly the enemy firing stopped as quickly as it had started. Slowly, we climbed to the safety of altitude with the team members dangling below. Once we got to altitude, the three of us headed back to Cam Duc. There we would unload the troops, refuel and then return home. Even though I appeared calm on the outside, my mind was gushing with excitement. I felt proud as I thought to myself, "Ken and I are doing better than we had in our

E&E training exercise."

The sun was breaking over the horizon as we shot our final approach into Duc Pho. It had been a long but productive night. Duncan and I headed to the mess hall to get some of that "good" army mess. Once we were finished with breakfast, we headed to our hootch for some much needed sleep.

Chapter 8

Missing In Action

One mission that our unit was assigned to fly that I thought was quite interesting was spraying of a chemical called Orange. Orange was a defoliant that we used to spray around perimeters to clear fields of fire. It was also sprayed on rice paddies to help cut down the enemy's food supply. After the war, there would be several investigations and studies into the affects of the chemical on the soldiers and the environment. It would be given the name Agent Orange.

Out west around Cam Duc, the ARVN (Army of the Republic of Vietnam) discovered several rice paddies out in the middle of what we thought of as nowhere since there were no villages or hootchs in the area. Our intelligence indicated that Charlie was growing this rice to feed his troops. It had to be destroyed and our unit was given the job of spraying it. To accomplish this mission, our unit rigged one of our slicks with chemical tanks and a spray boom. Looking at it, we all agreed that it was one of the "most wicked" crop dusters that we had ever seen. Our crews would take this Huey out, loaded full of Orange, and spray the rice paddies. The flying was fun and different from what we were use to and I really enjoyed it.

A few days following our night extraction from Laos, I

was flying resupply for the ARVN out at Cam Duc. It was shortly before noon. We were shooting an approach into the field when I heard a mayday call come across the radio. It was my good friend Ken Duncan, "Mayday, mayday, Cobra Seven's going down. We've been hit. Our coordinates are 24......north ...4....1......"

His radio was breaking up and mostly unreadable from our location. I knew that Duncan was out spraying the rice paddies along the Laotian border. Being on short final when his mayday call came in, I set down, and told the crew to quickly unload the supplies. I was in such a hurry to get headed towards Duncan's location, that I was pulling pitch before my crew had the last of the supplies unloaded from the bird. Once we got clear of the trees, I made a radio call to try to raise Duncan. "Cobra Seven, Cobra Two-Seven over. Cobra Seven, Cobra Two-Seven do you read me."

I keyed the intercom and told my copilot, "Johnson, I want you to look at our map and figure out a heading that will get us started towards Duncan's last known location."

I did a blanket call over our frequency to see if anyone else had gotten his coordinates. WO Snyder came up, "Cobra Two-Seven this is Cobra One-Six. We heard the call, but have been unable to make radio contact with Cobra Seven. We're headed towards the downed ship and estimate our arrival at seven minutes."

"Roger, Cobra One-Six, Did you copy his coordinates"

"Negative Two-Seven, his call was breaking up."

I was familiar with the general area where Duncan had been spraying because I had been spraying there earlier in the week. I picked up our estimated heading and headed in that direction, roughly calculating in my mind that we were about twelve minutes from his location. We could hear Snyder on the radio trying to make contact, but it was to no avail.

When Snyder arrived over the downed ship, he could

see a firefight taking place. He could tell that no one was in the ship. It was rolled over on its right side up against a dike with the aft section of the tail missing and the blades torn off. He made a couple of passes over the tree line where the fire was coming from with his gunners heating up their barrels, and then swung down alongside the downed bird to pick up the crew. The whole time Snyder was doing this, he was taking heavy fire. When he got his bird down alongside the crashed bird, to his shock and amazement only two crewmembers climbed aboard. They were Duncan's copilot Arnold and the gunner Terso. As they scurried on board his bird, they yelled for Snyder to get the hell out of there. The LZ was hot and he had no choice but to depart. I arrived on scene in time to observe Snyder's bird departing from the rice paddy.

Snyder gave control of the bird to his copilot then turned and drilled Arnold, "Where the hell's the rest of the crew?"

Arnold answered, "We were spraying across a rice paddy when suddenly we took a hit in our tail. I think it was from a RPG (rocket propelled grenade). We immediately lost our tail rotor and were both fighting to keep the bird flying. Duncan decided to try to put the bird down by doing a run on landing into the rice paddy."

Without the tail rotor on a helicopter to counter act the torque from the main rotor, the aircraft wants to spin in the opposite direction of the main rotor. It's called Newton's Third Law of Motion, "for every action there is an equal and opposite reaction." In the Huey at cruising speed, the vertical stabilizer normally allows you enough directional control to maneuver the bird to a more desirable landing area, but you have to be careful because as you lose your forward airspeed the streamline effect disappears and the aircraft will start to spin out of control. By executing a run on landing you can hopefully get the bird onto the ground at an airspeed high enough to keep marginal control of your yawing effect until on the ground.

Arnold continued, "The rice paddy was the only level land we could find and the bird was vibrating so badly, we were afraid of losing control. I agreed with Duncan and felt that we had no other choice. We had pretty good directional control coming into the field and got her down okay. We almost had her stopped when we hit the dike and the bird flipped over tearing the blades off."

By some miracle, they all survived the crash. They unbuckled themselves from their seats and crawled out from the mangled bird. Arnold thought he had broken his right arm as the bird flipped on its right side. Terso was thrown clear of the bird and was pretty bruised up. Initially after the crash, they weren't taking fire. Duncan wanted the crew to stay together but since he hadn't heard a reply on his mayday call, he wasn't sure if anyone would be coming to rescue them. He knew that Charlie would be coming after the downed bird and felt they had a better chance for survival if they got away from the ship. They had flown what he estimated was about a mile from where they took the hit to where they set down. Duncan said he figured they had about ten minutes before the enemy showed up. Duncan's crew chief Johnson agreed with him and wanted to get away from the downed ship, but Arnold and Terso felt they would rather take the chance of someone hearing the mayday call and rescuing them. Arnold said they spent about a minute deciding what to do. Duncan, being the AC, decided to give them their choice rather than order them to come with him. Arnold and Terso decided to stay with the ship. Duncan and Johnson decided to leave. Duncan grabbed one of the M60s and some ammo from the wrecked bird and headed west into the jungle, which was the direction away from where they figured the enemy would be coming. Terso grabbed the other M60 and a couple of ammo boxes and they set it up behind a rice dike and got ready to defend their position. Arnold said that Charlie showed up about eight minutes later. As Charlie came out of the tree line, they opened fire with the M60 forcing them back into the tree line. Thank goodness it was only a platoon of gooks and they had the M60. They had been in the fire-fight for about two minutes when they heard Snyder's Huey fly overhead and saw him dive down and do a couple of gun runs on the dinks (slang for the enemy). As Snyder shot his approach, they continued putting heavy fire into the tree line until they were able to make their run to the bird.

I was shocked when Snyder radioed that they had only recovered two of the downed crew. I flew down over the bird to get a good look, hoping to see some sign of Duncan and Johnson. During this low pass, we didn't draw any fire. I flew west of the rice paddy in the direction that Snyder had radioed us that he believed they had headed, but couldn't see any trace of them. We stayed on station as long as we could circling the area looking for any type of movement. Other than the open rice paddies, it was dense jungle and I knew that if they didn't come out into the open, we would never find them. As we flew above looking down over the jungle, I realized that it could take weeks to walk out of there. We radioed our battalion for some infantry support. It took almost two hours before we finally had some friendly troops inserted around the downed ship. The infantry secured the ship and our maintenance hauled it out, but the ground troops could find no sign of Duncan or John-son. They sent out a patrol in the direction in which they had entered the jungle but had no luck locating them.

By evening, I was devastated. Ken was my best friend. As I laid in my sleeping bag thinking about him being lost in that dense jungle, it haunted me. I kept asking myself, "Why Ken?" We had talked several times about what we would do if we were shot down. Would we stay with the ship? Would we hit the trail? Even though we talked about it, for some reason I never really believed that it would happen to us. That is what happened to other pilots, not Ken or I.

I could feel the war changing me emotionally. I was learning that to survive, I had to shove my feelings deep into my soul and not let them surface. I rationalized that there would always be time to think about it later. WO Ken Duncan and gunner Jim Johnson were listed as MIA. Unknown to me at the time, they would never be found!

Chapter 9

On the Ground

The following day, I was back in the seat flying. I learned quickly that you couldn't dwell on your loses or it would drive you crazy. You just continued forward, one day at a time. As the days passed, I noticed that the weather was starting to change. The temperatures were cooling down and the monsoon season was close at hand. When the monsoons finally arrived, the low cloud cover and constant rain forced us to change our flying tactics. We could no longer climb to altitude to get above the small arms fire. Low-level flying became our only avenue of transportation.

The weeks continued to slowly pass. Life in Vietnam was so different from life back home, that I felt as if I was living someone else's life rather than my own. I had gone from a seventeen-year-old high school graduate to a Huey aircraft commander in just over two years and felt as if I had lost my youth. I found myself missing the small things that I took for granted when I was home, like going to the Dairy Queen or stopping by McDonalds to get a few burgers. I promised myself, if I ever made it home that I would never again complain about being bored or having nothing to do.

It had been seven months since I had last seen a Caucasian woman, and I missed seeing and watching them. I didn't find the Vietnamese women very attractive and always said that the day that I did, I would know that it was time to go home.

The New Year started off just like the previous one. The war continued and we continued to fight it. There always seemed to be more flying than we could physically handle. We were getting fewer days down. I could feel it starting to wear on me both physically and emotionally. The more we flew, the more the guys drank. It seemed to be their only way to release stress. There was always someone going home and with their departure, new guys coming in. I tried not to think about going home and tried to stay focused on what I was doing. I found that thinking about home distracted me and the less I did it, the better off I was.

I was lying in my bunk one night almost asleep when I heard a bunch of gunshots. They sounded as if they were coming from just outside my hootch. I grabbed my pistol and headed for the door. Just then, I heard a bunch of screaming followed by a round of automatic weapons fire. As I flew out the door, Snyder yelled, "A couple of sappers have infiltrated our perimeter. We've killed one of them but the other one has ducked behind our hootch."

I could see that Snyder had an M16 rifle but the rest of us only had our pistols. We knew that being a sapper, he was carrying explosives and could quickly set up a booby trap for us, so we had to be careful. Three of us circled around our end of the hootch while the other guys went around the back.

We were staying low, trying to be cautious, when I saw a small, half naked man suddenly dash out in front of us. Seeing that he didn't have a rifle, I quickly jumped up and sprinted after him. He was about twenty feet ahead of me. I could make out Lt. Mason in my peripheral vision running right alongside. We were slowly gaining on him as we ran.

The sapper was stripped down, wearing only shorts and had a type of knapsack wrapped around his waist to carry his explosives. I was getting ready to dive for him when a load explosion went off to our left sending debris everywhere. Lt. Mason and I dove for cover. I yelled, "Mason, are you okay?"

"Yeah, where did that shit come from?"

"I don't know, but that was to close for comfort."

Somehow a third sapper had made it into our compound undiscovered and was setting off explosives. When the explosion went off, Snyder opened fire with his M16 on the sapper that we were chasing and shot him dead. As we were getting up, we heard more gunshots. Our perimeter guards located the third sapper trying to work his way back out of the perimeter and shot him. Mason and I walked over to the dead sapper. He looked so young. I would guess twenty at the most. As I stood there staring at his dead body, I really wished that we could have captured him alive. Everyone was excited from the action, but it was late and I was tired, so I walked back to our hootch and went back to bed.

I paused in my storytelling, sensing that Captain Donaldson wanted to question me more about what I had just told him. "Mr. Gray, what were your thoughts as you looked at the dead sapper's body?" Captain Donaldson asked."

"At the time, I felt as if I was being engulfed by death and that my whole life was spinning out of control. I thought about Ken and wondered if some gook had stared down at his dead body as I did at this soldier. I looked around at everyone else being all pumped up with excitement and wondered why I felt so different. If I could have, I think I would have ran away, but I knew there was no place to run to."

Colonel Donaldson probed deeper, "You said that you learned to shove your feelings deep into your soul. How have you handled those feelings since the war?"

"Well, I'm not so sure that I have? When I first got back from the war, I really had trouble sleeping. Late at night, I would go outside by myself in the back yard and cry, not understanding why. But then as the years passed, things got better."

"Mr. Gray, you realize that crying is a natural way of grieving for a lost friend and it is nothing to be ashamed of. I would be concerned for your mental health if you hadn't. I believe I've heard enough of your Vietnam experience to be able to establish an emotional and psychological baseline of your character. Listening to your adventures and how you convey them has given me a good insight into your psyche. Now I want you to explain how you met Com and what type of relationship you felt you had with her."

"Okay, let's see where I want to begin."

It had been a long hard year. I was beginning to see light at the end of the tunnel. With less than thirty days remaining in my tour, I was beginning to let myself think about going home. I was becoming what they call in the Army a "short timer". But even though I was getting short, I had heard stories of soldiers getting killed on their last mission, so I knew that I wasn't out of the woods yet.

Word came down from battalion that the Army was offering an early out program to the warrant officer pilots. This program had two options. The first option was to "reup," as it was called in the Army, and go indefinite. The second choice was to be discharged from the service upon arrival back in the States. I decided that I would take the second choice and leave the army when my tour ended. I had had enough of this man's Army. With Nixon's withdrawal of the troops from Vietnam, our operations were being affected immensely. As the old timers were going home, they weren't being replaced on a one to one ratio, so the aviation units were pulling the same amount of missions but with fewer pilots. It felt as if we were flying twenty-four hours a day. All we did was rotate between our sleeping bag and the cockpit.

One afternoon, I was flying in my aircraft with one of my favorite copilots, Lt. Rett. We didn't always fly our own aircraft because of the maintenance required on the helicopters. If your bird was down for repair, you would be assigned to fly someone else's bird who wasn't flying that day. I really preferred my own bird; I was familiar with her and knew exactly how much power she had and how she would perform in a given situation. Flying someone else's bird was like going out with a girl on your first date, versus going out with your girlfriend. On that first date, you never knew what was going to happen.

I had my regular crew chief Tim Growe and gunner Bob Grass crewing that day. They were both great guys, and I couldn't ask for a better crew. We called ourselves the G-machine because all three of our last names started with G. We were working out west of Cam Duc in the mountains, flying resupply, supporting infantry patrols. It was one of those clear blue-sky days. I was really enjoying the flying, executing high overhead approaches, down to the troops in the field. There had been a lot of enemy activity reported in the area but we hadn't taken any fire all day. It was around 1600 hrs when we located our unit and called for smoke. "Bravo platoon, Cobra Two Seven is inbound. Pop smoke."

"Roger Cobra Two Seven, red smoke is out."

The ground unit had done a no-no and called the color of the smoke. Looking down, I saw four different red smokes. Seeing this made me realize the extent of the enemy troops that were below us and confirmed that Charlie was monitoring our radio transmissions. It also made me realize how lucky we had been to have not taken any fire all day.

I radioed back, "Bravo platoon, Pop another smoke but

do not, I say again, do not call out the color of smoke."

"Roger Cobra Two Seven, sorry about that, smokes out."

We looked down and again saw four smokes, but this time I saw two yellows, one green, and one red. The green appeared the closest to where we had marked the unit's location on our map so I radioed, "Bravo platoon, we have a green smoke over."

"Roger Cobra Two Seven, we confirm a green smoke."

"Roger Bravo platoon, we're headed in."

We crossed over the LZ at fifteen hundred feet and did a high recon of the area. The LZ looked secure. Seeing that the soldiers had a good perimeter set up, I executed a high overhead approach to my left. Within seconds, we were rolling onto a short final. I flared the bird and pulled pitch. Bringing the bird to a hover, I carefully lowered her down into the LZ. My crew tossed off the ammo and C-rations as I talked to the sergeant through my side window. He yelled, "Thanks for bringing in the supplies. We've been making contact off and on for the last three days so be careful."

I yelled, "No problem, take care."

I turned and looked over my right shoulder and saw that the ship was empty. Pulling pitch, I pushed the cyclic forward. The light bird hit translational lift and started climbing towards the skies. We were two hundred feet above the ground when we started taking heavy fire. Keying my mike, I yelled, "Go hot."

I could feel the bird lurch, and then suddenly, as Growe was screaming, "We've been hit," the cyclic slammed into my left thigh as the helicopter rolled violently to the left. I heard someone yell, "Shit, there's transmission or hydraulic fluid blowing all over back here."

I yelled at Lt. Rett, "Get on the controls with me."

With the two of us fighting the cyclic, we were able to get it back where we could at least keep the ship from rolling into the ground. Our hydraulics were gone, but the ship was still flyable. We were taking heavy fire and both gunners were busy manning their M60s and returning it. I glanced back over my right shoulder and saw fluid leaking everywhere. As I turned back around, the turbine started to lose power. Glancing at the altimeter, I saw it read eight hundred feet. With the hydraulics gone we had no choice but to fly her straight in. We spotted a partially open field and decided to try to steer the damaged bird towards it. Our altitude was decreasing rapidly as Lt. Rett and I fought to keep control of the bird. Suddenly the engine quit. We slammed the collective down and tried to autorotate her into the field. At fifty feet, we tried to flare but the nose came up, then violently rolled to the left. We bounced into the rice paddy skidding across the field on the left side of the bird. We tried to hang on as she beat herself to pieces.

I don't know how long I was out, but when I awoke, Lt. Rett was pulling me from the wreckage. Once we were clear of the aircraft, I could see Growe walking around in a dazed condition. Grass had been thrown from the bird during the rollover and was laying about thirty yards from our location. I yelled at Growe, "Growe, Growe, get over there and check on Grass."

As I was yelling, Growe came to his senses and yelled, "Yes sir, sorry." and headed for Grass.

I was having a tough time breathing. My left side had been crushed and I could feel that several of my ribs were injured. I tried to stand but my left leg wouldn't support my weight. Looking down at my leg, I could see that it was bleeding. The outside of my pants leg, just above my left knee, was soaked in blood. My flight suit was ripped and there was a cut about four inches long across my thigh. "Curt, we need to get that bleeding stopped." Lt. Rett said as he took off his belt and applied a tourniquet to my thigh.

Growe rushed back to my side and said, "Mr. G., Bob is

dead!"

"Are you sure?"

"Yes, I think his neck is broken."

We had been so busy trying to control the chopper that we hadn't had a chance to make a mayday call. I yelled at Rett, "Try the radios. See if you can make a mayday call then destroy them. We have to get out of here fast."

I knew that no one else had been working in our immediate area, and after seeing all those smokes, I realized that Charlie would be upon us shortly. Rett scurried back inside the wrecked Huey but couldn't get the radios to work. He yelled, "Curt, they're dead."

"Okay, get out of there and let's go, be sure to grab the map and the medical kit."

Growe grabbed one of the M60s and some ammo. With my side crushed, I couldn't walk by myself. I threw my arm around Rett's shoulder and we hobbled out of the clearing and into the jungle.

I had never felt such pain in my life. My eyes were tearing up as we tried to put space between ourselves and the downed bird. We hobbled along for forty minutes before I decided that I couldn't go any further. I was having trouble breathing and was fading in and out of consciousness. As my eyes struggled to make out the jungle, all I could see were gray spots moving in and out. I had lost too much blood. My left pant leg was totally soaked with blood. The pain was too intense and I knew that if we were discovered, I would be like a sinking brick in water pulling Rett and Growe down with me. They would stand little chance of escaping.

After Duncan had gone down, I had played his scenario over and over in my head relentlessly, questioning if it had happened to me what I would do. I made my decision. I knew that I needed to stop the bleeding in my thigh or I wouldn't be able to remain conscious. To be able to do so, I would have to stop moving. I decided that we would all stand a better chance of survival if Rett and Growe left me and went for help. We stopped and crawled into some thick underbrush for cover. I explained my plan to them. They both disagreed and said that it was crazy to leave me. "Look," I said, "If I don't get medical attention soon, I'll die from loss of blood. You guys stand a better chance of making it to friendly forces without me. Working as a team, you can cover each other's back and I'll just sit tight and rest."

Lt. Rett responded, "We don't want to take the chance of losing you."

"You don't have to worry about losing my location, I'm not going anywhere. As long as I keep putting pressure on my leg, the bleeding stops. Lt. Rett, I want you to mark on the map where you think our present position is."

Growe and I watched as he drew a line between us and the coordinates where we made our last resupply then calculated a compass bearing. He figured our present position appeared to be about a mile and a quarter from the friendly unit. The only problem was it was rough terrain and full of gooks.

I had a canteen of water, a flashlight, and my forty-five. They wanted to leave the M60 with me, but I convinced them that it would be better for them to take it. With them moving, there would be a greater chance of them coming across the Vietcong than with me being stationary. I explained to them that it was more important that they made it back to safety, because without them making it, there would be no rescue for me. Also, if I didn't make it, they still stood a chance of survival.

"You guys need to get going. You still have a couple of hours before nightfall. Be careful and good luck."

I could still see the shock in their eyes from the crash and the death of Grass as we said our goodbyes. They quickly cut several branches and covered me and our trail. I felt exhausted and as I watched, I wondered if we would ever see each other again. I kept dozing in and out of consciousness and before I realized it, they were gone. By then, I was too tired to care and collapsed into a deep sleep.

A loud explosion jolted me from my sleep. I awoke in darkness and could see nothing as my eyes frantically searched for movement. It took me a moment to realize where I was. Looking down at my watch, it read 1948 hrs. I knew that Charlie had located the chopper by now and had probably blown it up. My leg had stopped bleeding, but my left side was killing me. I reached for the medical kit and searched through it for some pain medication. Even though they taught us in survival training that a man could live for thirty days with only water, my stomach was feeling hungry.

I never cared much for camping. When we were kids, my best friend and I once set up a tent in the woods north of our house and spent a night sleeping out. I didn't find it exciting and went home early the next morning. That was the extent of my camping experience before entering the service. Now that I was out in the jungle, by myself, I could feel this insecurity engulfing my senses. Laying there in the darkness, I listened to the sounds of the jungle, wondering if Lt. Rett and Growe had made it back to the friendlies. I knew and understood that even if they had made it, it was too dark to be rescued tonight, but hopefully by first light they would be on their way. My left side was constantly throbbing and I hoped that the painkillers would kick in soon. I pulled out my forty-five from its holster and held it in my right hand and eventually dozed off.

I was awakened by a dog, off in the distance, barking. When I opened my eyes, I was shocked to see a Vietnamese standing over me. At first, all I could make out was a silhouette in black pajama pants with a straw hat over its head. Then I saw my pistol in its hand. I must have dropped it in my sleep. "Oh shit," I thought to myself as I looked at the gook standing in the shadows staring at me. "What am I going to do now?"

My biggest fear since arriving in Vietnam was not of being killed, but being captured by the Vietcong then being tortured to death. We had two pilots who had been captured in our AO. The Vietcong paraded them through the villages at night in tiger cages for propaganda. Then after about a week, they tortured them to death. When we discovered their bodies, it was unthinkable what they had done to them. I promised myself right then; I would fight to my death rather than ever be captured.

I was soon to find out that what you think you will do and what you actually do in a given situation doesn't always match up. I thought about lunging at the gook but I was in no shape to put up a good fight. As these thoughts raced through my mind, I suddenly noticed that the gook had long black hair flowing down its neck. As my eyes focused in on the face, I realized that it was a Vietnamese girl. She appeared to be in her late teens or early twenties and stood about five foot four. I asked very slowly, "Do you speak English?"

To my surprise she answered, "Yes," and proceeded to ask me in broken English if I was from the downed bird that her villagers had discovered.

"Yes, I am." Then I looked her directly in the eyes and said, "I'm hurt. Can you please help me?"

My mind was racing with ideas on how to get my pistol back from her but she maintained her distance. I asked her, "How do you know English?"

She didn't answer and stood there in silence for the longest time. By the expression on her face, I could tell that she was in deep thought. I wondered if she was going to shoot me or turn me into the local VC.

When she finally spoke she said in broken English, "I not VC. I not turn you in. I help you." She handed my pistol back to me and said, "You stay here, be quiet. I be back." She then turned and ran off.

I yelled, "Wait a minute," but she disappeared into the jungle.

"Shit, Shit, Shit," I thought to myself. "What do I do now? If I try to move, I'll reopen my wound and I know I can't stand any more loss of blood. Also, if I move and my crew comes back to rescue me, they won't be able to locate my new position. If only I could have asked her a few more questions!"

Thank goodness she had given back my weapon. At least with my pistol, I didn't feel totally defenseless. Glancing at my watch, it was 0545 hrs. I realized I had to make a quick decision. During the night, my wound had scabbed over and had stopped bleeding. Deciding that it was best to try to move, I slowly lifted myself up on my right leg. When I tried to put some weight on my left, the pain was so excruciating that without some type of crutch the leg was useless. I carefully lowered myself back to the ground and looked around for a branch to use as a crutch. Seconds later, I heard voices. I quickly pulled myself back into my cover and grabbed my pistol. A patrol of Vietcong soldiers came walking down a trail about twenty yards behind my location. I lay there motionless, praying that they weren't coming to get me. I never realized how loud ones heartbeat was till that moment. Mine was so loud I was sure the enemy would hear it beating. Lying there, I counted eighteen VC as they passed by. To my astonishment, they never even paused. Maybe I could trust this girl, but was I willing to bet my life on it? Looking down at my leg, I saw that my wound had reopened and was bleeding. It would be best if I stayed put. Hopefully my crew had made it back to the ground unit and was on their way. I prayed that they would arrive before she did.

Minutes felt like hours as I lay there watching and waiting. I looked at my watch again expecting it to be close to noon but it was only 0710 hrs. A few minutes later, I heard people coming. I grabbed my pistol and got ready. As the voices got closer, I could see that it was the Vietnamese girl with a boy in his mid teens. Seeing that neither of them was armed, I felt relieved. As they got closer, the boy whispered, "Hello GI, hello."

I whispered back "Hello."

As they approached, the boy said, "Me Thong, This my sister Com. You okay?"

"No, not really."

I explained to them that during the crash I had crushed my left side. I showed them the cut in my leg. As we talked, Thong took some food that he had wrapped in a cloth and handed it to me. It was some type of biscuit. I hadn't eaten since noon yesterday and with all the excitement and stress in the last twenty hours I was hungry. Thanking him, I quickly ate it.

Thong explained, "You crashed into middle of VC stronghold. Not good. It not safe to bring you back to village. Our uncle big VC leader. He not like Americans. If he finds you, they kill you."

Hearing this didn't make me feel secure. I changed the subject and asked how he and Com spoke English. Com said that she worked as a hootch maid in Da Nang. She explained that she had learned English while working for the soldiers and had taught her brother. A couple of weeks ago her aunt had gotten ill and her mother asked her to come to the village and take care of her.

Looking at both of them, I could tell they were most likely French Vietnamese. Being Caucasian, I had never thought that the Vietnamese were an attractive looking people. Since Vietnam had been a French Colony, there were several Vietnamese that were part French. When you combined the two races, I thought it made handsome people. Com had fine features with long shiny, black hair. She appeared to be five foot four inches tall and had a slight built weighing no more than one hundred pounds. Thong appeared to be five foot six and weighed, at the most, one hundred and twenty pounds. He had a gaunt looking face but wore a big smile. As we sat there talking, I could tell that Thong was very curious about Americans.

Com looked at my opened wound and said that I had to get it closed or else I could lose my leg. We had been talking for about eight minutes when Com said, "It is not safe to stay here. If we find you, so can others. You only twenty meters from main trail between villages."

Com turned to Thong and said something in Vietnamese then he answered. They spoke back and forth but it was so fast and with my limited Vietnamese, I couldn't figure out what they were saying. I couldn't tell if they were arguing or not. Finally Com said, "We move you to safe place now. We fix leg."

"Com, can you get word to American soldiers to rescue me?"

"It too dangerous now. I go back to Da Nang in eight days. I get help then."

Listening to Com, I thought to myself, "Eight days is a long time to hide out without being discovered."

Chapter 10

Eight Days

Thong came over and helped me off the ground. He told me to wrap my left arm around his shoulder and use him as a crutch. I put my left arm around him and tried to walk. My ribs ached with every step and breath that I took. Com grabbed the medical kit and took it with her. I asked her, "Where are you taking me?"

"There's an old deserted village that you Americans attacked a few years ago. There's still a few hootches standing. In one of the hootches, there's a tunnel the VC use to use to hide weapons. It will be safe place for you to hide."

This village was located alongside a stream about a half-mile from our present position. Thong said that due to the numerous VC patrols in the area, we would have to stay off the main trail and be careful as we worked our way towards the abandoned village. As we slowly moved through the jungle, I kept hoping that we would come across a GI or ARVN patrol. Even though I flew over this area daily, I had never been down in it. It looked totally different than it did from above. I quickly got disoriented and had no idea where I was.

With every step that I took, I had to fight the urge to

scream. Earlier in the morning, I had loaded up on painkillers but they didn't appear to help. My wound had reopened and was bleeding excessively so we had to stop and tighten the belt around my leg. Up to now, I thought I was tough, but tears were rolling down my cheeks. I kept thinking to myself, "Will I make it?" Several times we stopped and took cover as villagers or enemy troops passed by. During the last forty minutes of our walk, I was so weak that Com had to help Thong carry me.

It was close to noon by the time we arrived at the village or should I say what was left of it. It was in shambles. Most of the hootches were gone, burned to the ground with the earth grown over. It didn't take long for the jungle to reclaim itself in Vietnam.

Thong and Com helped me into a partially standing hootch and laid me down. They were short of breath from carrying me, especially Com. Feeling exhausted, I pulled out my canteen and we shared a drink. As I sat there observing the hootch, I noticed that three sides of it were intact but part of the back and half the roof was missing. Inside the hootch, under a piece of old board, was the entrance to the tunnel. Com appeared nervous and after a few minutes said, "I go now, must get back and check on my aunt." She said something to Thong in Vietnamese and he nodded. She turned to me and said, "I be back later," and quickly left.

Seeing that my wound was filthy, I asked Thong, "Can you get me some water from the stream. I need to wash and clean my cut?"

"I try."

He got up and went off to scavenge through the grounds looking for a container to collect the water. I didn't want to give up what drinking water I had left in my canteen if I didn't have to.

While Thong was gone, I crawled over to the tunnel and

looked inside. It was larger than I expected. The entrance was a foot and a half across and tunneled down to a larger chamber that appeared to be six foot wide by five foot high and twenty feet in length. It would make a great hiding place. What concerned me was there was only one way out. I decided it would be best to stay above during the day and only go into the tunnel after dark or if someone passed by the village.

Within a few minutes, Thong reappeared carrying an old clay vase he had found and filled with water. By the big grin on his face, I could tell that he was proud of finding the vase. Not having any rags and having already used up the gauze from the medical kit, I removed my right boot and took off my sock. I soaked the sock in the vase while I unwrapped the bloodied dressing from the wound. The wound was swollen and dirty from the walking we had done, and I knew that I had to get the dirt out of the cut or infection would set in. I pulled the sock from the vase, wrung it out, and then carefully tried to clean my wound.

While I was cleaning the wound, I could feel the painkillers finally starting to take effect. Feeling light headed, I found it hard to stay focused on what I was doing. I picked up the gauze and searched for an area that had the least amount of blood. I took that part of the gauze, covered the wound and rewound the remaining gauze around my thigh to secure it in place. Now that the wound was clean, I needed to stop the bleeding. I carefully applied pressure to it. While working on my wound, I couldn't help but notice that Thong watched every move that I made with great interest. Being curious myself, after careful thought, I decided to ask, "Thong, Why aren't you VC?"

He laughed and said, "Me no fighter." He then told me that ever since he was a little kid, his sister had been taking him into Da Nang. When he was younger, the GIs gave him gum and candy. He said he liked Americans and one day hoped to go to America.

I asked him, "How old is your sister?"

"She twenty, me fourteen."

"Do you have any other brothers or sisters?"

"I had another sister. She seventeen but she and papa killed a couple years ago."

Hearing this, I decided it was best not to ask how and quickly changed the subject.

"Thong, is there any way you can contact the Americans who were patrolling in the area the other day?"

"No, it too dangerous for me to approach GIs in the field. When in field, Americans think all males are VC. I learn, whenever American patrols come close village, I go hide till they leave."

Listening to Thong, I realized and understood that he had seen too much violence in his life to risk taking the chance.

The grogginess from the painkillers was too much. I couldn't stay awake any longer. I crawled over into the corner of the hootch and fell asleep. When I awoke, the sun was disappearing over the trees. Thong was sitting next to me sound asleep. My thigh was throbbing, and I could feel a fever setting in. My flight suit was drenched in sweat. I grabbed the medical kit and searched for more painkillers.

Sitting there watching Thong sleep, I couldn't help but think how different his life was from mine. It had been only a few years since I was fourteen, but our life styles were so vastly different. Life wasn't fair. We had it so good back in the States but didn't realize it. I thought if all teenage Americans had a chance to catch a glimpse of a third world country, especially one torn with war, they would be more appreciative of what they had. My thoughts then returned to my crew and wondered if Rett and Growe had made it to safety and if so, did they send a patrol to rescue me?

It was close to dark when I saw a figure cross over the

stream and head towards us. I gently nudged Thong and whispered that someone was coming. He got up and went out to meet the advancer. Thank God it was Com. She had a large cloth sack strapped over her shoulder and was carrying in her right hand a small metal container hanging from small chains. It looked like an incense burner that a priest would use during a high mass. She took one look at me and said, "I afraid you get fever."

Com set the metal container down and pulled a lantern out of her shoulder sack. Since it was close to dark, she suggested that we go down into the tunnel where it would be safe to light the lantern. I grabbed my flashlight and crawled towards the entrance. Shaking uncontrollably, I tried to lower myself into the tunnel. What energy I had this morning was gone. I tried to stay on my back as I worked my way down the tunnel so I wouldn't dirty my wound. Once I was down in the main chamber, Com picked up the metal container and carefully crawled in, being careful not to spill the contents. Thong grabbed the cloth sack, pulled the cover over the opening and crawled in behind her.

As Com lit the lantern, I asked, "Did you have any trouble when you returned to your village?"

"No, but much talk among VC about trying to find helicopter crew. They know that one GI dead but not found no others."

Chills ran down my back as I listened. I had heard some shots earlier in the day and wondered if they had captured Rett and Growe. Com pulled some food out of her sack and set it along the wall. She pulled out a cloth that had something wrapped in it. As she unwrapped it, I was surprised to see that it was leaves and wondered why she would wrap leaves in a cloth.

Thong took some of the food and began to eat. I went to take a piece of bread when Com said, "No eat, not now, later."

I was surprised by her authoritarian tone and backed off. She had been so soft spoken up till now. She pulled a little bottle out of her sack and told me to drink it. When I pulled the cap off, it looked like green pea soup. I asked, "What is this stuff?"

"It medicine and you drink whole bottle," Com replied.

For some strange reason the thought occurred to me that it might be poison, so I decided I better ask her what she was planning on doing. She explained that she was going to seal my wound and that the drink would help ease the pain, and allow me to get some sleep. I asked her, "How are you going to seal the wound?"

"You ask too many questions. I busy and have to hurry. Coals in the container are cooling off."

Deciding that it wasn't poison, I took one final look at Com and Thong and downed the putrid drink.

Within minutes, I could feel the effect of the drink. My mind was fighting to stay alert. I tried to watch as Com took a knife and cut off my left pants leg above my wound and unwound the dressing. She pulled a tweezers out of her sack and set it next to the leaves already placed alongside my legs. She went over and picked up the metal container and brought it over and set it next to the leaves. She told Thong to get behind me and grab both my arms and pin them behind me. She said something to me, but I was too groggy to understand. Com picked up my canteen and poured what was left of the water over my wound then sat down on my knees. With my legs pinned, she took the tweezers and picked up a leaf and dropped it on the coals. Once the leaf was hot, she picked it up and placed it across the wound. I yelled and passed out. She took another leaf and did the same pressing it on top of the wound. Later she would explain to me that the heated leaves would cauterize and seal the wound preventing infection from forming.

When I awoke, my wound had what looked like mud

caked all over it. I felt weak, but my fever had broken. I had dry mouth and was thirsty. Wondering how long I had been out, I looked to see the time, but my watch was missing. The lantern was out and the cover to the tunnel was open. I whispered, "Anybody here?"

Within seconds, Thong's head popped into the entrance of the tunnel. He was smiling and asked, "How you feel?"

"I feel much better, but I sure could use a drink."

Thong crawled down into the tunnel carrying my canteen and some food. I knew that Com had used the last of my drinking water on my wound, but I didn't care if the water was contaminated or not. I took a quick drink. As I was drinking, Thong handed my watch back and said, "Since you sleeping, I not think you need it," then he laughed.

"Thong, how long was I asleep?"

"Two days."

At first I thought he was kidding, but as we talked, I realized that he was serious. "Thong, I'm starving. Do you have anything to eat?"

He dug into his cloth sack and handed me some bread that looked like French rolls.

Thong sat and visited while I ate. I asked him how his sister had learned to treat wounds like that. He explained that it was a tradition passed down through his family for hundreds of years. Even though he said it was no big deal, I thought differently. My leg was already feeling better.

"Have you heard anything about my crew?"

"I heard VC were hot on their trail Tuesday but crew lucky and joined up with ARVN patrol."

"What a relief!" I thought to myself then asked, "Have you heard or seen any helicopters in the last few days?"

Thong laughed and said, "Me see helicopters flying over every day."

It was late afternoon. We had crashed on Monday so I

reasoned that it was Thursday. As I sat there, I wondered what my company was doing to rescue me. After Rett and Growe's return, had they sent out a patrol yesterday to search my last known location? Had they put more troops out in the field? Without a map, I realized I had no way of returning to the position where I had last seen my crew. Besides, I was in no shape to do so. My side was still sore and it hurt when I twisted or expanded my chest. I hoped that my ribs were just bruised and not fractured or broken.

As we sat there talking, I learned all about Thong's family. They were from Quang Tri. Com had gone to school in Da Nang where she learned how to read and write. When she finished school, rather than return to Quang Tri, she got a job working for the Americans as a hootch maid. Thong had a little schooling in Quang Tri but after his father died, he stopped going and spent most of his time either with Com or out here with his aunt. He said he liked being out in the country rather than in the city and felt by staying out in the countryside, when he got older he could avoid having to join the Army. Com was here because their aunt had been sick with malaria and needed to be cared for. Thong said that his family was neither Vietcong nor on the side of the South Vietnamese government. They just wanted to be left alone. He said that his uncle on his mother's side was a big VC and hated the Americans, and that if he found out about me, I would be executed. Just then, we heard movement from above. Throng crawled up to the entrance as I grabbed my pistol. I could hear him talking in Vietnamese then I heard Com's voice. I relaxed as Thong crawled back down with a package in his hands. Right behind him was Com.

Com came over and kneeled down. She looked at my wound and said it looked good. She handed me the package that Thong was holding. I looked in and saw a shirt and pants. She said, "You need to get out of dirty flight suit."

"Thanks, I'll do it later."

"No, do it now," she ordered in a firm voice.

Realizing there was no modesty in Vietnamese families, I took off my Nomex flight suit and put on the clothes. I found myself liking Com's spunkiness. Com grabbed my sweaty, bloody flight suit and stuffed it in her bag and said that she would burn it. She also told me that she was still planning on returning to Da Nang on Monday. Once there, she would be able to get help by telling the officers where she worked about me and giving them my location. Hopefully they would send a chopper to my rescue. As I listened to Com, I thought, "Only ninety six hours and I'm out of here."

I thanked Com for all she had done and told her that I was already feeling better. She looked at me and smiled. The three of us sat and visited while I ate a little more. They asked me about my life back in the States. I told them all about home and how much I missed it. I tried to explain to them about winter and how we would get these big snowstorms back in Minnesota but I don't think they could grasp the concept of snow. I asked Com, "Do you have a husband or boyfriend?"

She giggled and said, "Me, no no."

Even though she was skinny, I found her quite attractive. Her skin was soft looking and her hands weren't callused. You could tell that she hadn't spent many hours out in the rice paddies like so many of the Vietnamese. I told her I thought she was pretty and hoped she found a nice guy. Hearing this, she blushed. I asked her how her aunt was doing. She said she had been worried about her when she first got here. Her aunt's fever had been so high that she had come close to dying but after a few days she got the fever to break and now she was getting better. Com then told me something that surprised me. "Thong stayed with you entire time you unconscious."

"How he could do that without someone from the village noticing that he was gone?" I asked.

"Who would notice him missing?"

She then explained that her aunt was sick in bed and no one really paid any attention to him. I thanked Thong for watching over me then asked why he would do that. He just smiled and shrugged his shoulders. Com said, "Wednesday afternoon, you running high fever and yelling in your sleep. Thong had to hold you down while I covered you with wet rags to help break your fever and keep you quiet."

As I listened to Com, I realized how fortunate I was that she had found me. I didn't know what more I could say but, "thank you."

It was after dark when Com and Thong left. Thong had wanted to stay but I was worried that his prolonged absence from the village might make someone suspicious. So, I talked him into leaving. Once they were gone, I crawled out of the tunnel and sneaked behind the hootch to relieve myself. It felt good to breathe the fresh night air. The tunnel's air was damp and earthy smelling. I was tempted at first to sleep above in the hootch, but my better sense told me to crawl back into the cave for the night.

I woke early and looked at my watch; it was 0558 hrs. My side was sore and sleeping on the ground didn't help. I decided to crawl up and get some fresh air. I wondered what time Thong or Com would arrive. I realized last night after they left that I felt safer with one of them with me. I knew that if any Vietcong showed up, they could possibly distract them from the tunnel, plus I enjoyed having their companionship.

Shortly after eight, Thong came walking across the stream. Upon seeing me, his face lit up with that big grin. I greeted him with a good morning and he handed me a cup of rice. I never cared much for rice but I was glad to have it and thanked him profusely. He told me there had been lot of activity in the village that morning so I shouldn't be surprised if I hear a lot of gunshots throughout the day. I thought "good," that means there must be friendly forces in the area. I decided that it would be best if I stayed above in case a friendly patrol came by our location. I definitely didn't want to miss an opportunity to get rescued!

It was close to eleven. Both of us were stretched out on the floor of the hootch lying on some thatch. I was dozing in and out when suddenly I heard voices. They sounded like they were right outside the hootch. I grabbed my pistol and cautiously crawled over to an opening in the hootch, being careful not to make any sound that would give us away. To my horror, I could see a patrol of Vietcong standing fifteen yards in front of the hootch. The patrol was gathered in a circle talking. I could see one soldier pointing upstream. I looked over at Thong. He was asleep. I gently nudged his foot and went shush as I covered my lip with my finger motioning for him to be quiet. I pointed to the soldiers out front. I knew Thong could understand what they were saying. He listened intently for about three minutes then motioned for me to stay down. He slowly crawled out the back of the hootch and worked his way approximately fifty yards upstream. From there, he came out of the brush and started walking down stream as if nothing was going on. He walked right up to the VC and started talking with them. Moments later, I could hear them laughing. I wondered what he was saying to them. They talked for about five minutes then the patrol headed upstream and he headed back towards his village. Once the patrol was out of sight, he reversed directions and came strolling back to me. I thought to myself, "What balls this kid has!"

Thong told me, "VC say a platoon of Americans maybe spotted in area. They wanted to know if me had seen them. I told them, I had run into Americans one mile upstream and they were lost. I told VC that Americans always lost and walk in circles all day. Since I know some of the soldiers, I knew they believe me."

"Aren't you worried they won't find any Americans and come back for you?"

Thong laughed and said, "There're always Americans wandering around this area. Sooner or later they will find some."

After the close call, I was anxious to get out of there. I figured that within a few more days, I would be in good enough shape to be able to walk without reopening my wound. I spent the remainder of the day with my eyes peeled, hoping to see some of our troops. Late in the day, I heard shooting off in the distance but no soldiers were ever sighted.

It was early evening, and Thong and I were sitting in the hootch talking. He told me that his sister had bought a little Honda scooter a few years ago that she used to travel between Da Nang and their village. As we were talking, I saw Com, through an opening in the wall, walking across the stream. She had a little sack hanging from her shoulder. Once she got across the stream, she looked in all directions to make sure that no one was following or watching her. Seeing that it was clear, she ran over to our hootch. I was glad to see her. As I said hi, she smiled and pulled some food out of her sack and handed it to me. She turned to Thong and told him that he needed to return to the village right away and spend some time with her aunt. She hadn't seen him for a couple of days and was asking about him. Com told her that he had been with some of his friends and was all right. Hearing this, Thong said he wanted to stay with me. Com then yelled at him in Vietnamese. I had no idea what she said, but when she finished yelling, he said he would go. I told Thong, "Go visit with your aunt for a few hours, then when you're finished, come back and spend the night."

I could tell by his smile that he thought it was a great idea. He said, "I be back later," then got up and left. After spending last night alone, I wanted the security of having someone with me who could act as a decoy if needed.

This was the first time that Com and I were alone. We talked as I finished eating. I told her that I had been trying to learn Vietnamese and knew some key phrases, but when I listened to her and her brother talk, I realized how little I knew. She said that during the next couple of days she would be willing to try to help me learn more. We spent the next hour reviewing what I had already learned. When I pronounced certain words, she would giggle saying, "No, no, no." Then she would pronounce it correctly having me repeat it several times.

While we were sitting there reviewing my Vietnamese, it started getting dark. We both knew that it would be unsafe to light the lantern above, so we crawled into the cave. Com said that she needed to check and redress my wound. I watched as she first took a wet cloth and carefully washed the top layer of mud from my thigh. After examining my wound for infection, she scraped some clay from the wall of the tunnel and mixed it with water and carefully applied it to my wound. It felt strange to be sitting in a cave with a Vietnamese girl who I had just met three days earlier. Watching as she cared for me, I wondered what she thought about Americans and the war. When she finished, she told me to stay still until the mud dried.

I told Com that I appreciated her help and would always be thankful to her. She crawled up along my right side and sat next to me. We sat there in silence for a few minutes. I was still weak and my left side throbbed. I looked at Com and realized that I was attracted to her. I knew that if I were back in the States, I would have asked her out. But this wasn't the States, and I knew there would be no dates. Just then, to my surprise, she asked, "You have wife or girlfriend?"

"No, there's no wife or girlfriend."

I explained that I had dated a girl for a while before joining the Army but it was nothing serious and we hadn't stayed in touch. I watched Com as I told her this. She didn't say a word, but when I finished, she leaned over and put her head on my shoulder. I slowly lifted my right arm and put it around her. It had been almost three years since I had last hugged a girl and had forgotten how good it felt.

Moments later, we heard footsteps above. I grabbed my pistol in time to watch the cover over the entrance pop open. Thank goodness it was Thong. I was surprised that he was back so soon. He was smiling as he crawled in and closed the cover behind him. He looked at me, then his sister, and started laughing. I asked him, "What are you laughing at?"

"Oh, nothing," he said as this big grin came over his face. He said something to Com in Vietnamese and she yelled back at him as he laughed.

We talked for a few minutes when Com said, "I need to get back to village before it to late."

I thanked her again for all her help and watched as she crawled out of the tunnel. I spent the next hour talking to Thong. I was feeling weak and tired from my injuries, and needed to get some sleep. Without a mattress, it was hard to get comfortable. I tossed and turned all night trying to find a position that didn't hurt my ribs.

It was after nine in the morning when I awoke. The entrance was open and light was shining in. I crawled upside and to my surprise found Com sitting there. She told me that she had come about six-thirty but knew that I needed my rest so she let me sleep. I asked her, "Where's Thong?"

"About hour ago we spotted a VC patrol coming down the stream. Throng went out and joined them. He wanted to distract them from coming close to village."

"Aren't you worried about Thong getting into trouble with the VC?"

"No, most of the local VC know Thong and like him. They're use to him hanging around and asking questions."

I eased myself down in the corner of the hootch being careful not to bump my leg or side. Com handed me a banana with some rice and bread. I asked her what she thought about the war. She said that even though her uncle was a big VC, she hated the communists. She told me that she had gone to a Catholic Missionary school and had converted. I was Catholic myself and surprised to hear that; so few of the Vietnamese were of the Catholic religion. In school, she studied how democracy and communism worked and said she didn't believe in communism or socialism. She told me she was smart enough to know that when she was out at her aunt's village she must keep her thoughts to herself. She explained that a booby trap set up by the VC had killed her father and sister a few years ago. I told her that I was sorry to hear that. The more we spoke, the more I realized how smart Com was. All the Vietnamese girls that I had previously met were hootch maids and had little formal education. I had always kidded with the guys that the day a Vietnamese girl started looking good to me would be the day for me to go home. I guess that day had come, for the more I got to know Com; the more I was attracted to her.

Around eleven Thong showed up. He said, "Yesterday, a couple of American patrols were spotted scouting around the location where we found you. Because of them, there be several VC patrols in area. It be best for us to keep our eyes open and you stay close to tunnel."

Hearing this, Com said, "I better get back to aunties or they might suspect that something is up."

I told her, "You be careful," and watched as she darted off across the stream.

Thong told me that several of the VC that he had been with were from his village, so he decided to spend the morning talking to them so they wouldn't suspect him of anything. We spent the afternoon talking quietly and staying close to the tunnel. Thong helped me practice my Vietnamese. After my Vietnamese lesson was over, I decided to teach him about American sports. I explained to him the games of baseball and football. Towards late afternoon, Thong caught me off guard when he asked, "Do you like Com?"

"Why do you ask that?"

"I can tell she like you. I hope you like her."

"Yah, I like you both very much."

Upon hearing that, he seemed content and smiled.

Around seven in the evening, Com showed up. She said her aunt was much better and for the first time since Com's arrival, she was up and walking around. Even though it was dark, it was such a beautiful night that we decided to stay above, I was tired of the damp smell of the tunnel. We sat on some thatch in the corner of the hootch with our backs against the wall. We spoke little and when we did, softly, knowing how voices carry in the night. Com was snuggled up on my right side and Thong sat kitty-cornered from us. It was so peaceful and pleasant that for once I wasn't worried about being rescued and felt as if this moment could last forever.

I knew that Thong liked me and didn't think he would mind, so I turned and kissed Com. As she kissed me back, I heard Thong whisper that he was going to crawl into the tunnel and get something to eat. As I held Com in my arms, I knew there was no future for us but it felt like the right thing to do. After about ten minutes, Thong popped his head out of the tunnel entrance and asked, "You finished?"

We looked at each other and laughed. We decided that it if we were going to be talking, it would be best for us to crawl down into the tunnel. Once we got down inside, Thong and Com started kidding each other in Vietnamese. I could pick up parts of the conversation and could tell it was about me. I told them both, that they had to talk slower and when I didn't understand a word; they would have to repeat it to me then explain what it meant. Before I knew it, it was close to 2200 hours and Com said she had to get back to the village to check on her aunt. She crawled over and gave me a hug and said she would see me tomorrow. I told her to be careful as she slid through the entrance into the darkness.

After Com left, Thong crawled over and sat close to me. He told me that he was glad that I liked his sister. As I listened to him speak, my mind was overflowing with feelings of confusion. I knew that I had been on an emotional roller coaster ride since being shot down. Both my body and mind had been beaten and were working hard to recover. I was seeing a different side to Vietnam that I would have never seen had I not been shot down. I really liked both of them and wondered how I could feel so close to them after having known them for such a short period of time. All through my life, I had lived for the future instead of the moment, where as Thong and Com seemed to live for the moment. Even though we had so many more material things back in the States, I wondered if we were not losing out on our daily lives by always working for tomorrow, rather than living for today.

Thong and I talked about his sister. I told him that I really like his sister's smarts and her spunkiness and independent attitude. As we talked, I could tell that he really looked up to her and wanted the best for her. I was both physically and emotionally drained, and Thong could tell. After about thirty minutes, he told me that he thought I should get some rest. He said that he would sleep above so that he wouldn't keep disturbing me with his many questions. I told him thanks, and went to sleep.

When I awoke, I was surprised to see Com lying next to me asleep. Checking my watch, it showed six thirty. I ran my hand over Com's soft hair and leaned over and kissed her on her check. She awoke and smiled. She said she had gotten up at five thirty and had wanted to see me before starting her day. Since I was asleep when she arrived, she decided to nap 'til I awoke. She said that she had some duties that she had to take care of for her aunt before returning to Da Nang, so she wouldn't be able to spend any time with me 'til late afternoon. I told her I understood. She gave me a big hug and kiss then said, "I have to hurry," then got up and left.

Thong was already up, so I crawled up and ate breakfast with him. I had realized a few days earlier that the chance of an American patrol coming by my location was slim to none. Com would be returning to Da Nang tomorrow, so I hopefully had only thirty hours 'til my rescue. Thong spent the day teaching me more Vietnamese and asking questions about America and my feelings about different subjects. I was amazed at how analytical some of his questions were and sometimes wondered if he was an adult in a boy's body. Shortly before noon, we had a torrential rainfall that lasted forty minutes then cleared as fast as it had come.

It was well after dark before Com arrived. I was looking forward to her visit and was worried and getting concerned that something had happened to her. She explained that she had been busy all day getting things in order before returning to Da Nang and had a hard time getting away from her aunt. Com said that she wanted to check and clean my wound one more time before she left. As she cleaned and redressed my wound, we talked about her trip back to Da Nang. She would be leaving early in the morning. I asked her how long it would take her to get to Da

Nang. She told me, that with her Honda, it would take about three and a half hours. I watched her carefully as she talked and cleaned my wound. Even though I wanted to be rescued, I found myself wishing I had more time to spend with her.

When she finished, she said she had something for me. She reached into her sack and pulled out a folded piece of paper and handed it to me. I was surprised as I unfolded the paper. Inside was a gold heart necklace and a small picture of her. The necklace had a big heart that was hollowed out in the center with a small one hanging inside it. I carefully took the necklace out of the paper and looked at it. Com crawled over and took the necklace and opened the clasp. She hung it around my neck then gave me a kiss. She said she always wanted to be in my heart. I thanked her and told her that I would always wear it. I took the photo and carefully tucked it in my wallet then gave her a big hug.

I had a little crucifix that I always wore around my neck. I took the crucifix off and placed one of my dog tags on the chain and placed it around Com's neck and tucked it inside her top. I told her, "The crucifix is a gift for you and the dog tag can be used to prove your story." I then instructed her, "I want you to go to the highest ranking officer that you work for. Explain to him what has happened. Be sure to draw the location of this village on his map. Tell him that I will plan on being extracted sometime early tomorrow afternoon. Also, tell him that I have done a visual recon of the area and there will be no problem getting a Huey in and out of my location. I feel that the best extraction is to use just one ship, a quick in and out. Have the pilot aim for the middle of the stream right across from the standing hootchs. I'll be ready."

The stream was the only area open enough to get a bird into, plus it was shallow enough that there would be no problem for me to reach the bird. I quizzed Com several times to make sure that she understood my directions. I had thought of writing a note for Com to give to the Americans but decided that it was too dangerous if someone was to stop and search her. I didn't want to put her in harm's way. I had her memorize my mother's maiden name and instructed her that if they didn't believe the story or thought I was already dead and it was a possible ambush; just have them verify my mother's maiden name. That would prove our relationship.

We spent the remainder of the evening visiting and before we knew it, it was time for Com to leave. I asked Thong, "Can you please give us a few minutes alone?"

He smiled and said, "Sure, I understand."

He took my flashlight and crawled out into the darkness. I took Com in my arms. We held each other tight. I didn't really know what to say or how to thank her for everything she had done. I told her that she had saved my life and I would always remember her and be grateful. I thanked her for the necklace and told her that I would treasure it forever. I gave her a kiss and noticed that she had a tear running down her check. After our kiss, we said goodbye. She quickly turned and crawled out of the tunnel knowing that we would never see each other again.

After Com left, Thong crawled back into the tunnel. I was feeling depressed and he could tell. We spent the remainder of the night quietly talking about what we wanted to do with the rest of our lives.

I didn't sleep much during the night. My side was sore and I was worried about Com making it safely back to Da Nang. It was close to five before I fell asleep. When I awoke, I was surprised to see that it was close to eleven. Thong was up above and had let me sleep. My first thoughts were about Com and wondered if she had made it safely to Da Nang. I knew that with my dog tag, the officer would believe her story and not think that she was setting them up for an ambush. I also knew that it would take time for them to contact my unit and verify that I had indeed been shot down. I wondered if my unit would send the rescue ship or it would come from the unit Com worked for.

I had some cold rice for lunch. My stomach was upset and I had diarrhea. Thong had been filling my canteen from the stream and who knew what kind of microscopic bugs were in the water. Even though I had only known Thong for a few days, I looked on him as a younger brother. I thanked him for everything that he had done. He just smiled with that big grin of his. I took off my watch and gave it to him. I knew since that first day after I awoke, that he liked it. He thanked me as he took the watch and put it around his wrist. I told him that if anyone asked him about it, just tell them that some stupid GI gave it to his sister hoping to get a little action out of her.

I explained to Thong, "I think it's best for your safety for you to be back in your village when the rescue bird comes."

"No, I want to stay and make sure you out okay."

"No, you've already done too much. I won't risk getting you into trouble."

We hugged each other and said goodbye. It was the first time since meeting Thong that I saw his smile disappear. He slowly walked out of the hootch with his head down and started crossing the stream. Half way across, he turned in my direction. He pointed to his watch on his left arm then thrust his arm up in the air with his fist closed and shook it like an Indian salute. I waved. A big smile came over his face. He turned and ran off. I was never to see him again.

Chapter 11

Rescued

A feeling of isolation and loneliness came over me as I watched Thong disappear into the jungle. I wondered if sending him away was the right choice. I knew it was the safest thing for Thong, but what if Com hadn't made it safely to Da Nang. Thong was a great decoy and if I was captured, he could translate and maybe save me from being executed on the spot. Thong told me that he would come back later in the day to make sure that I was gone. At least, I knew that if for some reason my rescue bird didn't make it, Thong could get me a fresh supply of food and I could start humping out in the morning.

It was close to 1400 hrs when I heard the familiar sound of whop, whop, whop, whop. The sound of the bird's rotor blades cutting through the air was music to my ears. I looked overhead and saw a team of Huey gunships with a single slick. The slick flew directly over the village and set up for a high overhead approach. My endorphins kicked in as I got up, crawled out of the hootch and headed for the stream. As the slick started his decent, I hobbled into the stream. Both my legs were splashing through the water as the bird completed his approach and pulled to a hover. The crew chief hopped out and gave me his hand. I lifted myself up onto the skid and into the chopper. Looking into the bird, I could see that our CO, Major Edwards was flying, Lt. Rett was his copilot. I gave them the thumbs up. Within seconds, we were out of the LZ. We didn't draw fire on the way out and if we had, our gunships were circling above ready to return it.

The crew chief handed me a spare helmet so we could talk. I strapped on the helmet and keyed the intercom, "It sure is great to see you guys." The whole crew greeted and welcomed me back. It sure felt great to see Lt. Rett again. He told me that when he heard that I was found, he rushed over to Major Edwards and pleaded with him to let him fly the extraction. Major Edwards said that he thought, under the circumstances, it was the proper thing to do and assigned him to the flight.

On our flight back, Major Edwards explained, "Monday when you went down, we weren't immediately aware of your situation since you didn't transmit a mayday call. The ground unit you were supporting didn't radio to headquarters until you didn't show up to resupply Bravo platoon. They needed to be resupplied before nightfall and were getting concerned when they hadn't heard from you and darkness was quickly approaching. When we received their radio call, we tried doing a radio check. It was at this point that we realized that you were missing. I assigned Cobra Two-Two to resupply Bravo platoon and ordered a team of gunships paired with a rescue ship to fly out to your last known location. By the time they arrived, it was getting dark and they were unable to locate your bird, and once darkness set in their efforts were fruitless."

He went on to explain that initially they figured the reason they didn't hear our mayday call was due to our low altitude and being in mountainous terrain. The following morning they located our destroyed bird and immediately inserted troops to search for us. They recovered Grass's body, but no one else was to be found. By late Tuesday afternoon, Lt. Rett and Growe had located some friendlies and were rescued. Upon receiving the coordinates of my location from Lt. Rett, Major Edwards sent a patrol to search the area. During their search, they came in heavy contact with the enemy and had no luck locating me. They formally had me listed as a MIA and by Friday had pretty much given up hope of finding me alive.

Major Edwards said he was surprised when a hootch maid showed up in Da Nang knowing my whereabouts. At first, they thought it was a trick until she showed them my dog tag and explained the situation to them. I asked Major Edwards to please make sure that she was rewarded for her efforts. He said he would take care of it.

They flew me to the Duc Pho hospital pad and dropped me off. Major Edwards said, "Someone from the company will be back later in the day to check on you, but right now we have a combat assault to attend to."

"Major Edwards, I just want to thank you again for pulling me out."

"No problem, we're just glad to have you back."

I was glad to be back in Duc Pho, but it was kind of scary that Duc Pho was starting to feel like home. They took me into the hospital where a doctor examined my wound and gave me a physical. The Doc said he was amazed at how good a job Com had done at closing and cauterizing my wound. He had never heard of using a heated leaf to seal a wound before and seemed dumbfounded by it. But after examining it, he decided to leave it as it was. He just cleaned the surface and re-bandaged it. They x-rayed my side and found that I had three fractured ribs. He wrapped my side and said I would have to spend the night there for observation and to make sure that everything else was okay. He gave me some antibiotics for my diarrhea and some pain medication to help with my ribs. It had been an exhausting day and a goodnight's sleep sounded pretty good, especially in a bed with clean sheets.

That night, our CO allowed several of the guys to come down from the unit to visit. It was good to see the guys. WO Snyder brought me my shaving kit and a clean flight suit. I hadn't shaved in over a week and was looking pretty scruffy. We sat around and talked. Lt. Rett explained what happened after they left me. Boy did he have a story to tell. "After leaving you, we made good time. We even thought we were going to make it back to the friendly troops by dark. We had covered over three quarters of the distance when we spotted some silhouettes while crossing an open rice paddy. It was getting dark, so it was hard to make out who they were. At first, we thought they were peasants until they opened fire on us, then we knew they were VC. We dropped down behind a rice dike and returned fire. We killed at least four of them, but were still pinned down when darkness came. Around ten o'clock, Charlie attacked again. We fought them off, and if we hadn't had the M60 we would have been toast. The second firefight lasted about thirty-five minutes. Then it got very quiet. Growe and I lay there against the rice dike wondering what to do next. I knew that we had to move or by daylight Charlie would bring in reinforcements and we would be goners. We decided to get down on our bellies, in the water of the rice patty, and slowly crawl away. We had to drag the M60 under the water as we went. Every time we came to a rice dike, we would slowly crawl over it and slide back into the water on the other side. Once we got to the tree line, we started making better time. We spent all night moving, and by the time the sun came up, we were a good distance from where we had been pinned down. Being up all night, we were exhausted, but realized that we had to keep moving. I lost our map while crawling through the water and after moving all night, we were lost. Luckily we still had a compass, so we decided to travel east, hoping that we would come across some friendly troops."

After walking for several hours they came across a trail that Lt. Rett recognized. He had resupplied this area often and knew it well. All they had to do was follow this trail. It would take them to LZ West. They were about a thousand meters from the fire support base when they saw some troops coming down the trail and took cover. As the troops got closer, they recognized them as ARVN troops and hailed them. At first, he thought the ARVN troops were going to open fire on them, because when they heard Lt. Rett yell, they all dropped to the ground and took a defensive stance. Once the ARVN realized that they were Americans, they greeted them and escorted them back to LZ West where they were picked up by one of our birds.

As we sat there talking, I couldn't help but think about Grass and wished that he had made it. He was a short timer with only six weeks left in country. I had spent a lot of time talking to Grass about what we were going to do when we got back stateside. He told me he had a girl back home and was going to propose to her when he got back. They had met in their senior year in high school and had been going together for over five years. He had shown me her picture often. She was a pretty girl and I always thought if I had a pretty girlfriend like her, I would show her off also. I really liked Grass and had always thought we would stay in touch after the war. Unfortunately, he hadn't been as lucky as the rest of us and now that wouldn't be possible.

With less than three weeks to go, I knew that the Army would be sending me home. I was glad that I was leaving, but I wished my last flight could have been under different circumstances. The following morning the doctor re-examined my wound and told me that there was nothing more they could do for my ribs. He issued me some pain medication, and then released me from the hospital. Major

Edwards sent his jeep to pick me up. It took me back to our company area where I would spend the day getting my paper work and belongings in order. I would have the night to say goodbye to all the guys and would ship out the next morning. That night, we had a little going away party at the O'club. I was still weak and tired from the experience so after saying my goodbyes to the guys, I went to bed.

Early the next morning, I caught a C-130 transport from Duc Pho down to Cam Ranh Bay. Within hours, I was onboard a Seaboard World 707 headed for McCord Air Force Base, Seattle, Washington. I couldn't believe that I was actually going home. Just a few days earlier, I was sleeping in a tunnel out in the jungles of Vietnam, and now I was sitting on this jetliner eating peanuts and drinking a cold Coke. I kept waiting for myself to wake up from my dream and find myself back in that damp tunnel, but when I heard the wheels squeak on landing at McCord, I knew that it was real. After exiting the aircraft, I caught a military bus that took us over to Fort Lewis, Washington, where I would spend the night. The following morning I would be discharged from the Army.

Chapter 12

Transformation

When I finished telling Captain Donaldson about my tour in Vietnam he said, "Let's break for lunch."

After lunch, he got right back to work probing my mind for more information. He asked several questions about my relationship with my wife Paula. I explained that I met her in 1974 and married her a year later. He asked, "Mr. Gray, do you considered yourself happily married?"

"Yes, I love Paula dearly."

I was a little surprised by his next question, "Have you ever cheated on her?"

"No, the thought of cheating on her has never crossed my mind." I went on to explain that we took our marriage vows seriously and had just finished celebrating our ninth wedding anniversary. Besides, with a three-year-old daughter plus Paula being pregnant, I had too much to lose.

After Captain Donaldson completed his questioning concerning my family, he said, "Mr. Gray, it's time to establish your new identity. We'll have to keep your first and last name the same, since that is how Com will remember you, but everything else will be changed."

He brought in a camera and took a photo to be used for

a new passport. They changed my middle name and assigned me a new social security number. My new passport would have a new address from a different state. After discussing with Captain Donaldson my knowledge of different cities and states, he decided to have me live in Birmingham, Alabama. I had flown corporate out of Birmingham in the 70's and had a good knowledge of the city and its suburbs. He felt that my familiarity with Birmingham would give me a good chance in convincing people that I lived there. He set my new identity up so there would be no traceable trail back to my real identity and family. This was done for the protection of both my family and the government if the mission failed and I was captured and held as a spy.

Captain Donaldson brought in a tape recorder and had me record several phone calls to my wife. He had the calls all scripted and I read them as he recorded. We made several phone recordings saying that I was fine and studying hard and that I loved them and missed them. Captain Donaldson explained that they would strategically place these phone calls to my house when they knew that no one would be home to answer the phone, allowing my answering machine to intercept the calls. Even though I would not actually be talking with Paula; just allowing her to hear my voice in the phone messages would give her the emotional security that everything was fine. He said he tried to plan for any changes or variables that might come up while I was gone. I would be allowed to call Paula for the last time late Tuesday afternoon right before I would board a plane to Thailand. I was instructed to tell her that school was hard but was going well. I was also instructed to tell her that I was in school through Thursday, and then I had a 48 (two days off) and then had classes again starting Sunday morning. Since I wanted to be sure that I did well in training, I decided to stay down in Dallas for my 48 and study, but would call her Saturday.

When I had started my training with Captain Donaldson, I was a married man with a three-year-old daughter and another in the hanger. When I finished with him, I was a single man with no living relatives. What a transformation!

For my cover story, Captain Donaldson set me up as a United Nations (UN) inspector overseeing the Red Cross relief in Phnom Penh. I would be there only to observe and inspect the Red Cross workers as they performed their relief mission. I would be flown to Bangkok, Thailand, where I would catch a Red Cross flight to Phnom Penh. The Red Cross workers would be expecting me. Once in Phnom Penh, I would be working on my own. I would spend the days observing the Red Cross team and have the evenings off to work on accomplishing my mission.

Once we had my new identity established, Captain Donaldson's next job was to teach me what he called "canned answers." These were answers to questions that he expected Com to ask me. He had worked them out himself and had an answer to just about any question that she could possibly ask, and now it was my job to memorize them. I spent the next two hours studying and memorizing them. When my time was up, Captain Donaldson started drilling me with his questions. We worked for the next two days on these questions. It was difficult, but I understood the importance of knowing the right answer when asked. He pushed me relentlessly, even yelling at me at times. At one point, I became so upset that I felt like knocking his head off. After two days of his continual questioning, I found myself starting to believe that my answers were the truth. During his questioning, he would insert, "Mr. Gray, do not trust anyone, especially Lee Thi Com."

Even though Captain Donaldson didn't know the exact details of my mission, he understood the importance of me being able to get Com to fall in love with me in the shortest possible time. He explained that the key to my success would be for me to use our past history from Vietnam and to expand and work off of it. He also stressed that Com had never married, and he felt that that was an asset.

Captain Donaldson taught me techniques in manipulation and told me how he felt would be the best way to romance her. He instructed me on how to analyze and read into Com's answers, and how to draw her feelings out from our past and make them more personal and loving than what they had really been. He told me, "Always remember that you are creating a fairytale love affair for Com, so work to find her emotional needs and fulfill them. Try to find out her dreams and become them. But always remember, this is Com's fantasy, not yours. You mustn't start to believe your own bullshit!"

Each session that I spent with Captain Donaldson was enlightening yet mind-boggling. I always left his sessions emotionally drained.

My next three days were spent busy in training and the nights were spent with Colonel Anderson at his personal residence. During my lunch break Tuesday; I was sitting in the briefing room by myself, eating a ham and cheese sandwich, when I came to the realization that since I had gotten on the plane early Sunday morning, there was no record of my existence. There were no airline tickets to be traced; there were no hotel rooms, no credit cards or check purchases. Come to think of it, I had never come in contact with anyone outside of the military. Even during my lunch and dinner, my instructors always brought my meals into my training sessions. I couldn't believe how my life had transformed itself in just three days.

Before I knew it, Tuesday afternoon arrived and my training was complete. The time had flown by. The training had been so intense that I hadn't really had a chance to think about my family. I received one final briefing from Captain Donaldson before I was allowed to call Paula. My phone call went as briefed. We talked for thirty minutes then it was time to go.

When I got off the phone, Colonel Anderson came in and spoke with me for several minutes. He said that even though he would be flying with me to Bangkok this would be the last time that we would be able to talk openly about the mission. He asked me how I felt. He wanted to know if I felt the training that I received was enough to get the mission accomplished. I told him that even though the training had been quick and intense, I felt that I was ready, given the time allowed, and would give it my best shot. He said that if there was anything that I thought I needed, now was the time to speak up, because once I walked out the door of the pentagon, that I, Curtis Gray of Minneapolis no longer existed in mind or body. It was my mission to immediately transform myself into my new role. I was to think, act and become my new identity.

General Mackie wanted to meet with me for one final briefing. Colonel Anderson escorted me to General Mackie's office where the general wished me luck and said that he would pray that I would have a safe trip. Upon completion of our meeting with General Mackie, Colonel Anderson and I left the pentagon in a military vehicle. We were driven to Andrews Air Force Base where an aircraft was standing by for our flight to Thailand.

Chapter 13

Cambodia Bound

It was shortly after 1900 hrs when our plane lifted off the runway at Andrews Air Force Base, destination Bangkok. There was a twelve-hour time zone difference between Washington and Bangkok. Even though it was Tuesday night when we left Washington, it would be close to midnight Wednesday by the time we landed in Bangkok. Due to the length of the flight, we would have to make a fuel stop. I would spend a short night in Bangkok then catch the Red Cross flight over to Phnom Penh in the morning.

The plane was stocked with several magazines and a current newspaper for our reading pleasure. I grabbed a magazine and sat back and tried to relax. Since I had been instructed not to talk about the mission after leaving the Pentagon, I had been pretty tight lipped. Once the aircraft leveled off at attitude, Colonel Anderson suggested, "Curt, why don't you go forward and visit the cockpit."

"That's sounds like a good idea."

As I got up from my seat to go forward, Colonel Anderson whispered, "Remember, UN worker."

When I entered the cockpit, it was already dark so there wasn't a whole lot to observe outside. Glancing at the altimeter, I could see we were cruising at an altitude of thirty seven thousand feet. I sat in the jump seat and visited with the crew. The captain was circumnavigating a towering cumulus cloud. I told him, "It's kind of late in the season for thunderstorms."

He laughed and responded, "Yeah, well tell the thunderstorm that."

Being a pilot, I always enjoyed learning about an aircraft that I wasn't familiar with and had never flown. But rather than being curious about this aircraft, I found myself wondering what lay ahead in the upcoming days.

We visited for forty minutes then I excused myself from the cockpit and went back into the cabin. I hadn't eaten since lunch and was starting to get hungry. Knowing that the aircraft had been catered with dinners, I asked Colonel Anderson, "Sir, would you like a bite to eat?"

"Yes, it's about that time."

I went to the galley, warmed two meals then loaded them along with drinks onto a tray and brought them back to our seats.

Since meeting Colonel Anderson, I hadn't had the chance to talk with him about anything other than the mission, and figured now was my opportunity to find out more about him. He already knew my entire life's story, yet I knew little of his. While eating dinner, I asked, "Colonel, did you ever serve in Vietnam?"

"Yes Curt, I did two tours. My first tour was from October 1966 through October 1967."

"Sir, what was your MOS (military occupational specialty)?"

"I was an infantry officer stationed down in the Delta. When I returned to the States, I decided to put in a request for military intelligence. Of course with my MOS change, I had to go back to school. After school, I was sent back to Nam for my second tour in January of 69 where I was based in the central highlands, as an intelligence officer."

He went on to explain, "During my second tour, I spent a considerable amount of time in the jungle. Our mission was to set up remote listening sites along the border. We would try to intercept and decode NVA radio transmissions."

"Did you ever spend any time in Laos?"

He laughed and said, "What do you think?"

I learned that Colonel Anderson was a West Point graduate. Most of the academy graduates that I had met during the years always wore those large rings, and tended to believe all the garbage they were fed in school about being a step above everyone else. Colonel Anderson was in that small percentage that didn't let it go to his head and, because of that, was a good soldier.

During our conversation, I told Colonel Anderson that I didn't like how the film and television industry had been portraying the Vietnam veteran since the end of the war. If you believed everything that you saw on TV and at the movies, you would think that every Vietnam vet was a drug crazed suicidal maniac. He said he couldn't agree more and started explaining the truths about several of the Vietnam myths that were now accepted as fact by the public. He explained that the myth about the average infantryman fighting in Vietnam being nineteen was incorrect. "Curt, the average age of the soldier in Vietnam was twenty-two. If you looked at the KIA reports, only 11,465 of the 58,148 KIAs were under twenty. I bet you didn't know that the average age of the warrant officers killed in Vietnam was 24.73 years old, and the average age of all the deaths, not counting the MIAs, was 23.11 years of age? This is a far cry from what most people believe and accept as the truth."

I mentioned the fact that some of my veteran friends, who had gone to the VFW clubs after the war, hadn't been accepted as true veterans by the veterans of WW II because Vietnam had never officially been declared a war. When Lt. Rett was told that by some WW II vets, he told them, "You may have fought in the big war, but I fought in the long war."

Colonel Anderson said that this type of mentality by some of the older vets really upset him. He told me, "That is another myth, that the fighting in Vietnam wasn't as intense as in World War II. It just doesn't stand up under scrutiny of the facts. Curt, of the 2.59 million Americans who served in Vietnam, 58,169 were killed. If you included the MIAs, and the 304,000 who were wounded, this makes one in every ten men who served a casualty. Even though this percentage is similar to past wars, did you know that the amputations and what they called permanent handicapped wounds were three hundred percent higher than in WW II?"

I was shocked when Colonel Anderson told me that close to seventy-five thousand Vietnam veterans were severely disabled. He went on to explain, "The average infantryman who fought in the South Pacific saw close to forty days of combat, which was spread over four years, where the average Vietnam infantryman saw close to two hundred and forty days of combat in one year. You can thank the air mobility for that. The helicopter allowed the infantrymen to be more efficient than in previous wars."

"Colonel Anderson, I keep hearing that there was a disproportionate amount of minorities that served in Vietnam, yet when I think back, I don't recall seeing that during my tour."

"Curt, again that is definitely untrue. If you look at the death statistics, 86% of the men who died in Vietnam were Caucasians, 12.5% were black and 1.2% were other races. The black casualty rate of 12.5% was proportional to the number of blacks in the US population during the time of the war."

Colonel Anderson told me that it was also a myth that the majority of the Vietnam soldiers were draftees and high school dropouts. The soldiers in Vietnam were the best educated soldiers that our nation had ever sent into battle up to that point in our history. I was surprised to hear that the more educated you were, the greater chance you stood of getting killed because the educated people tended to be pilots and infantry officers.

As we talked about the misconceptions of the war, I could tell that he had experienced many of the same emotions as I had since returning home. We talked about the anti-war movement and the protesters; how we understood what they were really protesting was not the war but the draft. It boiled down to the fact that they were afraid of being drafted. It was ridiculous to call it a peace movement because they were not concerned about peace but about being drafted. If it was indeed a peace movement, they would have continued to demonstrate after the Americans pulled out of Vietnam because the war continued until 1975. They would have demonstrated over the killings by the Khmer Rouge in Cambodia but they did not. Once the draft was canceled in 1972, the anti-war movement pretty much evaporated.

I told Colonel Anderson that after I got back from the war, I took some additional flight training to learn to fly fixwing and obtain my flight instructors licenses. One day, I was out at the airport and had just finished flying. I had my military flight jacket on and was getting ready to leave when some long hair hippie, who I had never seen before, walked up to me and asked, "Were you in Vietnam?'

I said, "Yes, I was."

I was astonished by the next words that came out of his mouth. He asked, "How many people did you kill?"

I couldn't believe that someone was that insensitive. Without even hesitating, I replied, "Seventy-Two," and stared right into his eyes. I could tell that it startled him. He quickly turned and left. I thought to myself, "What kind of asshole would ask a soldier who had just returned from war how many people he killed?"

Colonel Anderson laughed when I told him that one day Paula brought home a Jane Fonda exercise tape and I made her take it back. I told her that I wouldn't allow Fonda's tape to be played in my home after the treasonous escapade that she pulled. At first Paula didn't understand, as most people wouldn't, but after I explained exactly what Fonda did, I think she was actually shocked to think that someone would do such a thing while we had our own soldiers being held captive. She agreed to take the tape back.

We talked about this garbage documentary that had aired last year on TV called "Vietnam, A Television History." I told him how I watched all thirteen episodes and the more I watched, the madder I got. After the seventh episode, I called a friend of mine who had flown bird dogs over in Nam. I asked Larry if he had been watching the series and if the series was talking about the same war that we had fought in? Larry said he felt the same way as I did. That it was just a bunch of bullshit.

It really bothered us that a journalist and a film maker would get together and take their personal opinion of the war, then go out and seek only people who would reinforce their position, then try to pass it off as history. I was appalled when they spent fifteen minutes talking with a VC woman who claimed that she had been tortured by some Americans, yet spent about a minute breezing over the atrocities and the mass graves they found containing the bodies of men and women that the NVA had murdered during the TET Offensive in Hue.

The producers said they wanted to present a film with both perspectives, the Americans and the Vietnamese, but as I watched the film, I could tell that was a lie. I kept waiting for them to interview some AVRN soldiers for the South Vietnamese perspective, but they didn't. 223,748

ARVN died fighting for their cause and another 1,169,763 were wounded yet the filmmakers never bothered to interview one ARVN soldier or give the ARVN a chance to voice their side of the war. All they interviewed were NVA and Vietcong enemy soldiers or disillusioned American vets. Is that what you call an honest and accurate documentary? I was upset. I told Colonel Anderson that after watching that series, I take what I see on TV with a grain of salt. Of course, when I learned that the French had put up money to help back the film, I started to understand. I was glad when a group called Accuracy in Media (AIM) did a rebuttal, which aired on PBS called "Television's Vietnam: The Real Story" to correct the inaccuracies.

One thing that I learned while in the service was the importance of the gift of gab. With this gift, you could pass hours shooting the breeze. We had been discussing the war for quite a while, and I knew that it was getting late. When I looked at my watch, I wasn't surprised to see that it was close to midnight. Deciding that it was time to get some rest, we closed the window shades. I went and grabbed some blankets and pillows, then stretched out across three of the seats and went to sleep. I woke up a few hours later. I could tell by the silence of the engines that we weren't airborne, so I raised the window shade and looked out. We were sitting on what appeared to be an air force ramp, refueling. Colonel Anderson had left the plane. I was tired, so I went back to sleep. When I awoke again it was still dark. I looked at my watch. It read 0800 hrs, but I realized that I was still on Washington time. I had gotten a good night's rest and felt refreshed. Colonel Anderson was still asleep, so I pulled out the list of Vietnamese terms that he had handed me earlier and started to review them. My Vietnamese was pretty rusty. I sure hoped that Com remembered her English.

Thirty minutes later, I saw Colonel Anderson starting to

move about. "I don't know if I should wish you good morning or goodnight," I said.

He chuckled then got up and went to the rest room. When finished, he went forward to talk to the flight crew. He came back twenty minutes later and informed me, "Curt, we're two hours and forty minutes out of Bangkok. During our fuel stop, I brought some fresh food onboard and was wondering if you're ready for breakfast."

"That sounds good to me."

He went to the galley and brought back an assortment of fresh fruit and bakery goods.

While we were eating, Colonel Anderson briefed me that upon arriving in Bangkok we would clear customs then spend the night over at a local hotel. In the morning, I would report back to the airport by myself and check in for the Red Cross flight to Phnom Penh. He suggested that even though I had just woken up, I should try to get as much rest as possible in Bangkok because once I got up in the morning, I would have a full day's work ahead of me, and he wanted to make sure that I was as alert as possible.

We sat there killing time, anxious for our descent to begin. This wouldn't be my first trip to Bangkok. I had been there once before in the mid seventies after returning from the war. On that trip, I arrived late at night and caught a bus to go downtown to the Sheraton Hotel where I was staying. A young girl in her early twenties got on ahead of me and grabbed a seat. I remember watching her, wondering what a young girl was doing traveling in a third world country by herself, thinking that she was either brave or stupid or maybe a little bit of both. I also remembered being surprised when I saw the guards at the airport carrying automatic weapons. Seeing them had given me a feeling that I was back in a war zone and wondered if it would be the same this time.

I looked out the window of the aircraft as we begin our

descent into Bangkok. From the air, with all the buildings lit up, Bangkok was a pretty city. I wondered if Phnom Penh would look the same. After touching down, we cleared the runway, taxied over to a ramp where several Thailand Air Force aircraft were parked and shut down. A Thai officer came on board and greeted us. He seemed well acquainted with Colonel Anderson. They spoke for several minutes in Thai before asking to see my papers. I opened my briefcase and handed them to him. He skimmed over them and said, "Okay," and handed them back to me.

The Thai officer signaled for a car, which pulled up to the aircraft. The driver got out and loaded our luggage. We were driven over to the main terminal where we unloaded our luggage and took it over to their immigration and custom officials. Once we were clear of customs, we walked out front where the driver had relocated the car and climbed in. He drove us over to a small hotel, a short distance from the airport, where we would be spending the night. The driver talked to Colonel Anderson in Thai for a moment then drove off. We walked into the small lobby of the hotel and checked in. I observed that the clerk seemed to be acquainted with Colonel Anderson. We were given adjoining rooms down at the end of the hallway on the second floor. It was an old, rundown hotel probably built in the late thirties or early forties. There was one double bed in the room. There was no telephone or TV. In the bathroom, there was no bathtub, just a small water spigot hanging from the ceiling. Around this water spigot was a circular rod hanging down with a musty curtain attached to it. Below the curtain was a drain in the floor. There was a small sink and mirror off to the side of the commode. Seeing this, made me realize how much I had become spoiled over the years since returning from Vietnam.

I plopped down on the bed to relax. I was lying there staring at the ceiling when I heard a knock on my adjoining door. I got up and went over and opened it. Behind the door stood Colonel Anderson, "Do you have a minute?"

"Sure, come on in."

"Curt, I think it would be best if we keep the adjoining door open for the night. The reason I'm here is to make sure that you get on the plane tomorrow without any difficulties." As he said this, I wondered why there would be any difficulties, but decided it was best not to ask. He continued, "I suggest that you get up at 0700 tomorrow. This will allow you enough time to shower, shave and eat breakfast. I realize that with the jet lag, you will be up most the night."

He handed me a brown paper bag that contained breakfast and told me that I was to eat it in my room.

"I expect you to go downstairs tomorrow morning, by yourself, at 7:45 sharp, and check out of the room. The room has already been paid for, so basically you're just turning in the key. The driver from this evening will be waiting for you outside the lobby of the hotel. When you leave the lobby, I want you to walk directly over to the car and get in. If any other cab drivers try to get your attention, just ignore them. If the driver asks you any personal questions on the way to the airport, I want you to stick to your cover story. He'll take you to the airport and drop you off in front of immigration and customs. Once you're through customs, I want you to go into the terminal and look for a Red Cross employee. He'll be wearing a Red Cross nametag. He's expecting you."

"Does he speak English?"

"Yes, he does. Now, once you locate him, I want you to go up and introduce yourself as Mr. Gray with the UN. He'll then escort you out to their aircraft. Your flight is scheduled to leave at 1000 hrs. Do you have any questions?"

"No, I think I understand."

"I will be at the hotel in the morning to wish you luck but once you leave your room, I won't see you again until you return from Cambodia."

Colonel Anderson handed me some Thai money and told me how much to tip the driver. He gave me some Cambodian money and a credit card with my name on it. The credit card was only to be used in case something happened where I would need more money than what I had on hand. He reminded me that my hotel room in Phnom Penh was billed to the Red Cross and warned me to not let them con me into paying the bill. He explained that the average Cambodian thinks all Americans are wealthy and will try to take advantage of them. He also reminded me of what Major Stevenson had taught me about pickpockets, that there were hundreds, so be careful and always on guard. It was important that I didn't lose my papers or passport. We talked a little longer then decided to try to get some rest.

It was close to three in the morning when I finally drifted off into dreamland. The next thing I knew, Colonel Anderson was standing at the adjoining door. "Good morning Curt, it's time to get up."

"Good morning." I replied as I sat up and looked at my watch. It was 0700 hrs. Colonel Anderson was already dressed. I got up, shaved then got dressed and had a quick breakfast.

Before I knew it, it was time to begin my mission. Colonel Anderson wished me luck and said he would see me next Tuesday. We shook hands. As I left the room, I had a strange feeling that I would never see Colonel Anderson again. I walked down to the lobby, turned in my key then walked outside into the sunlight. Looking in both directions, I spotted the driver leaning against the front fender of his car. He was parked down the street to my right. When he saw me, he rushed over, grabbed my suitcase and greeted me. He spoke little English, so I didn't have to worry about conversation on the way to the airport.

I had no problem going through immigration, customs and locating the Red Cross worker. He introduced himself as Allen Green and said he was from Buffalo, New York. Mr. Green appeared to be five foot nine and weighed no more than a hundred and fifty pounds. I estimated his age as being forty-five years old. He was balding on top with his hair cropped tight around his ears. He informed me that he would be flying with me to Phnom Penh. Being the director in charge of the Cambodian relief, he wanted to make sure that I had a chance to see and understand exactly what they were trying to accomplish. As we talked, he indicated that he had expected someone older than me. Upon hearing this, I decided it would be best if I took control of the conversation and instead of having him ask me questions, I would do the asking and let him do the answering. I had been taught well by Captain Donaldson and knew exactly what to ask.

We walked out to the plane and got onboard. It was a medium size cargo plane loaded with food and supplies. I kept Mr. Green busy explaining every facet of his operation as we flew to Phnom Penh. When we landed at Phnom Penh, Mr. Green escorted me over to the communist officials where he explained who I was, and what I was doing there. They checked my paperwork then issued me an official looking piece of paper. What this paper authorized, I had no idea, since I couldn't read Khmer. Mr. Green spoke the country's language well, and within a few minutes I had all my papers in order and we were finished. By the time we returned to the plane, it was completely unloaded. Mr. Green instructed me to ride with the truck over to the orphanage where they would be dropping off the supplies. There, I would find the Red Cross team that I would be working with and observing. He explained that the team had a Cambodian driver who was responsible for taking them around to the different locations where they worked. He would be able to take me over to my hotel. I asked Mr. Green, "Will you be coming with me?"

"No, my office is in Bangkok and I will be returning with the plane. You be careful to keep a low profile, and make sure you always carry your papers with you. If for any reason the communist officials stop you, just show them your papers. That should take care of any problems."

I shook Mr. Green's hand and told him that I liked what I had observed so far and thanked him for his help.

It was close to noon when I climbed into the right seat of the supply truck. I could tell this truck had seen better days. Its body was dented and scratched, and it had a big crack across the center of its windshield. It looked as if someone had tried to throw a rock through it. I just hoped that it would get us to our destination.

The truck didn't have air conditioning and the temperature already registered in the low nineties. I could already feel the sweat running down my back as we drove off. The driver spoke little English, so I just sat back and took in the sights. The streets were full of bicycles and scooters. The city reminded me of the larger cities that I had seen while in Vietnam. Looking around, I could see a lot of damage caused by the war. As we got into the main part of the city, most of the buildings were intact even though they appeared old and dilapidated.

It took us thirty-five minutes to get from the airport to the orphanage. As the driver pulled into a small courtyard, several kids ran out to greet us. They seemed happy to see the truck. Most of the boys were wearing shorts but no shirts and the girls weren't dressed much better. Looking at the kids, I could see right away that several of them suffered from malnutrition. Their stomachs were swollen and their hair had turned red from lack of proper nutrition. Many of them had ringworm and open cuts on their bodies.

When I climbed out of the truck, several of the kids ran

over and greeted me. I liked kids and was happy to see them. As the kids surrounded me, I heard a voice from behind say, "I see that you've found some new friends."

I turned to see a young Caucasian woman in her late twenties. She wore khaki shorts and a blouse. Her hair was pulled back in a ponytail. "Yes, I have. Hi. I'm Curt."

"Well hello, I'm Nancy."

I went over and shook her hand. As we chatted, I grabbed my luggage. She escorted me into the orphanage where the other two team members were busy feeding babies. Scanning across the room, I could see at least forty babies lying there. Several were crying. Since the other two team members had their hands full, I went over and introduced myself to them. Their names were Jean and Jack Johnston, a husband and wife team from Des Moines, Iowa. Hearing that they were from Iowa, I almost blew my cover and said that I was from Minnesota. But in the nick of time, I caught myself and said I was from Birmingham, Alabama. Jack said, "Curt, You sure don't sound like you're from Alabama."

I responded. "When I went in the service, I learned very quickly that it was better to talk without an accent. Those drill sergeants liked to pick on the guys with the heavy accents."

He laughed and said, "Do you want to help feed the babies?"

I said, "Sure," and within seconds I was holding a little Cambodian baby in my lap with a bottle in my hand.

While feeding the babies, I briefed them on what I was trying to accomplish for the UN. I told them to carry on as normal and if I had any questions, I wouldn't be shy about asking them. We spent the next hour and a half feeding the babies. During this time, I learned what they were trying to accomplish in this war torn country and was impressed by their dedication. When we finished feeding the babies, I looked down at my watch. I couldn't believe it was already 1352 hrs. Anxious to get to the hotel and scout out where I would try to meet Com, I decided to leave. I briefly explained to the team members that I had been up most of the night and was ready to go to the hotel. Nancy said that their driver would take me over to where I would be staying. We set up a time to meet in the morning. I told the team members that I enjoyed meeting them and looked forward to working with them. The driver then drove me to my hotel.

Chapter 14

A Blown Opportunity

I positioned myself facing north at a little street café in the city of Phnom Penh. The café had five tables setup between the storefront and the side walk. The tables had umbrellas and were decorated with table clothes. I took the table closest to the sidewalk that allowed a clear view of the street. From this position, I could look up the street and see the front of General Samrin's headquarters. In my briefing, I had been instructed that Lee Thi Com left work at approximately 1800 hrs every Monday through Saturday. It was customary for her to walk down this street as she headed home for the evening.

As I sat down, I looked at my watch. It was only 1720 hrs. I had come early to make sure that I would be able to get a table situated close to the street where I would be visible to Com as she walked home. Also, I was extremely antsy and felt that some fresh air would do me some good. When the waitress brought the menu, I had a hard time figuring out what was what and ended up ordering some type of stuffed sausage roll. Having never learned to drink coffee, I ordered a Coke. Thank goodness for Coke, you can buy it everywhere and as long as it's bottled, it should be safe to drink. The last thing I needed to do was catch what they call in Mexico "Montezuma's revenge." I'm not sure what they called it in Cambodia, but I definitely didn't want it. There was enough to worry about without adding a case of the trots.

I thought to myself, as I wiped the sweat that was dripping from my brow, "This weather sure is different from the October weather in Minnesota." When I had left the hotel twenty minutes earlier, the temperature was 93 degrees, but as I sat there, I realized that it was as much the excitement as the high humidity that was causing me to sweat.

Sitting at the little café table, with its red and white checkerboard tablecloths, several thoughts kept running through my mind as I watched the minutes slowly tick by. First, would Com even recognize me? It had been almost 14 years since I had last seen her, and we had both been so young. Secondly, if she did recognize me, would I be able to convince her that this was an accidental meeting, and that I had no idea she was in Cambodia.

Finally after what seemed like hours, the hands on my watch indicated 1800 hrs. I immediately glanced down the street focusing my eyes intently on the front door of the United Front for National Salvation of Kampuchea headquarters building. Moments later I saw the door open and watched as several figures came out. They gathered momentarily in a small group, as if they were visiting with each other, then they dispersed. I could make out what appeared to be a young lady walking in my direction. My heart began to pound faster and faster as if it was keeping tempo with each step that this young lady took towards me. She crossed over to my side of the street and headed right towards me. I was anxious and could feel my palms starting to sweat.

Looking at her, I couldn't make out for sure if it was Com. I told myself, this is it. I am ready. This is what I had been sent here to do. As each step brought her closer and closer, my eyes searched her figure for some type of familiarity. Finally after what felt like eternity, I caught my first good glimpse of her face. Yes, it was Com but not the Com that I had remembered. Instead of being this young twenty year old girl that I had known, in her place walked a beautiful and mature woman. I instantly felt my stomach tighten as my heart rate exploded. My heart was pounding so rapidly and loudly that I instinctively looked around to see if anyone else at the café could hear it. Suddenly, I felt as if I was fifteen again. You know, the way you felt when you were trying to get up the nerve to ask that special girl out on your first date. Much to my surprise, as Com approached closer to me, I quickly turned and shielded my face so that she wouldn't see me as she walked by.

Why I reacted this way, I don't know. I hadn't expected this kind of reaction from myself and was totally surprised and caught off guard by it. My mind jumped from one thought to another, trying to decide what to do or say, but my body just sat there motionless. Then within seconds, it was too late. Com walked right past and continued down the street. I watched as she turned the corner and disappeared out of sight.

Realizing that I had just blown my chance to make contact with Com, I sprang from my chair, quickly paid my bill then ran down to the corner. Turning the corner, I scanned up and down the street, but she was nowhere in sight. I had really blown it. How could I have acted so childishly? How would I explain my actions to Colonel Anderson? I knew that time was crucial to the accomplishment of my mission, and I had just wasted my first day! I looked back down the street towards the café wondering if I had drawn attention to myself. Everything appeared normal, so I turned and headed towards my hotel. I would have to wait till tomorrow evening to try again.

Walking back to my hotel, I tried to analyze my surprised reaction to seeing Com. What was it that had caused me to react the way that I did? Could it be the moral implication of what I might have to do that scared me? I didn't know, but I would have twenty-four hours to think about it.

I pushed open the door to my hotel room and slowly walked in. The room was hot. The warm air felt stifling to my lungs with each breath that I took. I flung myself down on the old lumpy mattress. The ceiling fan was clanking as it did its slow rotation above my head. I laid there on my back staring up at the ceiling fan rotating, not unlike the rotation of a helicopter rotor blade, the type that had hung over my head during my tour in Vietnam. Slowly my mind wandered off into nothingness.

I awoke to a distant explosion off somewhere to the east of town. The ceiling fan was still clanking as it rotated overhead. I looked down at my watch. It was 0720 hrs. I had slept the whole night away. I promised myself that I wouldn't make the same childish mistake tonight as I had last night. Even though I had been caught off guard by my initial sighting of Com, I now knew what to expect, and I knew what I would have to do. My mind felt much clearer and calmer after my good night's rest. Our men's lives depended on me. I would not; I could not let them down.

Friday morning was spent observing the three members of the Red Cross team as they went about their duties. As we traveled through Phnom Penh, I tried to make myself as familiar with the surrounding streets and alleys as best I could. The more familiar I was with the surrounding area, the safer I would be if I had to make a quick escape. I was enjoying working with Nancy, Jack, and Jean. They were hard working, dedicated people and quickly earned my respect. Nancy spoke Khmer and would translate for Jack and Jean when necessary. The morning went by quickly and before I knew it we were eating lunch.

After lunch Nancy asked, "I need to do a quick inventory of supplies at one of our hospitals on the western edge of town. Do you wanna go with?"

"Sure, I would be glad to."

"Great, Let me tell Jack and Jean then we'll get going."

She went over and told them her plans then went looking for her driver. I walked over and got into the car. The car had two big Red Cross decals, one on each side, to identify it. Nancy sat in the front passenger seat and I sat in the back on the right side. "Nancy, how far a drive is it?" I asked.

"It's an 18 mile drive, and usually takes about twenty five minutes depending on traffic."

"Good, you can be my tour guide if you don't mind."

"Sure, no problem."

Our route took us right through the center of Phnom Penh. It was enjoyable talking with Nancy. She was a very interesting woman and besides, with her knowledge of the city, she made a great guide. She told me she went to medical school to become a nurse practitioner, but after graduation, decided to take a year off to travel and see the world. During her travels, she ran across two nurses who were doing mission work down in Haiti. They started talking and the ladies invited her to go out with them for the evening. During dinner, they told her how much personal enjoyment and satisfaction they were receiving by doing what they called "giving back" to the poor. Nancy said her chance meeting with these ladies would change her life forever. When she finished her year of traveling, she went back home and started working in one of the major hospitals in her hometown. She said she enjoyed the work but couldn't stop thinking about what the nurses had told her. To make a long story short, she quit her high paying hospital job and volunteered to work with the Red Cross and here she was five years later. I could tell as I listen to Nancy's story that she was dedicated to her new mission in life.

Riding through the city streets, I was getting a chance to see the city and at the same time learn about it from Nancy. As we entered the western outskirts of the city, the traffic slowed. Looking up the street, I could see two army vehicles partially blocking the road. The vehicles were parked at an angle, one on each side of the road forming a roadblock. Several Vietnamese soldiers were standing alongside them. The soldiers were stopping and questioning the occupants of each vehicle as they approached the roadblock. Most of the vehicles were turning around and heading back into town.

"Nancy, what do you think is going on?"

"Don't worry. We run into these roadblocks all the time."

When we got up to the roadblock, the Captain in charge came over to Nancy's window. He addressed her in Khmer so I had no idea what they were saying. I felt like a little child sitting there not understanding what was being said. When they finished speaking, Nancy had the driver pull over to the side of the road. She turned to me and said, "The Captain said there was some enemy activity about a mile down the road earlier in the day. He said they killed a couple of Khmer but he couldn't guarantee that the road would be safe to travel. I explained to him that we were with the Red Cross and told him that it was very important that we get to the hospital today to inventory their supplies. He said the decision to go or not was up to us."

"Is it that important that we get there today?" I questioned.

"I need to get an order in for their supplies before we leave Monday or they could run out of basic necessities like bandages, disinfectants, penicillin and so on. A lot of people could suffer if they run short of these supplies."

"Can't you rely on previous inventories checks and estimate your order?"

"I guess I can if I have to but I would prefer not to have to do it that way."

While we were discussing our options, the captain walked back over to Nancy's window and spoke to her. He told her that if we could wait about ten minutes he could have a few of his men escort us through the trouble spot. I could see a sigh of relief in Nancy's expression as she accepted his offer.

A few minutes later a jeep pulled up with three soldiers. The captain halted the line of vehicles and flagged our driver to follow his men. Our driver pulled in behind the jeep then slowly drove through the roadblock. I should have felt secure having the armed soldiers escorting us but for some strange reason I felt like a sitting duck.

We proceeded approximately nine blocks when the road made a tight sixty-degree turn to the right. As we came around the turn, I heard gunshots. The jeep in front of us veered to the right and crashed into a parked vehicle. Our driver observing this panicked and floored the gas. Our car spun out of control as we went around the turn. Before the driver could get the car back under control, our front wheel hit the curb flipping us over into a ditch located along the right side of the road. I yelled, "Nancy are you okay?" as I crawled out of the back seat. I could smell gas.

"Yeah, I think so."

"We got to get out of here quick, she might blow."

"I can't get the door open. It won't open. Oh my God, I can't get out. Help me. Help me. It won't open," Nancy screamed.

Hearing Nancy scream sent chills down my spine. It reminded me of a radio call I had heard while in Vietnam. We were flying up by the DMZ when we heard a mayday call coming from a pilot. He had been flying over North Vietnam when he was shot down and forced to eject. Unlike most mayday calls I had heard during my tour, this pilot was screaming hysterically over his survival radio. Unfortunately, all we could do was listen and relay his information because we weren't allowed to fly into North Vietnam. I remember feeling so helpless listening to him knowing that we couldn't rescue him.

At least this time I could help. I yelled at Nancy, "Don't worry, we'll get you out."

Looking across the vehicle, I saw our driver make it out unharmed. He quickly decided not to help and took off. The gunfire continued as I struggled to get Nancy out of the car. Her door was too smashed to open. The roof was crushed so she couldn't get to one of the other doors. I yelled, "Nancy, cover your face, I'm going to kick the window out."

Her window was already shattered, so I took my foot and started kicking it. After three kicks it gave way and crushed in. "Come on. Come on," I yelled, as I reached in and pulled her through the window. I was afraid the car was going to blow. Nancy was screaming hysterically. I pulled her quickly away from the car then to the ground. I rolled on top of her and hugged her close to me. "Relax. Relax. We're going to be okay. We need to crawl over to the soldiers. I know you feel like running but don't. Take a deep breath and relax. When I let go of you, don't get up and run. We need to stay low and crawl. Do you understand?"

"Yes, I think so, but I'm scared."

"That's okay, so am I, but we're going to get out of here. Okay."

"Okay."

I slowly released my arms from around her body making sure that she wouldn't jump up and takeoff. When I was sure that she wasn't going to make a run for it, I released her body and took her by the hand. "Okay, let's go."

Staying down low, we crawled over to where the soldiers were. One was shot in the arm. The other two were busy returning fire. Nancy, seeing the wounded soldier emotionally snapped back to her old self. She crawled over to him and went to work trying to stop his bleeding.

I took a moment to analyze our situation. We were located down in a ditch about fifteen feet from the jeep. The wounded soldier had dropped his AK-47 when he was hit. It was laying about three feet from this side of the jeep. With the continuous shooting, I knew I needed to get to that weapon. Our lives could depend on it. I yelled at Nancy, "Can you tell these men to cover me. I'm going to crawl up and get his weapon."

Nancy looked up at me then over to the weapon and the jeep. Eyeing a first aid kit in the back of the jeep she yelled, "I'll tell them to cover you, but when you're up there, can you grab the first aid kit. I need it otherwise this man is going to die."

"I'll try."

She yelled at the two soldiers. They looked towards me then opened fire while waving at me to make my move. I sprinted up and grabbed the weapon then dropped down behind the jeep. I unlocked the safety and popped up over the jeep and let off a burst while I grabbed the first aid kit. With the first aid kit in one hand and the AK-47 in the other, I sprinted back down diving into the ditch alongside Nancy and the other soldiers. Nancy grabbed the first aid kit and went back to working on the wounded soldier.

While catching my breath, I observed where the gunfire was coming from. It appeared that we were fighting four soldiers. With that small a number, we didn't have to worry too much about being overrun or outflanked. I figured it would be just a matter of time before the soldiers, who were at the roadblock, would hear the shooting and come to our rescue. At least, I hoped so.

The senior ranking soldier motioned that he was going to try to circle around and get behind their position. He wanted us to stay put and give him cover. We opened fire on the enemy's position as he crawled away. After emptying my clip, I reloaded and glanced back at Nancy. She was busy doing what she was trained to do. When I turned back towards the enemy, their shooting suddenly stopped. I glanced down the road and saw a patrol of Vietnamese with several vehicles coming in our direction.

I rushed over to Nancy's side. "Are you doing okay?"

"Yes, I got his bleeding stopped and I believe he's going to make it."

"That's good. I think we're all going to make it," as I pointed down the street towards the patrol.

When the Vietnamese troops arrived at our location, they spread out and searched the other side of the street for the ambushers but they had vanished. The officer in charge first spoke to his men then came over and spoke with us. Again Nancy had to do the speaking. She told the officer that it was imperative that they get the wounded soldier to the hospital immediately for surgery and she also convinced them to take us with them.

Nancy and I helped the wounded soldier over to one of their vehicles. To my surprise, just as we were about to leave, our driver came driving up. I don't know how he did it but he had somehow rounded up a replacement vehicle. Here, I thought he had run off in fear and we would never see him again. He jumped out of the car and ran over to Nancy apologizing for his actions. She gave him a hug and told him not to worry about it. After the hug, she turned and burst forth with tears releasing the stress that she had just experienced.

After recomposing herself, Nancy turned towards the officer in charge and told him that we would follow them to the hospital. When we arrived, Nancy and I went right to work inventorying their stock. I could tell she was quite shaken from the attack. She didn't talk and busied herself counting supplies.

It was close to three-thirty by the time we completed the job. I told Nancy that we needed to head back to the hotel. I knew I couldn't risk the chance of missing Com leaving work.

On our drive back, Nancy and I talked. She had never been shot at and was trying to digest everything that had taken place. I told her how I had felt the first time I was shot at and how personally I remembered taking it. As we talked, I tried to convince her that her feelings were normal and to not be so hard on herself for getting scared.

Thank goodness, our drive back was uneventful and we were back at the orphanage by four thirty. We dropped Nancy off then the driver drove me over to my hotel.

Riding back to the hotel, I couldn't help but think how ironic it was that I had actually been fighting on the side of the North Vietnamese in a small firefight. Who back in the States would ever believe that?

Chapter 15

Making Contact

Later that afternoon, I walked back down to the same café as last night. The table that I was hoping to get was occupied, so I went to the counter and purchased a Coke. I decided I would use a different tactic than I had initially planned on using. I would wait at the café counter until I saw the group exit the headquarters building. As they exited the building, I would get up and start walking towards Com as she walked down the street. When I was within hearing distance, I would stop and ask her for directions. Initially, I had wanted her to recognize me sitting at the café table, with hopes that she would approach me. But after last night, I knew that I couldn't take the chance of us not meeting again. Time was too crucial.

At 1800 hrs, I watched as the front door to the headquarters building swung open. I saw a small group of people step out. They said their goodnights then dispersed. A young lady from the group started walking toward the café. I got up, entered the street and slowly started walking in her direction. As I walked towards her, I rehearsed in my mind what I was going to say. Being a Caucasian, I knew that I would stick out. I was hoping this would give me the advantage I needed to help Com recognize me. We were about twenty feet apart when Com looked up and noticed me. As she glanced at me, I carefully studied her face. I could tell by the expression on her face that she recognized something about me. Her walk slowed as did mine. I smiled. As our approach grew closer, she looked directly at me. We were within five feet when suddenly a big smile lit up her pretty face. I could tell by her smile that she recognized me. I stopped and said, "Excuse me. You sure look familiar." I said this in English, hoping to jog her memory, if she still wasn't too sure who I was. We stood there, gazing into each other's eyes. Then she said, "Curt, is that you?"

"Yes," I replied, as I smiled and extended my arms out to her for a hug. As I did this, I realized that hugging was an American custom, not a Vietnamese custom and withdrew my arms quickly. I didn't want to come on too strong. The next words to come out of her mouth were, "What you doing in Cambodia?"

I knew that the next few minutes were the key to accomplishing or failing my mission. So I answered her question with my own question, "What am I doing in Cambodia? What are you doing in Cambodia?" She looked at me, and we both laughed. "It sure is great to see you. I never thought that I would ever see you again."

"It good to see you, but what you doing here?" she asked.

I ignored her question and said, "Wow, you look great."

She blushed. "Don't you know Phnom Penh dangerous place to be because of war?"

"Yes, Com that is why I'm here. I'm working with the UN and the Red Cross. I'm trying to get relief for the needy."

As I said this, I studied Com's face for any type of reaction. Would she believe me? "I just arrived in Phnom Penh yesterday afternoon."

"It best you not spend much time on streets by yourself."

"Com," I answered, "I know." Then I asked, "Can I walk you home?" She hesitated for a moment. As she hesitated, I thought to myself, "Curt you blew it. How would I know that she was headed home if I had just met her? I have to think before I speak."

After a few seconds and to my relief she said, "Okay."

As we walked down the streets of Phnom Penh, we reminisced about the time we spent together and caught up on the last fourteen years of our lives. Com told me about the fall of Vietnam and how it affected her family and their lives. She told me that right before Quang Tri fell, she had returned home from Da Nang to watch out for and help her mother and brother. When the city fell, they were forced to go south as refugees. The NVA stole her scooter so they literally had to walk from Quang Tri to Da Nang. I had flown that trip in a helicopter but had never dreamed of someone being forced to walk it.

She told me in a soft whisper, as she looked around to make sure no one could hear, that during the final days of the collapse of Vietnam, the NVA killed Thong, and that is why she had a deep hatred for the North Vietnamese, and would never forgive them. I was shocked to hear of Thong's death and felt as if I had just been told that one of my brothers had been killed. I had thought about Com and Thong often over the years and had always wondered what had become of them. I asked Com how it happened. "After government collapsed, my family sent to indoctrination center for questioning. During interrogation, sergeant in charge was rummaging through personal items when he noticed Thong's watch. He ordered Thong remove it. When Thong asked why, he got mad and struck Thong across head with pistol, knocking him to ground. The guard reached down laughing and yanked watch from Thong's wrist. Thong was bleeding badly from a gash across forehead. I rush over to try to stop bleeding and help him off ground. Once I got him off the ground and back to his senses, he mad. He valued watch dearly and started yelling at guard that he no better than common thief. I tried to quiet him, but too late. The guard yanked his pistol back out and without warning shot Thong in head. Blood splattered everywhere. I tried to catch him, but he dead. The guard laughed and quickly ordered two soldiers to drag his body out his office. Guard turned towards mother and me and threatened us, keep our mouths shut or he kill us too."

As I listen to Com tell her story, I could feel my hatred for the North Vietnamese building inside. My mind kept flashing back to Vietnam and my time spent with Thong and the friendship we had developed while I was living in the tunnel. Even though I had not seen him in fourteen years, I grieved his loss of life. I then thought of Com and realized how different our two lives had been. How fortunate I was to have been born in the United States and how unfortunate she was to have been born in Vietnam.

Walking down the side streets of a communist third world country should have been scary. But in some strange way, as I looked around at the dilapidated buildings built of cinderblock, plywood, even cardboard with their tin roofs, I felt as if I had been there before. When I looked at Com, I felt this unusual feeling of bravery combined with self worth and peacefulness all wrapped in one. It was a feeling that I hadn't felt for years.

Before I knew it, we were stopped in front of Com's house. Com turned towards me and said, "I have to go. I must make supper for aunt and mother. Will you be able to find way back to hotel?"

"Yes, you know, it sure was good seeing you again." I paused for a moment as I looked deep in her eyes then said, "I just want to show you one thing before I go."

I unbuttoned the top button of my shirt and pulled out

the heart necklace that she had given me fourteen years earlier. Com quietly stared at the necklace for the longest time. Then she slowly looked up at my face. I noticed a tear running down her cheek. She pulled me towards her and kissed me on my left cheek, then turned and ran into her house. As I stood there watching her run into the house, I could hear thunder in the distance or maybe it was artillery. I wasn't sure. All I knew for sure was there was a storm brewing.

As I headed back towards my hotel, I thought about my orders. It was already Friday night, and I had been given only five full days to accomplish them. My extraction was set up for first light Tuesday morning. During my briefing, I had been told that if I didn't accomplish my mission by Tuesday morning, due to the secrecy of the mission the extraction couldn't be changed. If I didn't make it to the extraction point, I would be on my own, and it would be my own responsibility to get out of Cambodia.

I had already wasted Thursday, my first day there, due to my unexpected behavior. Today had been fruitful, making contact with Com and walking her home. But where and how should I go from here? As I pondered my options, suddenly, I felt very tired. When I got back to the hotel, I went up to my room and went straight to bed.

Saturday, I woke to a constant pattering of raindrops. As I looked out the small window of my hotel room, my view was obscured by fog. Due to the rain, it was more humid than the last two days and quite cooler. Saturday in Cambodia was like any other work day so I knew that I wouldn't be able to get much accomplished until evening. I also knew that Sunday would be my big day, for I had been briefed earlier that Com always took Sundays off.

I got dressed, then left my hotel room and walked down the stairs that led into the lobby. As I was about to step outside, a little boy who appeared to be about ten years old ran over and tugged at my sleeve. I turned towards him and he handed me a note. He then ran out the door, down the street and hopped on the back of a little red scooter. Then he and the girl driver scooted off into the fog. I instantly scoured the lobby looking to see if anyone had seen what had happened or if anyone was watching me. Everything looked normal.

I wasn't sure whom the note was from. There was no writing on the envelope, so I stuffed it into my pocket and stepped out onto the street. I wanted to appear normal if someone was watching me and felt if I turned around and went back to my room, I might look suspicious. I had skipped dinner last night after my meeting with Com, so I was quite hungry. Yesterday, I had noticed a little café type bakery a few blocks from the hotel and decided I would try it out. I enjoyed the stuffed roll that I had my first night in Cambodia, so I bought what appeared to be some type of sausage stuffed inside of French bread. I walked over to a little green area and sat down to eat my breakfast. It had stopped raining, but there were still very few people on the streets. Once I finished the pastry, I took the note out of my pocket and opened it. It said, "Curt, pease met me tonight at my hous at 7 for meal." The spelling was bad, but I knew that it was from Com.

This note really surprised me, for I was expecting to have to make the next move. General Mackie had told me in my briefing that the seduction of Ms. Lee was left up to my own discretion. My orders were to do what was necessary to get Com to hand over the whereabouts of our men. I also remembered what Captain Donaldson cautioned me, "No matter how close you feel you have gotten to Ms. Lee do not, I say again, do not risk these men's lives or your own by telling her the truth. Don't trust anyone."

I folded up the note and placed it in my wallet then walked back to the hotel. By the time I got back to the hotel, my driver from the Red Cross was waiting to drive me to work. Having a driver made it a lot easier than trying to get a cab when you don't speak the language. I was glad that Colonel Anderson had set up the operation. He seemed to have covered all the bases and everything in my cover story was going as planned.

I was amazed at the amount of destruction in Cambodia and the extent of the work that would be required to repair it. Yesterday, Nancy told me that the Red Cross was trying to set up a program for passing out food beyond just the orphanages. She said they were working with the Cambodian hospitals trying to help set up facilities where they would be able to examine and take care of more patients. During our conversation Thursday, she had told me that they had been in Cambodia for one hundred and seventy-seven days and were returning to the US next week for a two-week break. I could tell by their appearance that they were tired and over worked and after what happened yesterday with Nancy, I knew she could use the rest.

The rest of the morning and into the afternoon was spent with the team observing and asking questions as I had been instructed to do. Even though I liked the three of them and found their work a blessing, I found it hard to keep my mind on the job at hand. By mid-afternoon, I decided it would be best if I left early and returned to my room to plan for the evening. I knew they wouldn't question my leaving early, since I was the inspector. Once I was back in my room, I repeated over and over in my mind different scenarios trying to figure out the best and most expedient way to accomplish what I had come here to do. I wanted to make sure that I completed it in the safest possible manner for both Com and me.

The sun was slowly hiding its rays behind the shanties as I walked down the street leading to Com's house. My thoughts were focused on my mission and how I was going to accomplish it. There was roughly sixty hours left till my extraction. America was over three thousand miles from here, and I was consciously tucking its memory and reality farther and farther into the recesses of my mind. I knew that I couldn't afford the thoughts and worries of home at this time. I had used this same technique while in Vietnam. I had trained myself to shove my thoughts of home and friends, with all of the memories, into the darkness of my subconscious and not let them surface 'til it was time for me to return home. It had worked well for me in Vietnam.

Walking down the streets of Phnom Penh, I was surprised that since I was Caucasian that the local inhabitants didn't pay more attention to me. They seemed to keep their heads down and go about their own business. I guess I could understand their timidness after having a ruler like Pol Pot during the seventies who executed anyone who even looked the wrong way at someone. I couldn't help but think about the stories that Major Stevenson had told me about Pol Pot and the Khmer Rouge. He told me about a massacre that took place in the last half of 1978 in a place they called the Eastern Zone. The Eastern Zone was an area located along the Vietnam border where the citizen's alliance was to Hanoi rather than to the Khmer Rouge. In what was the largest single massacre of their reign, the Khmer Rouge killed two hundred and fifty thousand people!

While walking, I looked at some of the vegetation in front of the houses and wondered if any of the trees were the Kabok tree (Ceiba pentandra). Its name in Khmer is "Koh" a word that means mute. During the Pol Pot reign there was a saying, "If you want to live, grow a Koh tree in front of your house." This phrase was directed at the people who had fled from the cities into the countryside. It warned them to remain silent about the things they had seen, heard, and felt.

When I arrived at Com's house, I walked up to the door,

took a deep breath and knocked. Two elderly Vietnamese ladies greeted me at the door. They spoke little, if any English, so I greeted them in Vietnamese. I could tell that they got a kick out of my Vietnamese, because they both giggled as I said, "Xin chao co (hello)." They were both short in stature and very thin. Their faces were weathered and worn with a leathery look, giving them an appearance of being much older than their years. They invited me in. As I entered the room, I noticed that it was extremely bare by American standards. The walls were constructed of cinder-block and covered with a light coating of stucco, painted light pink. There was a table with four chairs situated next to a door that led down a short hall to a small kitchen and one bedroom and bath. Off to the right side of the front room against the wall was a sofa with an oriental painting above it. In the center of the room was a fan hanging from the ceiling. There were no TV's or radios that I could see. The house was small compared to the houses back home, but very clean.

The ladies motioned for me to sit down on the couch, and then disappeared into the bedroom. A few moments later the bedroom door opened and Com walked out. As I stood up to greet her, I was astonished by her appearance. Yesterday when I had talked to her on the street, she had been dressed in the standard Vietnamese garb, which consisted of black, what I called pajama pants and top with a straw hat. She was now dressed in a beautiful satin red dress with dragon designs embroidered in gold across the front and down both sides. Her dress had a high tight collar around the neck with the back low cut and open. The dress fit tightly around her bosom down to her waist then hung three quarter length down her legs with a slit, thigh high up her left side. Under her dress she was wearing nylons. It definitely showed off her nice figure!

When I was stationed in Vietnam, the only time I had

ever seen nylons on the girls was when I was at the Tan Son Nhut Officers Club. The normal Vietnamese couldn't afford to wear nylons so I knew this signaled that this was a special occasion to Com.

I immediately greeted her with, "Wow, you look great."

Com walked over to me and took my hand. "Curt, I'm glad you come. I think of you all day. I never thought I would ever see you again."

She sat down on the sofa and I sat next to her. I couldn't believe how beautiful a woman she had become. I had never thought the Vietnamese were an attractive people, but Com being part French with that mixture of Oriental made her pretty. She had an exotic look to her. All I could think of was how beautiful she was. I replied, "I never thought that I would see you again either. I'm so glad that we ran into each other, I just can't believe we're together again."

Within minutes, Com's aunt and mother came out of the other room. Com introduced them, "Curt, I want you meet my mother Mrs. Lee and my aunt Ms. Lee.

I stood up and greeted them both.

"I've made supper and thought we eat with mother and aunt. We have much to talk about."

"Sounds great to me. What can I help with?"

She told me to be seated then they busied themselves putting the meal on the table.

While sitting at the table, this huge cloud of guilt started pouring its rain down upon me. I had been briefed to be very careful and guarded about my emotions. I was to keep them contained. Just get in, accomplish the mission then get out. I could worry about the guilt later. I reminded myself of what Captain Donaldson had taught me during my training; under no circumstances was I to tell Com about my wife and child. I was to play on her emotions and telling her about my family would blow all chances of any emotional involvement and without it, there would be no chance of completing my mission.

As I sat there watching Com and her family, I realized that I was emotionally way in over my head. I felt as if I had been out hiking and had stepped into a soft bog and was slowly getting sucked in, and there was nothing within my reach to grab and pull myself to safety. I had always taught my daughter not to lie, that lying was wrong. Now, I was already trapped in several lies, and I could see no end in sight. Finally my thoughts were interrupted by Com's voice, "Curt, what you thinking so hard about?"

"I've thought about you often over the years and have always wondered what happened to you. I just can't believe I'm here with you now." I paused for a moment then added, "You're so beautiful."

Com blushed as she lit two candles at the center of the table.

Our supper consisted of a dish of white rice with fresh fish cut up in strips laid across the top. Mrs. Lee had made some homemade bread, and there was some type of greens and tea to drink. Sitting there trying to talk to each other was quite funny. Com was talking in both broken English and Vietnamese. I was mainly speaking English, with a little broken Vietnamese, and then her mother and aunt were speaking only Vietnamese. I don't know how we were doing it, but we were all able to stay in the conversation and communicate quite well.

At first, our conversation consisted of small talk. But as the evening went on and we started to relax, we all opened up and started talking about the war, the Americans, the Vietnamese. We talked about the differences between Cambodian, Vietnamese and American traditions and customs. While we were talking about American families, the question that I had been dreading since I had accepted the mission came up. Com's aunt asked me why I had never gotten married. I had run this scenario though my mind a thousand times since I had agreed to take the mission. I knew that this would be one of my biggest tests. Looking right into Com's aunt's eyes, I said, "I've never met the right woman."

As Com translated my statement to her aunt, I looked at Com and smiled. She smiled back. When she finished translating, I asked, "Com, how come you never got married?" She just smiled and didn't say anything then our conversation drifted off in another direction.

They questioned me about the Red Cross and how long I had been an observer. I responded with the canned answers that Capt. Donaldson had beat into my brain during my training sessions. The answers seemed to be working.

Glancing down at my watch, I couldn't believe the time. It was already 2125 hrs. Since the Vietnamese occupation, a 2200 hrs curfew had been enforced. The order stated that all civilians must be off the streets by 2200 hrs. Anyone caught on the street after that time would be considered Khmer Rouge and would be treated as such. The Lee's home was a good ten-minute walk from the hotel where I was staying and due to the curfew, I didn't want to be late.

Just as I was about to mention something about the time, Com's aunt and mother got up from the table. They said how much they enjoyed the evening with me then disappeared into the other room. This was the first time that I was actually alone with Com since I had made contact with her on Friday. I nervously glanced down at my watch; it was 2130 hrs. I looked across the table at Com and smiled. I wasn't sure what to do or say next. Here I was in Cambodia with this beautiful woman, and I actually had military orders to seduce her. No one would ever know. There was only one problem. I had a beautiful, pregnant wife and a daughter back home who thought I was down in

Texas training at American Airlines.

I stood up from the table and walked towards Com. She got up and walked straight into my arms. I told her, "Thanks for the dinner and this evening. I really had a great time."

"Me too," she answered, as she reached up and kissed me. I returned her kiss. "Don't stop and talk to no one on your way back to hotel. These dangerous times."

"I won't," I replied as I picked her off the floor with a big hug. "Com, can I see you tomorrow?"

"Yes, I send you note in morning, now leave quickly. It late."

I gave her another quick kiss, turned and went out the front door.

Walking at a brisk pace, I went back up the street that led to my hotel. The streets were empty. There was no one in sight, not even a stray cat or dog. This made me nervous. I checked my watch again. It was 2145 hrs, so I picked up my pace. I felt like running, but I knew that running would draw attention to me and that could be dangerous.

Tomorrow was Sunday. I was counting on being able to spend most of the day with Com, which hopefully would allow me to get emotionally closer to her. I had only four more blocks to walk to reach the hotel and was in deep thought about how I would handle myself. As I came around the corner, I saw four men up the street to the right, leaning against one of the buildings. They were in their early twenties. I instinctively crossed over to the left side of the street. As I crossed the street, I watched as they came off the building and started walking towards me. I looked directly at them to let them know that I was aware of their movement plus to quickly evaluate their size and perceived strength. Their dress and haircuts indicated that they were not soldiers. Observing this gave me some relief, for I didn't want a confrontation with soldiers this close to curfew. When they got within ten feet of me, they yelled for me to stop. They were speaking in Khmer so I understood the stop but not the rest of what they were saying. I thought to myself, "I don't have time for this shit now" and decided it would be best to keep walking. I had just increased my pace when I heard them yell stop again plus something about American. When I heard this, I realized they weren't going to let me continue, so I abruptly stopped, turned and face them. Grinning and laughing, they came right up to me and got in my face.

I quickly looked each one directly into their eyes and decided that the second one from my left was the most dominant and aggressive one. He was most likely their leader. Just as I was coming to this conclusion, he stepped up and shoved me backwards with both of his hands. Rather than block his shove, I allowed him to push me. I stepped back with his shove, yelling, "Okay, okay."

I was trying to judge exactly what they wanted; was it to harass, to rob, or worse, to physically harm me. I had always taught in my self defense classes that until physical contact is made, it is not a life threatening situation, but once the situation turns physical you have to treat it as life threatening and do what you deem necessary to protect yourself.

As I yelled, "Okay, okay," the man who shoved me reached into his pocket and pulled out a knife. The knife had a six inch blade and I could tell by the way he was holding the knife that he had used it before. I knew that by not reacting to his shove, I had created a psychological advantage. He would take my passive response to his shove as a sign of weakness and cowardice and would not expect me to fight back. I took one look at his knife and another quick glance at the three other attackers and decided that this was indeed a life threatening situation. I couldn't afford to let the situation deteriorate any further. I knew that since I didn't speak their language, I would be unable to talk my way out of this mess. I raised my palms up in front of my chest as I said, "Take it easy guys." As I did this, the man with the knife stepped towards me. He extended his right arm with the knife thrusting it towards my throat in an attempt to either scare me or cut me. I sidestepped to my left, taking my right arm and crossed it over to my left in a clockwise circle and hooked his right arm from the outside. I simultaneously hit his right elbow with my left hand as I pulled back with my right, breaking his elbow. He let out a loud scream as he dropped the knife. I continued holding his right arm with my right, forcing him towards the ground between myself and the two attackers on my right. I kicked him in his throat with my right foot and pushed him towards the two. I could tell that this violent reaction momentarily shocked his friends. After shoving him towards the two on my right, I quickly turned towards the one on my left. He threw a punch at me with his left hand. I did an outside Moi Sao with my left hand to block his punch and hit him with a Gawk Sao (hammer strike) to his Triple Heater 23 point located a little bit forward and below the temple. I went to follow it with a palm strike to his chin but the previous strike had rendered him unconscious. His body went limp and crashed to the ground. I spun back around to my right in time to take a glancing strike to the right side of my skull. I blocked the next punch with an inside Moi Sao and hit him with a Gau Sao to the top of his nose. I quickly followed up with a short power palm strike to his face, which kinked his neck back, knocking him out. Upon seeing this, the fourth attacker lost his nerve, turned and ran.

My heart was thumping like a kettledrum, as I looked at two of my attackers unconscious on the ground with the third rolling around holding his throat. I instinctively looked around to see if anyone had seen what had happened. Thank goodness, the streets were empty. I glanced at my watch and realized I only had a few minutes to get to the hotel. I quickly turned and headed towards the hotel. My hands were still shaking from my adrenalin as I walked.

Entering the hotel lobby, I checked my watch again. It was 2158 hrs. I thought to myself, "This is too close. Don't push your luck, Curt; you want to make it home."

My shirt was damp with perspiration from my attack and near panic walk back to the hotel. When I got up to my room, I decided to change shirts. It was then I realized that someone had been in my hotel room. I noticed the toothpicks on the floor. I had placed a toothpick on a corner of both my suitcase and attaché case before I left the room earlier this evening. Thank goodness, I hadn't brought anything to the hotel that would compromise my mission. I wondered who and why they had been in my room. Had I messed up?

Suddenly my whole being, body and mind felt drained. I walked over and locked the door and flopped onto the bed. What to do next? I wasn't sure. I couldn't be concerned about it now. I was too exhausted to worry about it. It could wait till morning. I switched off the light and fell asleep.

Chapter 16

Best Day

Startled, I bolted out of bed. I was halfway to my hotel room door before I regained my senses. Standing there drenched in sweat and out of breath, I was gasping for air. The room was hot, and the air was heavy and humid as I struggled to catch my breath. It was a nightmare but what a nightmare. I hoped that no one had heard me scream. It was just a nightmare I told myself as I crawled back into bed. I had been dreaming that I was alone with Com. The dream still seemed so real. We were passionately making love when, suddenly, I noticed that Paula and my daughter Janelle were watching us from the door. When they realized that I saw them, they turned and walked away. That's when I bolted out of bed, towards the door, screaming for them to come back. I needed to reach them. I needed to explain...

Looking at my watch, it was still the middle of the night, so I rolled over and tried to go back to sleep.

Sunday would be the big day. This would be my chance to succeed or fail. Our military intelligence had discovered that Com always took Sundays off. Having this information, Colonel Anderson arranged so that I would also be free Sunday. There would be no duties or meetings for me to attend or observe today.

I was lying in bed trying to plan out Com's seduction when I noticed a note come sliding under my door followed by a knock. Having just gotten out of the shower, I was undressed. I yelled, "Just a sec," as I scrambled to pull my pants on. Rushing over to the door, I unbolted the lock and swung open the door. To my surprise, no one was there. I glance down the hallway but it was deserted except for a brown paper bag lying on the floor next to my door. I reached down and grabbed the bag. Stepping back into my room, I picked the note up off the floor and closed the door.

After locking my door, I opened the bag. Inside the bag was a pair of Cambodian work pants and shirt, along with a straw hat. I set the bag down on the bed and sat down on the corner of the mattress to read the note. The note was in broken English but readable. The note directed me to dress in the clothes from the bag. Then at 1000 hrs, I was to go down in front of the hotel and look for a girl sitting on a red Honda scooter. Once I spotted her, I was to walk over and say in Vietnamese, "Hi, are you Sang." If she answered yes, I was supposed to climb on the back of her scooter and leave with her. The note was signed Com.

It was 0915 hrs; I had forty-five minutes to decide what to do. Was this note really from Com or could it be from the people who searched my room last night? It would be so easy for someone to kidnap me then take me out of town and shoot or hold me as a spy. Suddenly, I remembered I still had the first note from Com stuffed in my pants pocket. I pulled out the first note. It was pretty wrinkled, but I unfolded it and laid it on the bed next to the new note. After several minutes of close examination, I decided that it was Com's printing.

I tried on the pants and shirt from the bag. The pants fit pretty well, but the shirt was a little large. I walked over in front of the mirror and tried the hat on. The clothes definitely helped me look more like a Cambodian. I decided that as long as I kept my head down, I should blend in pretty well with the locals.

At exactly 0958 hrs, I left my room. I walked down the stairwell then through the lobby out onto the street. Looking up and down the street, I noticed that the activity on the street appeared to be the same as any other day. Across the street, I saw a young girl sitting on a red scooter. She couldn't have been more than fifteen or sixteen. Crossing over to her side of the street, I approached her and asked in Vietnamese, "Are you Sang?"

"Yes," she said, as she smiled.

She cranked up the scooter as I climbed on the back. To keep my face concealed, I tucked my head down as she pulled out into traffic.

Riding through the streets of Phnom Penh, I noticed that Sang backtracked several times along our route, as we headed out of town. Once, she went completely around the block. She definitely wanted to make sure that we weren't being followed. As I rode on the back of the scooter, I wondered whom Sang was. How did she know Com and could she be trusted?

Approaching the edge of town, I noticed the buildings getting shabbier and farther apart. As we got out of the city, rice paddies started to appear. After about ten minutes of riding, Sang pulled off the main road onto a dirt road that led further into the countryside.

Approximately a half-mile or so on the right, I spotted a big old temple or monastery. It was sitting up on a knoll surrounded by trees. Its structure was rundown, looking very worn and tired. In its day, it must have been a grand temple, but it was in need of great repair. Even though it appeared dilapidated, it was still a magnificent piece of architecture. When the Khmer Rouge had taken over in 1975, they defrocked all the Buddhist monks and forced them to work in the rice fields. Several of them died from overwork and starvation. Since the Vietnamese occupation, the remaining monks had been allowed to return to their temples, but it would take years for them to get the temples back to the way they were, if ever.

As we approached the dirt trail leading up to the temple, Sang steered her scooter onto the trail. She drove up to the steps in front of the temple and stopped. As I climbed off the back of the scooter, Sang instructed me to walk up the steps and go over to a small red door located on the right side of the temple and knock. As I walked up the front steps of the temple, I heard the scooter start up. I turned in time to see Sang scooting off down the dusty dirt road headed back towards the city.

I walked over to the little red door and knocked. An elderly monk opened it. He appeared to be in his late sixties and stood about five foot two. His head was shaved. He was dressed in a worn but clean rusty orange robe. I said, "Xin chao chu." He returned my greeting with a slight bow then motioned for me to come in. I stepped through the door, and he immediately closed and locked it behind me. He led me down a long, damp, musty smelling corridor. Being unlit it was quite dark but as my eyes adjusted, I could see that it was decorated with beautifully painted murals depicting the countryside. There were flowers, streams, waterfalls and even a tiger in the paintings. We walked about two hundred feet down the corridor then made a ninety-degree left turn into a hallway that led to a set of large wooden doors. He motioned for me to open the doors then turned and disappeared around the corner.

The double doors led outside into a private courtyard. I stepped through the doors and closed them behind me. As I looked around the courtyard, I could see that at one time it had been an immaculately groomed garden. There were flowing shrubs and bushes all around its edge. They were no longer groomed but were in bloom and looked pretty.

There was an old pond running through the garden that probably once had fish in it, but was now dry.

In the center of the courtyard garden was a big grassy area. In this grassy area, I could see Com sitting on a blanket with a basket beside her. She was dressed in a grayish silver Vietnamese dress. The top came down below her knees like a dress but had slits up both sides. Then underneath, she wore pants that matched the top.

I waved as I walked towards her. She smiled and waved back. "Come sit here," she said as she gestured for me to sit down alongside her.

I said, "Good morning," as I sat down next to her.

She leaned over and kissed me on the cheek then giggled as she said, "I like your outfit."

"I like yours too, you look great."

"Let me explain about the clothes and Sang. Yesterday at work, one of my comrades said he saw me talking to a white man while I walking home Friday night. I told him you were with the Red Cross team and that me knew English but didn't get to speak much. So I thought it fun to talk to you. After seeing you last night, I think it better if no one sees us together too much."

"Com, someone was in my room last night going through my stuff!"

"Don't worry, that okay. When foreigners come, they think you all spies," she answered as she laughed.

"A spy, what would I be spying on? That's crazy," I answered as I faked a laugh.

"Many times, they put tail on outsiders. I not sure if they put tail on you yet, so I play it safe. I tell Sang to be very careful, to make sure that no one follow you when you come here. Anyways, I think you look better with these clothes."

"Are we safe here, being out in the country? How about the Khmer Rouge?"

Com smiled, "Yes, since Vietnamese occupation, temples and monasteries have been free of fighting and violence. The monk that greeted you is my aunt's cousin. His name is Lau. He would give his life to protect me, we safe."

"Com, I have something I want to show you."

I reached into my wallet and pulled out the photograph of her that she had given me back in Nam and handed it to her. She giggled as she studied the photo then remarked, "I look so young."

I looked at her and smiled. She smiled back. I told her how she had grown into a beautiful woman. As I told her this, I realized that I wasn't just acting my part but actually meant it. Suddenly it felt, as if it were only yesterday that she was nursing my wounds.

We sat on the blanket and talked. We reminisced about our old times together in the tunnel and talked about our dreams for the future. I explained to her what it had been like to come back to the States after my tour in Vietnam. She talked more about her refugee days when Quang Tri had fallen and how they had moved south. She confessed again how much she hated the communists after what they had done to her brother. I told her how I had really taken a liking to Thong and was saddened by his death. We talked about the reeducation camps. She explained how being literate allowed her to move up fast in the so-called new government. Com said her education had made the difference between being a professional versus working in a rice paddy for the rest of her life. She explained how she had worked her way up to where she was now and knew that in order to have a good lifestyle she would have to play the part. I believed she did it well.

Com told me that when the communists found out that she could read and write they assigned her a job in Da Nang as a secretary working for one of the generals in the party. This general was in charge of restructuring the city into a communist community. She quickly discovered that by playing the part she could have a better life for herself and her family.

As I sat there listening to Com tell her life's story, I couldn't help but admire her. I hadn't known she was so strong. The morning turned to afternoon as we giggled and played together. We ate the picnic lunch as we talked. Com made me feel as if I was twenty again.

The time was racing by quickly, and I found myself not wanting the day to end. I felt a spiritual connection with Com that I had never felt before.

I thought to myself, "Who is seducing whom here?" I knew that my time was running out and that I needed to make my move soon, but I found myself putting it off. I couldn't lie to myself. I was falling for Com. It wasn't as if I had just met her a few days ago. We had our past history together, which made me feel like I had known her for years. It was as if I was a different person, in a different world, in a different life, and I couldn't relate my old life to this new one. I knew now that it was possible to love two women at the same time. I glanced down at my watch. It was already 1805 hrs. It was time to do my duty for God and my country. Though I wasn't too sure if God would approve!

I said a little prayer to myself then said. "Com, Thursday when I was visiting one of the hospitals, one of the nurses pulled me to the side. She whispered to me that she had seen some American POWs in a work camp outside the city. Do you think that's possible?"

I had made up this scenario, but I thought that it sounded plausible. I studied Com's face closely as I asked her this. Her smile instantly disappeared and a faraway look came over her eyes. I knew instantly by her reaction that she knew something about the POWs.

Com sat there quietly, in deep thought, for what

seemed like a lifetime. Then in a very soft voice she said, "I have seen documents in General Samrin's office about these men."

"Why would they be holding American POWs this long after the war?" I asked.

She went on to explain that these men were pawns in a high-level chess game. She said something about war reparations promised by the Americans but never received. Due to her soft voice and broken English, I had a hard time understanding everything that she was telling me.

Earlier in the day, I told Com about my friend Ken Duncan. I told her how much it had troubled me over the years that we were unable to rescue him and that he had never been found. Even though this was true, I had purposely done it to set her up for this scenario. I asked her, "Do you think any of those men might be Ken or his crew chief?"

"I not know."

Hearing this, I decided that my best approach would be to sit there in silence and stare off as if in deep thought.

Sitting there in silence, I pondered what would be my next step if she didn't respond? After what seemed like a lifetime, Com slowly and gently took my hand and said, "Curt, I can find out, but it be very dangerous, especially if they suspect anything between you and me."

Without thinking, I pulled her close to me and said, "Com, I love you."

She reached up and gently kissed me on the lips and said, "I love you too."

We lay there on the blanket, embraced in each other arms, as the sun slowly sank beyond the courtyard walls. My seduction had worked, only one problem. I had spoken from my heart, without thinking, when I told her that I loved her.

I had told Com earlier in the day that the Red Cross

team was leaving Monday afternoon. They were to fly to Thailand, then back to the States for a well deserved vacation. I would be staying until Tuesday afternoon to finish up my reports and when finished, I would be flying back to Bangkok. In reality, that would not be the case. Once I had the information, it would be too dangerous and slow for me to wait till the afternoon to take the flight back to Bangkok. I would be extracted at first light Tuesday morning. The air force would launch a Super Jolly Green helicopter to arrive at our predetermined PZ (pickup zone) at daybreak to extract me. I needed the information by then. That left me with less than thirty-six hours. During my briefing, I had been told there would only be one attempt to get me extracted. This was due to the location of the extraction and the seriousness of causing an international incident.

I told Com, "I will be busy tomorrow observing till 1500 hrs after which I will be free. Can I please see you again tomorrow night?"

"Yes, I want to see you too. I arrange it."

I hesitatingly asked, "Do you think you will be able to find out that information by tomorrow night?"

"I not sure but will try."

"Since I work with the Red Cross, could you possibly find out the location of these men? Maybe I could see them?"

I was startled by Com's outburst. "No, no, no," she shouted. "They never let American see these men. They will kill you. They will kill me if they think me give this information out. It too dangerous!"

"Okay, okay." I said as I pulled her close to me. "I know it's dangerous. I don't want you to put your life in danger. I just thought if one of these men were one of ours, it would be nice to know where he was. Anyway, who would believe me if I told them that there were live POWs in Cambodia?

They would laugh and tell me that I was crazy. I just thought that when you found the document, you could write down their location and no one would ever know."

Rising to my knees I said, "Com, I'm sorry for asking. Please forgive me." Then I kissed her hand.

Com looked at me with a stern look and said, "I hate the War and the killing. I hate the communists. I live with war all my life. These men shouldn't give their whole lives for nothing. If they your friends, maybe you can help them. I try to find their location."

Hearing this, I was torn with emotion. I realized that I had fulfilled my mission, yet felt like I was betraying my own character. Once I was gone and these men were rescued, what would become of this pretty little girl? Especially when they figured out what had happened.

We sat in silence and watched as the sun closed its tired eyelids for the night. Looking up at the clear sky without any distraction from the city lights, I could see the stars making their grand entrance. It made me think back to when I was a little kid and of an old nursery rhyme. I asked, "Com, have you ever heard the rhyme, star light, star bright, first star I see tonight, I wish I may I wish I might, have the wish I wish tonight?"

Com turned towards me and said, "No I haven't, but what that wish be?

I looked deep into her beautiful eyes and said, "I would wish that everyday could be as good as today," then asked, "What would your wish be?"

Without even a hesitation Com answered, "I'd wish that me and my family be like you, free."

We were packing up what was left of the food and wine into the basket, when I noticed that it was well past 1900 hrs. Just as I finished folding up the blanket Com said, "Curt, you spend night with me, now."

I was surprised and didn't know what to say. I pulled

her close and said, "Com, I really would love to, but I can't tonight." Then I lied, "We have a briefing set up for 2100 hrs tonight at the hotel to discuss tomorrow's agenda. If I don't show up, they'll think that something is wrong and might call the authorities. It's too dangerous for you to come to my hotel, and I can't get out after curfew." As I said this, I could see her rosy coloring vanishing from her face. At first, I thought she was going to start crying. Again without thinking I said, "Tomorrow night, we have tomorrow night. We can spend the whole night together." Then I hugged her.

"Promise me, you must promise me."

"I promise."

Walking out of the courtyard, I was worried that maybe I had blown my mission by putting Com off. She had caught me off guard. I was the one that was supposed to be doing the seducing, not her.

We left the courtyard through the same wooden doors that I had entered through. Com led us back through the musty smelling corridor to a small room where Lau and a few other monks were sitting. She went over and gave Lau a hug and kiss. They spoke for a while in Vietnamese then I heard her thank him and say goodnight. I gave him a slight bow and said, "Cam on," which means thank you, and then we left the room through a different door. Com led me down a little hallway, out through another door, which led outside. Sitting there next to one of the pillars was Com's Honda scooter. I thought to myself, "Does Honda rule the world?"

Com explained to me that she would drive us to within two blocks of the hotel. She would then drop me off, and I would walk the remainder of the distance by myself. This would also be the place that she would pick me up tomorrow night at 1845 hrs. She instructed me to make sure that I entered the hotel from the back entrance. She then cranked up the scooter, and off we went into the night.

It felt strange to be riding on the back of a little Honda after riding Harleys, especially with a woman driving it. But for some unknown reason, scooting down the road, holding onto Com felt right. I kept my head down with my hat on so I would not be recognized. The ride back was much quicker than it had been coming out and seemed like it took half the time to get back to the city.

When we were two blocks from the hotel, Com made a right hand turn onto a side street and pulled over to the curb. Saying goodbye, I got off. She immediately drove away. I quickly walked to the back entrance of the hotel and took the aft stairwell to my room. I didn't meet or see anyone on my return. Opening the door, I quickly scanned the room and my belongings. Nothing looked out of place. The bed had been made, but my belongings hadn't been moved. I went in and took a shower then went right to bed.

Tomorrow would be a big day. I wanted to be well rested, but deep down, I knew that I was too excited to fall right to sleep. My mind kept reviewing over and over the day's affairs. As I lay there in bed, I couldn't help but wonder how deep I would fall into the dark abyss into which I felt myself being drawn!

Chapter 17

Ajax Cleanup

I spent Monday morning and early afternoon observing the Red Cross team. We visited, first a hospital, then an orphanage that was requesting Red Cross assistance. The difference between this orphanage and the one I had fed the babies at last Thursday could easily be seen. Observing firsthand the tremendous suffering and poverty the Cambodians were having, I felt guilty that I wasn't there to help these people and that possibly I was a wolf in sheep's clothing. By what I was observing, I could tell they were really in need of the help they were asking for. I thought about back in the States, where most people haven't seen or didn't understand what real poverty was. I kept reminding myself as we viewed these facilities that it wasn't my idea to be a Red Cross observer, so I shouldn't feel guilty, but I did.

By the time we got done at the orphanage, it was 1500 hrs and time to say good-bye to the team. Nancy came over and gave me a big hug. I told her that she should really be proud of what she was doing. I went over and shook hands with Jack and his wife Jean and wished them luck. Jack told me that he hoped I would give them a good report. I told him, don't worry about it. They were hard workers and I was impressed with what I had seen. Their driver had picked up their luggage at the hotel and was standing by to drive them to the airfield for their flight to Bangkok. Due to the small size of his car and their luggage, I wouldn't fit and would have to take a taxi back to the hotel.

I had arranged to meet Com at 1845 hrs. She would pick me up with her scooter, at the same location that she dropped me off last night. We were going to go back to the Temple for the night. It would be getting dark by then, and we felt the darkness would give us a better chance of getting out of town without her comrades seeing us.

Com told me yesterday that if she located the documents, she would copy them and put the copy in an envelope. She would have Sang bring the envelope to my hotel after 1600 hrs and slide it under my door. I had to make sure that I would be there. It would be too dangerous to have her hand them to me in person. If someone saw her handing an American an envelope, they might suspect something was up and report it. Com would instruct Sang to walk by my hotel room making sure that no one was watching and quickly slide the envelope under the door and keep walking. As soon as I viewed the information, I would commit it to memory and immediately burn the paper. It would be a death warrant for anyone to be caught with such information. Com said she couldn't risk being caught with this information or they would execute her and her family.

Sang was an orphan girl that Com had befriended when the Vietnamese first occupied Phnom Penh. She was about ten or eleven at the time, living on the streets, begging for her existence. Ironically, the Vietnamese had killed her parents. Com had noticed her on the streets and had taken pity on her and decided to help her. She found her shelter and as she got older, arranged for her to be an errand girl for Com's office. Com told me they loved each other like sisters. The red scooter we had ridden on yesterday morning belonged to a major in the Vietnamese army who worked with Com. He would let Sang use his scooter to run the various errands that the office assigned to her.

All day, while I was observing the Red Cross Team, I kept wondering if Com found the information and if she did, did she do it without getting caught. I was surprised by my strong feelings for Com and kept trying to understand how I could feel this way when I had a loving wife and child back home. If I hadn't gotten along with Paula, I could understand but we did, and I always thought of her as my best friend. When training for this mission, I thought that I would have no problem seducing Com without getting emotionally involved. When I first met Com in Vietnam, as I got to know her, I found myself being attracted to her. She had been a skinny little hootch maid and even though I thought she was pretty, it was not her body but her personality that I was drawn to. I realized now that she was what you would call a late bloomer. But just because she was good looking wouldn't make me feel the way I was feeling about her. I had once gone out with this beautiful girl back in the States, and I hadn't fallen for her. After a few dates, I realized that she might have been good looking, but that was the extent of her good attributes and stopped dating her. I wondered if it was pity that I was feeling for Com, but I didn't think so. She was healthy and seemed to have a great job considering her position in life. Her mother and aunt seemed to love her, and they were living well compared to most of the Cambodians I saw. I believe that over the past few days, as I learned more about what she had been through in her life, I developed an even stronger admiration and respect for her than I previously had. I saw attributes in her that I had seen in very few women during my life and I really loved that side of her. When I was younger, and my father passed away from cancer, I watched as my mother raised our family. I admired the courage that my mom showed. She was a strong take-charge woman unlike most of my friend's moms. As I grew up, most girls I met weren't like my mother. Instead, they appeared weak and gossipy and I wondered how they would ever survive by themselves.

I had learned in the past, that when you have a set amount of time to spend with someone, relationships tend to form and adjust within that perimeter of time, and what might normally take a few months to happen could accelerate and happen within a matter of days. I thought back to Vietnam when I had been shot down and discovered by Com. I had only known Com and Thong for seven days and I had slept almost three of those days, yet I had formed a close loving relationship with them. I had kept them in my prayers ever since and I don't think a day passed that I hadn't thought about them and wondered what became of them. Could it be this daily thought of Com that so intensified my feelings for her?

Even though I knew my UN job was a sham, I still needed to keep up my disguise so I wouldn't have someone suspect that something was amiss and blow my cover. I worried all day about making it back to the hotel in time for Sang's drop off. If she delivered the information, it was imperative that I was there to receive, memorize, and then burn it.

The cab ride from the orphanage took longer than expected. Feeling antsy, I kept glancing at my watch. I wanted to make sure I was there in case Sang showed up a few minutes early. As the cab pulled up in front of my hotel, I glanced at my watch. I had made it back with ten minutes to spare. I entered the lobby of the hotel and went straight up to my room. Positioning a chair next to the door, I sat down. "Please God," I prayed, "please let everything work out safely."

To come this far and then not be able to complete my mission would haunt me the rest of my life. I was too close to fail. I sat there watching as my clock slowly ticked off each second. It was as if I somehow entered a time warp. In this time warp, as each minute passed, the next minute would grow longer and then longer. Sitting there in complete silence, I could hear every sound, every voice, and every footstep in the hallway. Still, no envelope appeared.

Finally, I couldn't stand it any longer. My nerves were shot. I looked at my watch. It read 1700 hrs. I had never been good at waiting, just sitting, doing nothing. It would be better if I could see what was happening rather than just staring at the door. I decided to leave my hotel room. I would exit through the back door and go down the street about a block to an abandon storefront that I had noticed the other night while walking home. Posting myself there, I would have a good view of the entrance to the hotel and yet be out of sight. This way, I would be able to watch what was going on in the street. Also, I would be able to see Sang, if she came.

It took me approximately six minutes to exit the hotel, walk down the alley, cross the street and walk down to the abandon storefront. I slid into the store and hid behind some wooden crates, which prevented anyone from seeing me. From this position, I had an unobstructed view of the front of the hotel. Once I was in the storefront, I felt better. Instead of just sitting behind a closed door, at least now I could see what was going on in front of the hotel. Plus, I didn't feel so trapped if something was to go haywire. "This is much better," I thought to myself as I tried to relax.

The sky was overcast and gray. It had started to sprinkle as I repositioned myself from my hotel room to the storefront. I knew if Sang didn't show up by 1800 hrs, it meant that either Com couldn't find the documents or even worse, heaven forbid, Com had been caught.

As I stood there watching the movement on the street, I kept wondering what had happened? Then suddenly, I realized that I might have screwed up. I left the Cambodian work clothes that Com had given me in my room. I should have brought them with me. That way, if Sang didn't show up, I wouldn't have to go back to the hotel to change.

Looking out across the street, I noticed something that appeared strange. There were two men hanging out in front of the hotel. They were in their late twenties, maybe early thirties and dressed in civilian clothing. I had never noticed them there before. When it started to drizzle, they didn't seek shelter from the rain like everyone else on the street had done. They just stood there in the drizzle as if on guard duty. Looking at them carefully, I noticed that one of them was wearing military combat boots. Was I getting paranoid?

Moments later, I saw Sang come driving up on her scooter. She pulled up in front of the hotel and parked. My heart leaped from my chest as I watched her hop off the scooter and head for the door. I couldn't believe we had done it. I had to refrain from screaming out for joy. It was time for me to get back to the hotel. As I started sliding out of the storefront, to my horror, I watched as those two men approached Sang. I could hear their voices. They were yelling, but I was too far away to make out what they were saying. It was shocking to watch as they threw Sang up against the wall and started to body search her. Just then, a military vehicle pulled up and several soldiers jumped out of the back. Two of the soldiers ran over to where Sang was while the others rushed into the hotel. I quickly slid back into my cover. There was a lot of screaming and commotion going on.

"Shit, shit, oh shit," I thought as I watched them pull an envelope out from under Sangs undergarments. Then one of the soldiers struck Sang across her face with his rifle butt and down she fell to the sidewalk. How did they know? We had been so careful. Had Com been caught? Should I dare go to Com's house? As I stood there hidden from view, I slowly took several deep breaths and told myself, "Curt, don't panic." A feeling of helplessness came over me as I watched them pick Sang up and drag her into the hotel.

After approximately ten minutes, the soldiers came back out of the hotel. One of the soldiers was carrying my suitcase and attaché case. Another one was carrying the clothes that Com had given me. Even when I was flying combat in Vietnam, I never felt the sickness that was now engulfing my body and spirit. Multiple sensations were running through my body. I felt like running. I felt like vomiting. I felt rage, and I felt confused. I was deeply concerned about Sang and especially Com. I knew not to panic and that I was safe for the moment.

The soldiers all piled back into the army truck. They literally dragged Sang by her hair and threw her up into the rear of the truck then pulled away. I noticed that the two men who had been out front stayed. Now, there was definitely no reason for me to go back to the hotel. My only option was to wait and see if Com would show up for my pickup.

In the darkness of the abandoned storefront, I sat waiting for Com to arrive. I was just a block and a half from where we had arranged to meet. It would take me about three minutes to get there. I would wait until 1840 hrs then walk casually over to our pickup point. I prayed to God that Com would show up. If Com didn't make it, I would have to figure a way to get to my extraction point by myself. I wondered, as I sat there feeling isolated and depressed, "How did they know?"

A steady drizzle fell as I crawled out of the storefront. I headed down the street away from the hotel towards our pickup spot. As I turned the corner, I could see Com's scooter sitting on the side of the street, but no Com. I nervously scanned the surrounding area. Due to the rain, the streets were empty, and I could see no one. I decided that I wouldn't stop and just kept walking in the direction that I had been headed. If anyone were watching, this would draw the least attention to me. I walked right by the scooter and was about twenty feet down the street when I noticed a little alleyway on my right. As I approached the alleyway, I heard a voice calling my name. I looked behind me to make sure that no one was following. Seeing no one, I ducked into the alleyway.

It was Com. She had ducked into the alleyway to get out of the rain. I could tell by looking at her that she had been crying. She said, "We have to get you out of here quickly. They put orders out to follow you and if anything looked suspicious, to pick you up for questioning. I thought that maybe they picked you up already."

"No, I'm okay but do you know what happened? They got Sang and they took my belongings."

Com explained how she had gone into her office early in the morning. She had no problem locating the documents. They were in the same file cabinet where she had filed them previously. She made a quick copy of them and put the copy in an envelope. She then returned the original to the file cabinet. At lunchtime, she went into the bathroom with Sang and gave her the envelope. She told Sang to hide it and make sure that no one saw it. Sang took the envelope and stuffed it in her panties. She told Sang to deliver it to my hotel room after 1600 hrs and told her to slide it under my door, making sure that no one followed or saw her. They then returned to the General's office, where Com gave Sang several other documents to deliver as usual. This would keep Sang busy and out of the headquarters for the rest of the afternoon. Com knew that it was too dangerous to have Sang stay at headquarters with the document on her.

Everything went well, and Sang left as planned.

Yesterday morning there had been a bombing by the Khmer Rouge on the outskirts of the city. Six soldiers were killed. At approximately 1500 hrs this afternoon, military intelligence interviewed a witness that said she had seen a young girl on a red scooter drive by and throw a grenade into the military checkpoint killing the six men. She also said that she thought it looked like our errand girl. As they continued to question more people, someone said that they had seen her go to your hotel several times in the last few days.

"I in office when they gave orders to pick up Sang. General Samrin said to put tail on all Americans staying at your hotel. I knew that other Red Cross workers had left country this afternoon and that you still here. So I knew that they put tail on you.

"It was Sang that brought you note the other morning and she also brought you the clothes. I knew that once they found Sang with the information, they would come for you."

"Do they suspect you?"

"No, I not think so, but if they find envelope on Sang they kill her."

"I'm sorry Com, they've already found it. I saw them in front of the hotel strip searching Sang and watched as they pulled an envelope out from her pants. Thank goodness, I wasn't in the hotel at the time or else they would have gotten me. They searched my room and took my belongings."

Com grabbed my hand and said, "Come, we go to temple. You be safe there. I know people who will get you to Thailand, but will take day or two."

"No, I don't think it's a good idea to go to the temple. Someone might have seen me and Sang together yesterday. That could put Lau in danger. I won't do that to him. It's too dangerous.

"Com, I need to know one thing. Do you remember any of the information that you gave Sang?"

"Yes, there were five of them." She then named the men by their rank and names. She told me that they were located in a work camp outside a little village that was northwest of the city of Kampong Cham. As I stood there listing to Com name off the POWs, I couldn't believe what I was hearing. These names were different from the ones that I was sent to find. Were their more American POWs alive than we expected? I knew that my mission was crumbling, but at least I had the location of five live men and with the help of God, maybe we could rescue them. But first, I had to take care of Com and myself.

"I need you to take me to an abandoned village north-east of Phnom Penh called Vin Dau. Do you know how to get there?" I asked.

"Yes, but why?"

"Let's go, I'll explain when we get there. The sooner we get out of here, the safer we'll be."

Com ran over to her scooter and started it up. I carefully watched the street looking for anyone who might be following us, but no one was in sight. She drove over to the alleyway, and I hopped on the back of her scooter. She handed me her hat, told me to put it on, and off we went.

It was raining hard by the time we got out of Phnom Penh. Once we were out in the countryside, I took off Com's hat and placed it on her head to help shelter her eyes from the raindrops. Outside of the city limits there were no lights and with the rain pouring down we were engulfed in total darkness, except for the little beam of light radiating from the front of Com's scooter. I was glad that Com knew where she was headed, because I was totally disorientated.

The village that we were headed for had been used by the Khmer Rouge to torture and kill, not just Cambodians but also Chinese and Vietnamese. Of the estimated 1.7

million people who had died during their reign, several thousand had died there. The locals considered the village cursed and wouldn't live there anymore. Our intelligence had picked this village for that reason, figuring that no one would be living in the area, thus, making it a good extraction point.

Riding through the rainy countryside, I could feel Com's body shivering from the cold rain. Thirty minutes after leaving Phnom Penh, we entered what had once been the village. I instructed Com where to turn. Thanks to our satellite photography, even though I had never been to the village, I knew where to go. I had seen a great photo of the village and had committed its layout to memory. I directed Com to pull her scooter up to a hootch situated on the northwest side of the village. The hootch was located in the middle of a line of hootches, which backed up to a tree line. On the other side of the tree line was an open uncultivated rice paddy. This hootch was where I was briefed that my supplies would be.

Com pulled up in front of what was a rickety old bamboo hootch. I hopped off the back of the scooter as Com shut the scooter off. With the overcast skies and the rain pouring down, the night was so dark that as soon as her scooter headlight went off, I lost sight of her. Once my eyes adjusted, I grabbed Com's hand and led her toward the hootch. We were both soaked to the bone. Our bodies were shivering out of control as we entered the hootch.

Due to our hasty departure from Phnom Penh, we didn't have a flashlight. As we entered the hootch, we found it even darker than outside. I still had the matches in my pocket that I was going to use earlier to burn the documents but with my pants being so wet, I wasn't sure if they would light. I pulled the matches out and took a strike. "Curt, tell me what we do here," Com demanded as the match lit.

I surveyed the room and saw a broken table lying on the ground over in the corner. I handed Com the matches and said, "I need to find something, then I will tell you everything."

I walked over to where the broken table was lying on the ground. I leaned over to flip it up when my match went out. We were again engulfed in total darkness. "Com, light another match and hold it over here." While she lit another match, I bent over and lifted the broken table from the ground and threw it into the center of the room. Underneath, where the table had been, was a box dug into the ground. The box was about the size of a footlocker. I reached down and pulled open the box as the match went out. "Com," I yelled. "Light another match."

As the match lit up the darkness, I looked into the box. The first thing I saw was a combination lantern flashlight. I grabbed it and turned the lantern on just as Com's match went out. I set the lantern by the edge of the box. With the lantern shooting its rays out along the ground, I could see a survival radio. I also saw a nine-millimeter pistol, and a M16 rifle. Underneath the M16 was a manila envelope, which contained my final orders. I grabbed the pistol. It had the kind of holster that you wore across your shoulder and chest.

I knew that I had already violated the number one rule. I had been instructed several times during my three days of training to not do it. But I had done it. I had brought my enemy source into the knowledge of my mission. I had been told no matter what you feel or think is happening, "YOU TRUST NO ONE!"

Looking up, as I put the holster on, I saw that Com had backed away from me. I quickly thought, "Truth or deception!" In a split second my decision was made. "Com, it's time to tell you what I'm doing here." I walked over to Com and took both her hands. They were wet and cold and I could feel her shaking uncontrollably. I guided her over to a corner of the hootch and told her to sit down. As we sat down on the ground, we were both shaking from our wet cloths. I pulled her close to me in a hug trying to warm both of us.

I explained to Com, "The Red Cross is always concerned about the safety of their inspectors in third world countries. Since I'm a Vietnam Vet, they were doubly concerned about my safety in Cambodia, so they arranged for me to have a backdoor, so to speak, to get out if something went wrong. For instance, if the Khmer Rouge had launched an attack on Phnom Penh and captured the airfield, I would still have a way of contacting my country, allowing me a chance to get out of Cambodia alive. Com, this is standard operating procedure every time I go into a dangerous country. That's why there's a survival radio. The weapons are for my protection and the envelope contains coded instructions on how to call for an extraction." As I told Com this outlandish lie, I almost started to believe it myself. I knew that I had to make her believe it and I did.

I told Com to take her wet clothes off so that I could ring the water out of them. As she removed her wet blouse and pants I couldn't help but think how beautiful she was. I took her clothes and wrung the water from them as best I could. Then I removed mine and did the same. I checked the time. It was close to 2200 hrs. I knew that with the curfew it was too late to send Com home. I also knew that she wouldn't leave, even if it were possible.

After I settled Com down, it was time to read my final orders. I crawled over to the box and grabbed the manila envelope and crawled back to the corner to be with Com. I knew that even though Com spoke English that she didn't know how to read it. I opened the envelope. It contained a sheet of paper and a little pillbox. I opened the pillbox and looked in. There was one pill that reminded me of a Vitamin

E soft gel pill. I unfolded the paper and decoded the order. To my shock and dismay it read: Once you have obtained desired information: YOU MUST TERMINATE YOUR SOURCE. No loose ends allowed. Our men's lives are at stake, signed General Mackie.

I couldn't believe my orders. How could I do this? Com had saved my life in Vietnam and had risked her's to get this information for me. Sang was being held captive, if they hadn't already executed her. Now Com was willing to risk her life again to help me escape to Thailand, and I was supposed to kill her. I threw the pill across the room onto the muddy floor. Now I understood why I had been instructed during my briefing to make sure that I took Com to the deserted village. I thought the reason was to keep her busy and not allow her time to think about what she had done and possibly have remorse. This also explained why the President had been so concerned about an untrained civilian doing this mission.

While I was sitting there in shock and disbelief, staring off into nowhere, Com crawled over and threw her arms around my neck and said, "Don't worry, everything be okay." She then kissed me and said, "At least we're together."

I hugged her back. I was thankful that Com didn't know what the orders said. As we huddled in silence, the light from the lantern cast an illuminating ray over her beautiful body. I closely watched her as we sat there embraced in each other's arms wondering what I would do next. Then slowly I saw this smile come across Com's face. It was a soft loving smile that went right to my heart telling me that everything was going to be okay. When I looked into her eyes, suddenly I was fourteen years away. I was no longer a man in search of information for my country. I was transformed back into that twenty year old wounded soldier, isolated in a cave in Vietnam, falling in love for the first time. I was experiencing emotions that I had never felt before and would never feel again. As I pulled Com closer, time appeared to stop. There was no yesterday or tomorrow just the present. As we caressed each other, the touch of her hand made me feel as if we would never part. I knew and understood then that I was Com's soul mate and she was mine. We loved as if we had never made love and would never be able to again, knowing that our lives would forever be changed.

We spent the night huddled in the corner of that dilapidated hootch. I was worried about Com and told her that I wanted her to come with me in the morning. I would worry about explanations to my family later. I didn't care. This was my life now, not that other life miles away. Com told me that she had never loved any man except me, but she knew that she couldn't leave. If she left, her comrades would put two and two together. After what happened with Sang, and with me disappearing, if she showed up missing it would be signing a death warrant for the members of her family. She knew that she couldn't live with that. I admired her for her strength and level headedness and told her that I understood.

Com assured me that Sang would never compromise her during her interrogation. The communists knew that since Sang was in and out of the military headquarters daily, she had her own access to the information that she was caught holding. Since they knew that she had gone to my hotel several times in the last few days, and now that I had disappeared, they would figure that we were in it together. She also told me that since I was nowhere to be found, they would end up moving the POWs. They couldn't take the chance of an American knowing the whereabouts of American POWs in Southeast Asia.

As I listened to Com talk about the POWs, I was hoping that we could beat them to them. I would have the information to Colonel Andersons before 0700 hrs in the morning. How long it would take them to launch a rescue, I did not know.

Around 0300 hrs, Com fell asleep in my arms. I was too anxious to sleep. I had already decided to disobey my final orders. I just couldn't do it. I kept my earlier promise to Com that we would spend the night together, but I'm sure it wasn't the way she had imagined it. Huddled in a corner of an abandon old hootch with damp clothes was definitely not what she had expected. As I sat there looking at Com asleep in my arms, I felt closer to her than I had ever felt to anyone. Wiping the tears from my eyes, I knew then and understood that I would never be the same.

The hootch we were in backed up to a tree line. Beyond the tree line stood the uncultivated rice paddy that was designated as my pickup zone. A dirt road, seventy meters to the left of the rice paddy, led out of the village. To the right of the paddy stood another row of trees. I was to hide in the tree line behind the hooch until the rescue chopper was within one minute of the PZ. At exactly one minute, I was to sprint out into the rice paddy as the chopper shot its final approach so as to meet in the middle of the paddy. I would climb in and we would be out of there within seconds.

First light was forecasted to be at 0546 hrs. My watch read 0500 hrs, so I woke Com. I had already hidden Com's scooter. I turned on the survival radio and locked and loaded the M16. I told Com, "I think it will be best if you wait at least a good hour after my extraction before going back to town. You don't have to be at work till eight o'clock. That will still allow you enough time to make it home to change and get to your office on time." I wasn't sure how much attention the chopper would attract, and I wanted to make sure that no one saw her leaving the area.

"Com, I'm really sorry for all the trouble I've caused

you. I want you to know that I would never intentionally hurt you. I want you to always remember one thing." I reached down and took the heart necklace that she had given me years ago and hung it around her neck, "I love you so much. I wish we had had more time together. Don't ever forget, you'll always have a special place in my heart."

Com replied as tears ran down her cheeks, "I never forget you." She then said, "You know, Sunday was the best day of my life. As long as I live, I could never have a better day."

"I know, I know," I said as I hugged and kissed her one last time.

I told Com to stay down and out of sight. I grabbed the survival radio along with the M16 rifle, took one final look at Com, and quickly exited out the back door.

I sprinted over to the tree line and flopped down into a small ditch behind two big trees. I had extracted many soldiers from the rice paddies of Vietnam and had been extracted myself, but I never dreamed that it would be happening again. Unknown to us, when I had not returned to the hotel by 2000 hrs last night, Com's commander sent out a dispatch for all patrols to be on the lookout for an American. I hadn't seen or heard one vehicle all night. Then at 0528 hrs, I saw a military vehicle slowly drive down the dirt road that ran along the left side of the rice paddy. Lying in the ditch on my belly, I watched as the vehicle slowly crested the hill and disappeared from site. I thought to myself, "This is a bad omen."

I looked at my watch. It was 0540 hrs. I knew it was now or never. At 0543 hrs my survival radio crackled, "Ajax Man, Ajax Man, over."

"Roger Cleanup, go ahead." I responded. "We're three minutes out."

"Roger."

I got up on one knee and grabbed the M16 and unlocked the safety. My palms were sweaty, and I could feel my adrenalin pumping. I took one final glance back towards the hootch. I could hear the whopping of the rotor blades as they cut through the damp morning air. Scanning the horizon, I noticed some headlights returning down the dirt road. Had they heard the chopper too? It was 0545 hrs. The radio shattered the silence. "Ajax Man, Ajax Man, we're one minute to clean up."

"Roger" I answered. I took one final look at the vehicle coming down the road and estimated its distance at a quarter mile. I could tell with the help of first light that this was the same military vehicle that had just passed by a few minutes earlier. I got up and started my dash into the rice paddy. Due to the heavy rains from last night, the water was deeper than I had expected. After running approximately twenty yards into the paddy, I stumbled and fell, crashing to the ground. As I picked my soaked rifle and myself up from the rice paddy, I could hear the chopper getting closer. I also could hear the Vietnamese soldiers screaming. Out of the corner of my eye, I saw the truck stop abruptly and several soldiers flying out of the back with their AK 47s. They raised their rifles and took aim.

All at once, all hell broke loose. I could hear gunshots from the direction of the soldiers. I felt the rotor wash from the chopper pushing me down as she pulled pitch onto short final. The water from the rice paddy was drenching the air. Suddenly, the chopper's machine guns open fire, screaming a deafening roar. There was shouting coming from everywhere. I could hear the Vietnamese soldiers screaming, but I could also hear the helicopter crew chief screaming, "Give me your hand, Give me your hand, now jump."

As I flung myself into the chopper, I could hear lead piercing the side of the helicopter next to my head. The bullets were ricocheting everywhere as the pilot pulled pitch and we started our climb away from the hell below. I had just gotten myself inside the chopper when I felt a sharp striking pain to my forehead. The pain was coming from right above my left eye. I fell forward onto my face. I was stunned, but through my blurred vision, I could make out the rice paddy as it rapidly disappeared from sight.

Chapter 18

Initial Debriefing

Blood was running down the left side of my face as we low-leveled across the rice fields of Cambodia. The gunner yelled at me, "Are you okay?"

"Yea, I'll make it." I yelled back.

"Here's a cloth. Hold it against your wound to stop the bleeding."

My heart was still pounding from the run across the wet rice patty. I could feel my arms shaking as I grabbed the cloth from the gunner and pressed it firmly against my left eyebrow. Once again, I had been lucky. The shot had barely grazed my forehead cutting right across my left eyebrow and was embedded in the side of the helicopter. We had taken four hits during the extraction. Thank God, none of them were critical.

Once I got my bleeding under control, I put on a spare helmet they had on board and keyed the intercom. Not knowing if the extraction crew knew the nature or extent of my mission. I said, "Hey guys, thanks for the lift."

The AC responded, "Hello Mr. Gray. I hope you're okay? That was pretty hairy down there."

I couldn't agree more, and said, "It sure was. Thanks again."

The AC turned towards me and said, "I have instructions to give you this envelope," and passed it back to me. As I opened the sealed envelope, I could feel my pulse returning to normal.

Inside the envelope were instructions from Colonel Anderson. They read; if I accomplished my mission, I was to radio the location and number of POWS as soon as possible to Ajax Ops using their discreet frequency. They would be standing by ready to launch a rescue team. The rescue helicopter had a secure radio on board that scrambled the transmissions so that the Vietnamese couldn't intercept them. In addition to the instructions, the envelope contained a map of the outlying areas of Phnom Penh. Taking the map, I quickly located the small village where Com had told me the POW work camp was located. I asked the crew for a pen and jotted down on the envelope the grid coordinates of the village. As I rapidly did this, I kept thinking how critical time was to the accomplishment of our mission. Hopefully, we could launch the rescue raid before General Samrin and his men figured out exactly what took place last night. I quickly called the AC on the intercom and asked him to set the frequency on the secure radio and to verify that I would be transmitting on the correct radio. I wanted to double check that I didn't broadcast my message on the wrong radio and end up having it intercepted by the Vietnamese. He instructed me to switch my intercom switch to radio transmitter number two and said I would be ready to transmit.

"Ajax Ops, Ajax Ops, Ajax Man over."

"Roger Ajax Man go ahead."

"Roger I have five paxs at 11^0 50'N, 105^0 07' E over."

"Roger Ajax Man we copy, five paxs at 11^0 50' N, 105^0 07' E over."

I came back with, "Ajax Ops, That's affirmative." As I unkeyed the mike, I realized that I had completed my job.

Now it was time for them to complete theirs. Hopefully, it wasn't too late. I had gotten little sleep in the last few days and with all the stress, I was starting to feel its effect. Within minutes, I fell asleep.

In my sleep, I was dreaming about Com. She was trying to get back into Phnom Penh without being spotted. There were soldiers and roadblocks everywhere. Suddenly, I felt a push against my shoulder from the crew chief. I opened my eyes and saw that we were on final approach to what appeared to be an old American air force ramp in Thailand. As my eyes scanned across the ramp, I was surprised to see Colonel Anderson along with a Lieutenant Colonel standing at the edge of the ramp. I expected Colonel Anderson to be back in Washington. The aircraft commander hovered the bird over to where they were standing and set her down. As he rolled back the throttle, Colonel Anderson and his subordinate ran over to the chopper to greet me.

I whipped a quick salute to Colonel Anderson. Returning it, he said "Glad to see you made it back Mr. Gray. Are you okay?"

"Yes sir. I think I'll make it."

He quickly introduced me to the Lieutenant Colonel standing next to him. "Mr. Gray, this is Colonel Jim Sizemore. Jim will be helping me with your debriefing. That looks like a pretty nasty cut on your forehead. Let's get you over to the infirmary and have them stitch it up."

Even though the infirmary was only a few blocks from the ramp, we hopped into a jeep to save time. As I was getting in the jeep, Colonel Anderson leaned towards me and asked in a whisper so that the driver couldn't hear, "Curt, How sure are you of your information?"

"One hundred percent, sir," I responded.

He then explained, "When I received your grid coordinates; I instantly relayed them to an SR-71 spy plane that we had airborne. He proceeded to the location to take reconnaissance photos of the area. You understand how important it is to our rescue effort to have as much detailed information as possible before launching a rescue attempt."

"Yes sir, I do."

"We'll have only one chance and I want to make damn sure that it goes right. The plane is due back shortly. As soon as they land, I will have matters to attend to, but I'll leave you in the good care of Colonel Sizemore."

I had once seen a SR-71 flying over in Vietnam. It was a radically shaped aircraft manufactured by Lockheed and was nicknamed the Blackbird. The aircraft has quite the history behind it. It was initially called the RS-71 but when President Lyndon B. Johnson announced it on February 29, 1964 he accidentally switched the RS to SR in his announcement, which caused Lockheed to instantly change the name to the SR-71. It had a wingspan of 55.58 feet with a length of 197.42 feet and a height of 18.5 feet. It had a two pilot crew with a surface ceiling of 85,000 feet and a combat range of 2982 miles. It held two world records for absolute speed of 2,193.167 MPH and absolute altitude at 85,068.997 feet. The Blackbird was one of the first stealth aircraft built using radar absorbing materials, which gave it a low radar signature. Another unique feature of the SR-71 was the airframe was built using titanium. The amazing thing to me was this titanium was purchased from Russia.

When we arrived at the infirmary, a Thai nurse took me immediately into one of the medical rooms and started to clean my wound. As she cleaned the wound, she explained, "You're a very lucky person. If this wound had been an inch lower, you would have lost your left eye for sure and possibly your right."

She gave me a shot to anesthetize the left side of my eyebrow. Once it was numb, she proceeded to close my wound by putting five stitches into my eyebrow.

Sitting there in the infirmary, my mind was running

wild with questions. What had become of Com? Did she get out of the abandon village without being seen? And if she did, was she able to make it back to work without being discovered? Had Sang told them anything during her interrogation? Did they break her? How would the photos of the work camp turn out? How could they tell if there were Americans there? Had I copied down the correct coordinates? Would my mission turn out to be a success or failure?

My thoughts were interrupted by the sound of a jet landing. Colonel Anderson popped his head in the door and said, "Curt, our bird has landed. I need to go. Colonel Sizemore will stay with you. Once she is finished here, a doctor will come in and give you a quick examination then Jim will bring you over to my office to start your debrief. I'll see you shortly."

He turned and left the room. As he walked away, I realized that everything was now out of my control. All I could do was pray and wait.

Once I was done with medical, Colonel Sizemore took me over to Colonel Anderson's office located in the old headquarters building. As I walked in, I could tell by the decor and the photos on the wall that this was a Thai officer's office, not Colonel Anderson's, and that he had commandeered it for the time being. Colonel Sizemore told me to have a seat and asked if I wanted something to eat or drink. Even though I hadn't eaten since lunch yesterday, the thought of food had never entered my mind. I said, "That sounds good, what do they have to offer?"

"Curt, after what you've been through, anything you want."

"Okay, I'll take a hamburger and fries. Can you get them to throw some bacon and barbecue sauce on it along with a Coke?"

"No Problem," Colonel Sizemore answered as he picked

up the phone and ordered my meal.

When Colonel Sizemore finished ordering my meal, he pulled up a chair and sat down. He opened his briefcase and pulled out a notepad. He explained, "Curt, I'm a psychologist. I specialize in working with special operations personnel. My job is to debrief you. I'll be working with you much the same as Captain Donaldson worked with you prior to your mission. My objective is to prepare and make sure that you're ready to reenter society. We'll be discussing what you've just experienced and hopefully, with honesty on your part, be able to prevent any emotional scars from forming. We have learned since Vietnam that anytime someone goes through a traumatic experience, as you have just experienced, it is best to talk about it. We have found that if you try to ignore your experience and not talk about it; it can come out years later in what we call Delayed Stress Syndrome (In the nineties, it would become known as Post Traumatic Stress Disorder, PTSD.) We are now just beginning to understand the effects of delayed stress and how to deal with preventing it from happening."

Colonel Sizemore then told me an interesting story about Audie Murphy who was the most decorated soldier in World War II. Audie Murphy received every decoration for valor that our country offered, including five decorations from the countries of Belgium and France totaling thirty-three awards. He fought in the European theater in nine major campaigns and was wounded three times. He was credited with killing 240 enemy soldiers and capturing and wounding several more.

After Audie Murphy's discharge from the service, he became an instant celebrity and eventually started making movies. They said that he was the only movie star that was actually braver and more heroic in real life than what he portrayed in the movies. In 1955, the studio decided to make a movie about his combat experiences called *To Hell* and *Back*, which was based on his autobiography. The studio cast him to star as himself. Back then, they didn't understand that PTSD existed and called its effects "Battle Fatigue." Due to Audie's battle fatigue, he already suffered from insomnia and depression. When he started studying the script and filming the movie, his PTSD affected him so badly that he started sleeping with a pistol under his pillow, and with the light on. His friends were worried that he was becoming emotionally disturbed and possibly insane, when in actuality it was the delayed stress coming out from having to relive the traumatic experiences that he had suppressed since coming home from the war.

Colonel Sizemore went on to explain that even though he was a doctor he was still in charge of my military debriefing and his goal was to accomplish both at the same time. In my initial mission briefing, I had been told that only four people knew about the mission and Colonel Sizemore was one of the four. I asked him if he knew Captain Donaldson. He said yes, they were good friends and often worked together. He told me that he understood that I was very tired but there was some basic information that he needed to confirm as quickly as possible. He also explained that it was his responsibility to make sure that I was ready to intermingle with civilians without giving in to the urge to tell them what had just happened. He went on, "Curt, it is a natural tendency when experiencing something exciting to want to tell someone about it. This tendency to talk about your adventure, especially to your wife and loved ones is hard to overcome. If you want or feel the need to tell someone about what you just experienced, I'm the one to tell."

As I listened to Colonel Sizemore talking, I heard a flight of four Sikorsky HH-53C, known as Super Jollys', takeoff. These aircraft were used for combat search and rescue (CSAR) missions. These were the largest built helicopters in the free world and could obtain a top speed at sea level of over 189 mph and were equipped with a fuel probe for airborne refueling. As they flew over, I wondered if they were the rescue team.

Our debriefing was interrupted by a knock at the door. Colonel Sizemore got up, went over and answered it. In walked a Thai sergeant carrying a tray with my hamburger, Coke, and fries. He brought the tray over and set it on the desk then quickly turned and left. Colonel Sizemore poured a cup of coffee as I popped open the can of Coke and took a drink. "Are you ready?" he asked.

"Yes sir"

"Okay, the first thing I want you to do is relax and please forget that sir shit and call me Jim."

"Yes sir," I said with a loud laugh.

"Curt, on this question, I want you to rate your information on a scale of one to ten with ten being the highest. How certain are you of your information regarding the five POWs and their location that you radioed in?"

"Jim, I would rate it a ten."

"Are you that positive that your information is correct?"

"Yes, there is no reason to believe otherwise. I'm sure that Com was telling me the truth."

"Did you get any names?"

"Yes, I did, and I committed them to memory. I don't think I will ever be able to forget them."

Colonel Sizemore grabbed his pen and wrote the names down as I listed them. "Major John Jameson, Captain Robert Hughes, Lt. James Decker."

"Wait a second." I could see the look on his face expressing the same thought that I had when Com first listed off their names. "Are you sure these names are correct?"

"Jim, I know what you're thinking. I thought the same thing when Com gave me their names; there are more live American POWs in Cambodia than we first thought."

"God, this is unbelievable!"

I continued, "The other two are Captain John Ballinger and Sergeant Edward Morris."

When Colonel Sizemore finished writing down their names, he jotted down a quick note. He sealed it in an envelope, then called in the Thai soldier from the front office and ordered him to take the envelope to Colonel Anderson ASAP. He then said, "Curt, did you complete your mission as directed in your final orders?" I felt a chill run down my spine as I listened to his question. My mind raced with thoughts about what to say. "He then asked very sternly," Curt, did you tie up all lose ends?"

At first, I didn't want to admit that I had disobeyed my final orders. I thought about saying yes, but I knew that I had to tell the truth. "No, I did not."

"Why in the hell didn't you follow your orders when you know these men's lives are at stake?"

"Because there were extenuating circumstances," I said raising my voice. "Things didn't go as planned. I wouldn't be sitting here now if it weren't for Com," I tensely answered, almost shouting.

"Okay, okay, settle down and tell me what happened."

Being tired and anxious, I had over reacted to his statement. I could feel the tension in my body. I took a deep breath trying to relax then continued. "Everything was going pretty much as planned until late yesterday afternoon when I was to receive the information. Com had arranged to send it to me through an errand girl named Sang. Sang was carrying the information on her when she was stopped and searched by a Vietnamese patrol. They stripped searched her and found the document on her."

"Curt, wait a minute," Colonel Sizemore interrupted. "If they intercepted the messenger, how did you get the information?"

"I had previously arranged to meet Com at 1845 hrs.

When I met her, I told her about Sang being taken and asked if she remembered the names and location of our men. She said yes and gave them to me. Later that night, I questioned her again to verify her information and she gave me the exact same names and location as earlier."

"Okay, Com gave you the information herself; now tell me more about this errand girl and why they grabbed her?" Colonel Sizemore probed.

"It seems that someone fitting Sang's description had thrown a grenade into a guard stand on Sunday as they drove by on a scooter. The explosion ended up killing six soldiers. Mid afternoon yesterday, someone came into headquarters and identified Sang, their errand girl, as the attacker. Headquarters immediately put out an alert to pick her up, and when she showed up at the hotel to drop off the information, they intercepted her."

"Explain to me how you know for sure they found the document?"

"I was hidden down the street in an abandon store front waiting and watching for her to come. I saw her ride up on her scooter. She parked it then crossed the street to go into the hotel. As she tried to enter the hotel, I saw two men grab her. They slammed her against the wall and started searching her. I saw them pull an envelope out from under her clothing. I immediately assumed the envelope contained the information and later Com confirmed that it did. They also went up and searched my room and grabbed my belongings."

"They grabbed your belongings, why?"

"Com told me that the person who turned in Sang, said that they had seen her coming and going to my hotel the last few days, and since my hotel was where the Americans were staying, they were putting a tail on all Americans? Thank goodness, the three Red Cross workers who I had been working with had left earlier in the day, and I was the only American still registered that I know of."

"Does Colonel Anderson know that your information was possibly compromised?"

"No, I didn't think it would be appropriate to say anything over the radio about it, plus, I wanted them to at least try to rescue these men."

"Curt, it's not that simple. Is there anything else that we need to know?"

"Yes, Com said she believed they would move the POWs as soon as they discovered the list on Sang. I was hoping that we could get to them before they were moved."

Colonel Sizemore looked shocked. He quickly picked up the phone, called Colonel Anderson and told him that he better get over here ASAP. I was hungry and took a bite of my hamburger while he made his call. Within minutes, Colonel Anderson came rushing through the door. He appeared excited and said, "The photos we took show a guarded compound that appears to be a work camp. We can't tell for sure by the photos if there're any Americans located there. But I felt that the photos along with your information, was enough justification to launch a rescue attempt. I ordered a launch. They took off about twelve minutes ago and should be there within two hours."

Colonel Sizemore interrupted, "Curt just told me that his information could possibly be compromised."

"Compromised, what do you mean compromised?" Colonel Anderson questioned.

I quickly explained to Colonel Anderson what had happened to Sang and how they found the information on her. I told him that since they had intercepted the information before it was delivered to me, I was hoping that they wouldn't tie the two together before the rescue could be completed. This was the first time that I saw Colonel Anderson look startled. He said, "Even though the team is already launched, we cannot afford to do an assault on the camp without being positive that we can rescue at least one POW, otherwise the political ramifications could be disastrous. I'm not giving up hope, but we can't afford to gamble. I have no choice but to abort the mission."

My heart sank as I heard his words. He picked up the phone and called mission control. They patched him through to the air mission commander. I listened as he ordered them to abort the mission and return to base. When he hung up the phone, he turned and said, "Curt, don't give up hope yet. What we're going to do is insert a special ops team tonight and see what they can find out. With any luck, they'll still be there and we can pull them out first thing in the morning."

"Colonel Anderson, can I please stay here until the mission is complete? I really need to know what happens. I could never return home without knowing the outcome. It would drive me crazy."

He turned to Colonel Sizemore and asked, "Jim, what do you think?"

Colonel Sizemore thought for a moment then said, "I believe it will be crucial for Curt's emotional health to know what happens. Under the present circumstances, it will take longer to complete Curt's debrief than planned. I'll contact Captain Donaldson and have him develop a cover that will allow us a few extra days before Curt needs to return home." Hearing this, I felt relieved and thanked them both.

Colonel Sizemore suggested we take a break. We would resume my debriefing at 1400 hrs. He gave me instructions to talk to no one including the guards. After finishing my burger, I was escorted over to some old barracks where I was assigned a room. The Thai guard that escorted me to the barracks didn't leave but remained in the hallway outside my door. I was too exhausted to worry about anything further. I undressed, crawled into bed and within minutes fell asleep.

Awoken by a pounding on the door, I yelled, "Yeah, just a second." I pulled my pants on, went over to the door and opened it. Standing in the doorway was the Thai guard. "Mr. Gray, your briefing is in twenty minutes."

"Okay thanks, let me take a quick shower and I will be with you shortly."

I took a quick shower and got dressed. The short nap had really helped and after my shower, I felt refreshed and ready to continue my debriefing. My guard escorted me back to Colonel Anderson's office where Colonel Sizemore was waiting. "Did you have a good rest?" he asked as I walked through the door.

"Yes, I feel much better."

I closed the door behind me and took my seat.

Colonel Sizemore went on to explain, "I talked with Captain Donaldson. He came up with a cover that will allow us a couple of extra days if needed. You'll have a chance to call your wife later tonight. When you do, I want you to tell her that everything is going well in school, that you're working hard and learning a lot about the systems of the Boeing 727. I also want you to tell her that both your roommates stayed down in Dallas with you on your 48 (Friday and Saturday) and that you got a lot of studying done."

"What happens if she starts asking me names or where I'm staying?"

"Don't worry, I'll be furnishing you with names of your roommates and instructor in case she asks, plus the hotel where you are supposedly staying. You'll tell her that you will be coming home Thursday night after class. Also, be sure to tell her that you're sorry that you missed her the last two times you called."

It would be Tuesday morning in Minnesota when I placed my call. This would leave me three days. If this wasn't enough time and they decided that we needed more, I would call Paula back and tell her that I was walking down the steps at the flight academy, when I tripped and fell hitting my head. I needed to be taken to the hospital where I received five stitches in my forehead. Since the accident happened on American Airlines property, American requested that I be admitted to the hospital overnight for observation. They wanted to make sure that I didn't suffer a concussion. This would explain why I had five stitches in my left eyebrow when I came home from school. If we didn't need more time, I would tell Paula the story about tripping on the steps and just leave out the part about being admitted to the hospital overnight for observation.

After Colonel Sizemore finished explaining my new cover story, he gave me a quick briefing on tonight's insertion. "Colonel Anderson will be launching a Special Forces team this evening by helicopter to arrive at the LZ at 2200 hrs. They'll take off from here and fly down over the Gulf of Thailand till they are due south of Phnom Penh. At that point, they will aerial refuel then head north into Cambodia. They'll be inserting a team twelve clicks northwest of the compound under the cover of night. Due to the darkness, the helicopter pilots will be using night vision goggles. Colonel Anderson has surveyed the aerial photos and has determined the safest insertion and extraction points. He understands that it would be too dangerous to use the same LZ twice, so he has handpicked two LZs, placing a good distance between the two. This will make it harder on the team, because they'll have more distance to cover, but it is necessary to protect the security of their extraction point. The team's orders are to locate the compound then try to determine if there are American POWs there. If they're lucky enough to have a chance to return an American POW they'll do so. If they can't determine that there are Americans

POWs, they have orders to kidnap one of the compound guards and interrogate him to obtain the needed information. They must arrive at their PZ no later than 0500hrs. This allows enough time for their extraction before sunup."

As I listen to Colonel Sizemore talk, I knew that the teams were good, but that good? I wondered.

It was time to get back to my debriefing. "Curt, I want you to tell me everything that happened starting with your arrival in Phnom Penh."

I told him about my arrival, explained how I met the Red Cross team at the orphanage and fed the babies. I told him how I went to the hotel early and checked in. He chuckled when I told him about my initial reaction to seeing Com and how I had turned my face away so that she wouldn't see me. He explained to me that was actually a normal reaction and to not feel bad about it. I told him about the guilt I felt while observing the Red Cross workers knowing that I was a fraud and was only there to develop my cover. He asked me about the pain and suffering that I saw at the hospitals and how I felt about it. I did most of the talking while he sat there and listened asking an occasional question.

When it came to talking about my feelings for Com, I found myself wanting to change the subject instead of talking about how I felt about her. Colonel Sizemore sensed my reaction right away and kept asking me question after question about what we did, what we talked about, and how I felt? I told him that I felt ashamed that I could fall in love with one woman while being married to another whom I loved. He explained, "When your mind experiences such drastic changes in your life style from what is the norm, it can compartmentalize your feelings as if you were actually two different persons and react accordingly. The love that you feel for Com most likely is real but this love does not distract from the love you feel for your wife. You need to come to terms with your feelings and understand that it was okay to love Com, but at the same time you need to return back to reality, which is your life in Minnesota not the past few days that you spent in Cambodia."

I could already sense that would be the hard part. As we talked, I realized that Colonel Sizemore understood my feelings and didn't look down upon me for allowing it to happen. When I explained why I hadn't taken Com's life and had actually tried to talk her into coming with me, he said that after learning that the information was compromised and how Com helped to save my life, if he had been in my shoes, he would have reacted the same way. Hearing this made me feel relieved, because I knew I couldn't have taken her life.

He went on to explain, "You will have tremendous feeling of guilt when you first get home and the natural tendency will be to confess to your wife what you have done. I warn you, do not do it. If you do, it will break the trust that your wife has in you and put doubts in her mind. Besides, she wouldn't believe you." I was surprised by the next piece of advice he gave. "Curt, if the guilt ever gets too heavy to bear, you can seek out a priest in a confessional and confess to him. Canon Law binds him to whatever is told in the confessional, stays in the confessional. And you can be assured that he will abide by this law."

This would be the best advice that I would receive from the colonel; only I didn't realize it at the time. He also reminded me of the statement that I signed and reiterated how important that document was. He explained to me in a gentle way that the government could destroy my life and that of my relatives by using the IRS. He listed several things they could do to make my life miserable. He then reiterated, "Curt, I want to make sure that you fully understand that once you get off the airplane in Minneapolis, you will be on your own and that this mission never took place. Think of it as a dream and treat it as such. As far as anyone is concerned, Colonel Anderson and I never existed."

We spent the remainder of the afternoon talking. At 1700 hrs we stopped for the day. I would have my first chance this evening to make a phone call to Paula. Due to the time zone changes, it was still the middle of the night back in Minnesota. We scheduled to meet in the morning at 0900 hrs to continue my debriefing. Colonel Sizemore said he felt that I was okay to be by myself. He suggested that after dinner, I should try to relax and unwind, maybe even watch a movie. He arranged to have a TV with a VCR and several videos put in my room. We ate dinner together then I returned to my barracks to relax until it was time to call Paula.

During my debriefing, I asked Colonel Sizemore where we were located. He answered that the less I knew the better off I was. As I looked around the surroundings, I could tell that at one time this had been a good size US military installation but now most of it was closed down and the Thai's were using what was open. I had been asleep on the flight in and didn't get a good view of our location until on short final. I knew that during the Vietnam War, the US had several airbases in Thailand, which were used for flying bombing missions into Vietnam. After the war, they were closed. I wasn't sure, but I felt that I was at an old base called U-Tapao, which was located just a few miles east of a town called Sattahip. I figured this location was the closest to the water and Phnom Penh. If I was correct, we were 275 statute miles from Phnom Penh.

When I got back to my room, I went through the videos and chose one that I thought I would enjoy. I sat back and started watching the movie but quickly realized that I couldn't stay focused on it. I couldn't stop thinking about Com and wondered what had happened to her after I left.

Before I knew it, my clock read 2150 hrs, so I left my barracks and walked back over to meet Colonel Sizemore and call Paula.

Colonel Sizemore reviewed what I was to say, placed the call then handed the phone to me. Janelle answered the phone and said, "Hi Daddy, I miss you." It felt good to hear her voice. I spoke with her for a few minutes listening to her tell me what she had been doing since I had left. Then I asked to speak to mommy. Paula got on the phone and started asking me questions about school. She asked how school was going and if I liked and got along with my roommates? I felt bad having to lie to her but what other choice was there? Colonel Sizemore stayed in the room while we talked and monitored every word that I spoke. He wanted to make sure that I didn't compromise my mission. We talked for about twenty minutes then Paula said she had to get going because she had to take Janelle to the dentist. I told her I was still planning on coming home Thursday night and would call before I got on the flight to confirm it. I reminded her that she would have to come out to the airport to pick me up. When I hung up the phone, Colonel Sizemore complemented me on doing well and explained that after a few weeks, once the lies stopped, it would become easier. I felt bad about having to lie to Paula. I had never done it before Colonel Anderson came into my life. I told Colonel Sizemore that I would see him in the morning then walked back to my barracks. It had been a long day and after talking to Paula and Janelle, I was more tired and confused than ever.

Chapter 19

Final Debrief

When I got back to my room, I undressed and crawled into bed. The last twenty-four hours felt like a bad nightmare from which I couldn't awake. I prayed that Sang hadn't talked during her interrogation and that Com was okay and hadn't been caught. It was hard to keep alive my hopes that we would still be able to rescue some of our men. When Colonel Anderson aborted the initial rescue attempt this morning, my hopes were diminished. I knew the longer it took to confirm their location, the less chance we had of a recovery. These thoughts raced through my mind as I tossed and turned for several hours before falling asleep.

I woke up to a bright sunny morning. Looking at my clock, I was surprised to see it was 0830 hrs and that I had slept so late. I was due down at Colonel Anderson's office in less than thirty minutes for the continuation of my debrief. After a quick shower, I got dressed. It felt good to have fresh clothes on. Colonel Anderson knew that I had left Cambodia with only what I had on my back, so yesterday afternoon, when they delivered the videos, he had them leave some clean clothes for me.

I reported to the office at 0900 hrs. Both Colonel Anderson and Colonel Sizemore were there waiting for me. They greeted me, and asked if I had slept well. I told them yes I had, once I fell asleep. There was a tray with juice and rolls waiting for me on the desk. Colonel Anderson told me to be seated and have some breakfast. I took a roll and poured some juice then sat down. Colonel Anderson started by briefing me on last night's mission. "The insertion went smoothly. We had the team on the ground by 2200 hrs. Due to civilian foot traffic and rough terrain, it took the team two hours and twenty minutes to travel the twelve clicks between the LZ and the work compound. Once they located the compound, they set up a listening station and inspected the perimeter for any strengths and weaknesses. We equipped the team with night vision goggles and listening equipment to help with their night reconnais-sance. While surveying the compound, they were surprised to find it so well guarded. This indicated to our team leader that the commander was expecting a possible rescue attempt. After careful study of the perimeter, the team leader felt that it would be too risky to try to infiltrate the compound. He said since the prisoners were already asleep, they were unable to establish if there were any Americans among them. He was forced to make a tough decision. He decided the only way they would be able to confirm for sure who was inside the camp was to kidnap one of the guards."

Colonel Anderson continued, "After careful reconnais-sance of the compound and its perimeter, the team leader decided that the best course of action was to set up an ambush outside the main gate. They had been observing soldiers coming and going through the main gate since they had arrived. The team leader said the main gate opened to a trail, which led down to a road that ran into town. Due to the lateness of the hour, they realized that the chance of someone leaving the compound was diminishing and they would have a better chance of grabbing a soldier who was returning to the compound. Their main problem was selecting whom to kidnap. The team leader wanted to make sure the person they kidnapped would be knowledgeable about the prisoners. At 0120 hrs, they observed a Vietnamese lieutenant coming down the trail. He was by himself, and they could tell by his slow and wavering pace that he had been drinking. The team leader quickly decided that he was the one they had been waiting for. They watched him as he strolled along, singing in an almost incoherent voice. Due to his drunkenness, it was one of the easiest snatches that the team had ever done. Once they grabbed the lieutenant, they removed him from the immediate vicinity of the compound and tried to interrogate him. When they tried to speak to him, they found that he didn't speak English and even though he was dressed as a Vietnamese lieutenant, he was actually a Cambodian soldier and spoke only Khmer not Vietnamese. Unfortunately the team's interrupter spoke only Vietnamese and not Khmer, so they had to drag him with them as they worked their way to the PZ for their extraction. They made it to the PZ by 0400 hrs and radioed for an early extraction.

"We lifted the team out at 0435 hrs. The extraction went without a hitch and the team along with their captive was back in Thailand shortly after 0600 hrs. We immediately took the prisoner into a room with a Khmer interrupter and started interrogating him. He confirmed that Com's information was correct. During the interrogation, the prisoner confirmed they had been holding five American POWs at the work camp. He said they had been there for the last three weeks, and that yesterday morning, around 0800 hrs, the commander of the camp received a call to relocate the Americans' ASAP and to reinforce the security of the compound. Under further questioning, the prisoner admitted that there had been some other Americans at the prison compound a few months earlier but they were sent back to Vietnam. He told us that it was not uncommon for them to move their prisoners of war monthly."

I interrupted, "Colonel Anderson, did he know where they moved them."

"No, he stated that the commander told him that they were sent by truck to a little village fifteen kilometers away. There they were turned over to another officer who took them away and he had no idea where they were taken. Sorry Curt, it looks like a bust. I don't want you to feel bad about it. Jim briefed me last night on everything you went through. I am very proud of what you accomplished" As I listened to Colonel Anderson, I could feel my eyes tearing up as I thought about those poor men.

"Jim wants to work with you for the remainder of the morning, then after lunch, we'll board a plane to head back to the States. I'm sure you're ready to get home."

"Yes sir, I'm ready to go." I responded.

Colonel Anderson smiled and said, "Oh by the way, I have some good news for you. You've been hired by American Airlines. Jim will fill you in on the details. I have some business to attend to." He then turned and left the room.

Colonel Sizemore said, "Well Curt, let's get back to work and finish your debriefing."

He started by asking more questions. The first question he asked was, "How do you feel about not being able to rescue any of the POWs?"

With tears in my eyes, I replied, "I feel sick to my stomach, but mostly disappointed for them. I was so hoping that we would at least be able to return one of them home."

He went on to explain, "Curt, the POWs didn't know that we were coming, so there was no emotional letdown or disappointment on their end." I hadn't thought of it that way and just hearing that lifted a little weight off my shoulders. He asked, "Do you feel it was your fault that the mission didn't succeed."

"No, I don't feel any personal guilt or responsibility. I

know I did everything on my end possible to obtain the information, yet at the same time, I understand that I have no control of outside circumstances, like Sang being fingered as the grenade thrower. I think my biggest guilt is coming from getting Com emotionally involved with me knowing that I would never see her again."

"Do you think you would feel this way if we had been successful and had rescued several of the POWs?"

"No, I don't think so."

He went on to explain that I hadn't gone into the mission expecting failure, and that is the way I should look at it. The chance of rescuing several American POWs far outweighs the feelings of one girl. He also reminded me of the guilt I would have felt if I had refused the mission.

When we finished talking about our failure to retrieve any POWs, it was time to discuss my cover story. "Curt, your injury actually works to our advantage. You'll be flown to Dallas where you'll catch an American flight to Minneapolis where your wife will pick you up. It will be best if you tell her to meet you at the gate. This will help reinforce in her mind that you were down in Dallas in flight training." He went on to explain the good news that American had decided to hire me, but they didn't have a class date open till the beginning of February. I would tell Paula that due to my head injury, I had missed some classes and got behind. American suggested that I take some time off to make sure that I was all right. Since they were so busy with hiring and training, the first class they could get me back into was February. The good news was I would get to keep the seniority number that I would have been assigned upon graduation of my initial class so the delay wouldn't affect my career. As he told me this, I wondered if Colonel Anderson had anything to do with me being accepted by American Airlines, but under the circumstances, I decided it was best not to ask. Colonel Sizemore explained, "I think your February class date works out well, because it allows you time to readjust and come to terms with what you have just been through before jumping into an intense airline training program."

Colonel Sizemore reviewed again the importance of not telling anyone about what had happened. It would be my secret and mine alone. By the time we finished, it was time for lunch. He shook my hand and said, "Mr. Gray, I've enjoyed working with you. I wish you the best of luck in your new career."

"Jim, thank you for all your help and advice. Will I see you again before I leave for home?"

"No Curt, this is it. Try to remember the advice I gave you, and don't worry, you'll be all right"

I was expecting him to return to the States with us, but he said he was headed up to Bangkok. He told me that Colonel Anderson would be along shortly, and I was to stay there until he came. I snapped to attention and gave him a salute. He returned it, then turned and walked out the door.

Moments later, Colonel Anderson walked in appearing more relaxed than he had been earlier and asked, "Are you ready for lunch?"

"Yes sir."

"Well, let's do it."

Chapter 20

Going Home

Our flight from Thailand back to the States dragged on for what seemed like days. I read, slept and talked with Colonel Anderson to help pass the time. Even though I already knew the answer, I had to ask the Colonel, "Sir, can you please let me know when you find out about what happened to Com?"

"Curt, you know that due to the nature of this mission that will not be possible." Then looking me straight in the eyes with a stern voice, he said, "There will be no further discussion on this matter." I knew then that I would never know what became of Com.

Due to the time zone changes, it would be 1800 hrs Wednesday evening when we arrived back at Andrews Air Force Base. Colonel Anderson arranged to have a driver meet us at the airfield and chauffeur us to the colonel's private residence. Even though I had spent three previous nights at the colonel's residence, he took me aside and reminded me, "Curt, be careful not to mention anything to my wife about what had transpired."

"What if she asks me what I've been up to?" I questioned.

"She understands the nature of my job and will not

question either of us about our work."

Upon arrival at his home, Colonel Anderson's wife greeted us at the door and welcomed us back. She ushered us into their dining room where she had a delicious dinner waiting. After dinner, Colonel Anderson escorted me into his den and closed the door. "Curt, it's time to phone Paula. I want you to tell her that you tripped on your way to class this morning and cut your head. Make sure she understands that you're okay, and not to worry, but you had to go to the hospital and get five stitches in your left eyebrow. Tell her that you will be catching a flight home tomorrow afternoon and will call her when you find out what time your flight will arrive."

When he finished briefing me on what to say, I phoned Paula and told her my big lie. She was concerned about my cut, but I told her not to worry, that I was feeling okay, just a little upset about missing class. Colonel Anderson had instructed me not to tell her about the change in my training dates 'til I got home and she could visually see the stitches in my face. When I finished my phone call, Colonel Anderson and I sat in his den and talked for the rest of the evening. He explained that in the morning we would be flying into Naval Air Station (NAS) Dallas located just south of Dallas/Fort Worth International Airport. From there I would be driven up to Dallas/Fort Worth where I would catch my flight home.

I told Colonel Anderson that even though it had been only eleven days since I had left Minneapolis, it felt like a lifetime ago. He said he understood, and then confided in me that his last few years of working in special ops had been an emotional roller coaster ride, but for some unknown reason, he thrived on it. With the adrenalin rush that I had been living on for the past week, I think I understood what he meant. At 2300 hrs, we went upstairs and went to bed.

Upon arrival at NAS Dallas, Colonel Anderson took me into an office for my final debriefing and farewell. He handed me what looked like the suitcase and briefcase that I had left in my room in Cambodia. His men had gone out and purchased an exact copy of them along with all the clothes that I had taken with me. The clothes had been washed several times to take away their newness. They even scuffed up the suitcase to make it look like my original one. Colonel Anderson handed me an American Airlines ID tag and a kit bag full of 727 manuals and study guides. He explained, "Curt, this ID Tag along with the manuals and study guides would have been issued to you on your first day of class. I threw in the kit bag as a thank you gift for what you have done. I know it's not much after what you've been through."

I thought it was a nice gesture and said, "Thank you sir, I really appreciate it. I needed a new one; my old kit bag is pretty shot."

Colonel Anderson suggested, "Since you have a couple of months before starting class and now have the study guides and manuals, I would take this opportunity to study and get well prepared for your training."

"Yes sir, I'll make good use of the time."

"Now, I need you to return your fake passport and driver's license."

I reached into my back pants pocket, pulled them out and handed them to him. "I hate to do this to you Curt, but we need to body search you to make sure that you haven't taken anything that could collaborate what you have just gone through if you make the drastic mistake and decide to go public."

"No problem, I understand." The thought had never occurred to me about trying to sneak something home. I had already decided that I was going to stuff this whole adventure into a small box and file it in the dark caverns of my mind where hopefully it would get lost forever.

I was allowed to keep the picture of Com that she had given me when I was in Vietnam. I had been holding this photo for years. When my search was complete, Colonel Anderson handed me a sheet of paper and said, "Here's a list of general information about American's flight training. It explains where the new hire pilots stay and what topics you would have covered during your first two weeks of training. I want you to take a few minutes on your flight home to familiarize yourself with the information. It should help fill in any gaps you might have about your hypothetical training. Even though it's written on American Airlines stationary, I would suggest you destroy it before getting off the plane." He handed me my ticket to Minneapolis and said, "One of these days, we're going to return some of our men home and when that happens, you can be proud to know that you were part of the team that accomplished it."

Of all the personnel I had worked with during the last twelve days, I admired Colonel Anderson the most and told him so. He thanked me. We shook hands and said our farewells then walked out to the waiting car. As I approached the car, I stopped and turned towards Colonel Anderson. I snapped to attention and saluted him. He returned my salute.

Within minutes, I was being dropped off at the upper level of the American Airlines terminal A. After checking in at the gate, I went over to the newsstand to purchase a paper. I figured it would be wise to get caught up on what had been happening while I was gone.

Sitting in the back of the MD-80, I found myself anxious to get home. I reviewed the sheet that Colonel Anderson had given me so that I would be able to answer the general questions that my family and friends might be asking about my training. In my final briefing, I had been told that I would receive one more contact from Colonel

Anderson. He would place a phone call to my home when he knew I was gone. He would introduce himself as Mr. Blackwell then explain to Paula that he had lost the funding for his Vietnam documentary. He would apologize for any inconvenience he might have caused, then tell Paula that in the future, if he had an opportunity to make his film, he would keep me in mind.

The flight from Dallas to Minneapolis seemed short compared to the flight from Bangkok, and before I knew it, our aircraft was pulling up to the gate in Minneapolis. Paula and Janelle were waiting at the gate as I deplaned. A strange feeling came over me as I got off the plane. I felt as if I was instantly transformed from the person I had been living the last twelve days back into my old self. It was hard to explain--- as if indeed I lived two lives. I had felt this feeling once before when I had first returned home from Vietnam. When I got off the plane in Minneapolis and saw my mother and one of my brothers waiting for me, I felt myself being transformed from a hardened combat pilot with all the responsibilities that went with that position back into a normal twenty year old kid with no responsibilities. I think I was beginning to understand what Colonel Sizemore had explained to me in my debriefing about compartmentalization.

It was good to see Paula and Janelle again. I ran over and hugged and kissed them both. On our drive home, I felt bad every time Paula asked me about training. Hating to deceive them, I would try to say as little as possible while changing the subject. I would really be glad once I started training at American Airlines and wouldn't have to lie every time someone asked me a question about training.

My first few weeks back were emotionally hard. Several times when I was making love to Paula, I would think of Com then later feel like scum for doing so. I tried to forget what had happened, but couldn't. As the weeks passed into months, I would find myself making it through a day without thinking about Com, and then night would come and I would have a nightmare.

In February, I started training at American Airlines Flight Academy. I was assigned to the Boeing 727 as a flight engineer. Training was intense, but I had two good room-mates whom I got along with well. We were careful not to take the training too seriously and get all stressed out over it, as so many other new hires were doing. We studied hard, but we made sure that we took a short break every night to relax and have fun. By doing so, we had a good time while training.

After completion of training, I was assigned to New York's LaGuardia Airport for a few months. In June, I was awarded MD-80 training and found myself back down in Dallas for training. I always enjoyed training and was glad to be doing it. After completing my MD-80 training, I was assigned as a copilot to American's base at Chicago's O'Hare Field. We continued living in Minneapolis, and I commuted to work.

Due to the airlines work schedule, over half the pilots at American Airlines commute to work along with hundreds of flight attendants. The average airline schedule has you flying three days on and three days off. The better sche-dules have you working three days on with four days off. Since I was a new pilot, I didn't have the seniority to hold a schedule, so I had to sit on reserve. When you're assigned reserve, you have twelve days off. On your reserve days, you're on call and must be able to report to the airport within two hours by ground transportation. With this two hour restriction, I wasn't allowed to stay home in Minne-apolis and wait for a call. Because our duty days ran from midnight to midnight, on the evening of my second day off, I would catch a flight down to Chicago to position myself for work. I subleased a room in an apartment from another pilot who I had met while in training. I had a beeper and would hang out waiting for the beeper or phone to ring. As a commuter, reserve wasn't fun, but it was part of the job, and I accepted it without complaining.

My family life was good. My second daughter was born shortly after finishing flight training at American. As my daughters grew, Paula and I grew even closer together as we spent our time with the kids. I loved being a daddy. Colonel Sizemore was right about the urge to want to confess to Paula what had happened. At first it was almost unbearable, but as time passed, so did the urge. I came to realize that the love I had felt for Com was different from the love I felt for Paula and the one did not subtract from the other.

As the months turned into years, I got off reserve. The first schedules that I held were all nighters. We would leave Chicago at 2140 hrs and fly out to Oakland. From Oakland we would fly to Sacramento where we would stay overnight. We would arrive in Sacramento about three o'clock in the morning Chicago time. I would go to bed and get up around 1000 hrs Sacramento time, then spend the day walking around town, going to lunch and reading the paper. We would leave Sacramento late that night and fly back to Chicago arriving around 0430hrs. These all-nighter schedules had you flying two days on and two days off. They were a nightmare for commuters, because by the time you caught a flight home and drove home from the airport, it would be close to noon before you got to bed. After a month of flying all nighters, you were worn out. Thank goodness, I only had to fly them for eight months before my seniority allowed me to bid better schedules.

Flying for the airlines was my dream job. I got to travel, yet at the same time had a lot of time off to spend with the family and do my martial arts. As the years passed by, I found the flying starting to become boring. There just wasn't the excitement there had been flying helicopters in combat. I did have one incident happen when I was still a copilot on the MD-80 that gave me that old familiar adrenalin rush. We were finishing the third day of our trip. I was flying with Captain Bob Fulbright. We had flown into O'Hare earlier that morning, and all we had left to fly was a Minneapolis turn. We departed O'Hare and headed towards Minneapolis. The weather was good in Chicago, but as we headed northwest, we entered a cold front that was causing low ceilings.

By the time we arrived in Minneapolis, the winds were out of the east, and they were landing runway 11R. I was flying the leg. Bob contacted Minneapolis Approach. "Minneapolis Approach, American 524 level niner thousand with information Alpha."

"Roger, American 524, turn left heading two seven zero, descend and maintain five thousand, expect ILS 11R."

Bob read back the clearance, "Left, two seven zero, we're out of nine for five, expect ILS 11R, American 524."

We were being vectored onto a downwind for the instrument landing system (ILS) for runway 11R. When we were abeam the outer maker, we received our clearance, "American 524, turn right three six zero, descend and maintain three thousand."

"Roger American 524, turning right three six zero, we're out of five for three thousand." I pulled back the throttles and started our descent while rolling the aircraft into a right hand turn. I rolled out on the three six zero heading. When I started to bring the power back in to level off at three thousand feet, several of the instruments and lights started flashing. This was immediately followed by the aircraft wanting to yaw to the right. I pushed left rudder in and quickly scanned the engine instruments. The loss of the right generator caused the electrical system to changeover to the other generator causing the lights to flash. I could see right away that we had lost our right engine. "Bob, I think we just lost our right engine."

Bob observing the instrumentation replied. "Yep, it sure looks that way. Curt, I want you to keep flying the aircraft, and I will work the radios and the checklists." Just then, the flight attendant rings on the interphone. Bob reaches down and answers, "Flight deck, Bob."

"Bob, this is Kathy in back. When you lowered the gear we heard a loud thump in back on the right side of the aircraft."

"Can you see any damage? Are there any signs of smoke or fire?"

"No, not that I can see."

"Okay, stand by, and I'll get back to you."

I called for the engine failure checklist. Just then, approach called, "American 524, turn right heading 070, cleared for the approach."

Bob keyed his mike, "Minneapolis Approach, please be advised, we just lost our right engine and would like to declare an emergency. We would like a wide three hundred and sixty degree turn to our left with radar vectors back on to the approach."

"Roger, American 524, that's approved. We'll have the emergency equipment standing by. We'll need your fuel and number of pax (passengers) on board when you get a chance."

"Roger Minneapolis, American 524."

This wide turn would give us time to complete our checklists and prepare the cabin. After Bob completed the initial radio call, he started reading the checklist.

We could tell by our engine indications that the engine was seized up so we didn't bother to try a restart. Instead, we pulled the fire handle and discharged both engine fire extinguishers into the right engine as a precautionary measure. With the fuel that we were carrying on board, any fire could light us up like fireworks on the 4th of July.

Once we completed the engine failure checklist, we started the single engine landing checklist. While we were completing the checklists, I wondered if Bob would let me land the aircraft. This is what we practiced for in the simulator during our recurrent training at the American Airlines Flight Academy. In reality, I had never landed a commercial airliner on one engine, and this might be my only chance to do so. It was a challenge that I wanted to accomplish, but at the same time I understood that since Bob was the captain, he might want to land it himself. Once Bob got the checklists completed, he chimed the flight attendants and went through his TEST items. Test was an acronym we used to cover all required items for the flight attendant briefing. The first T stood for the type of emergency. The E stood for evacuation and if we felt they should prepare for one after landing, The S stood for the signal we would use if we needed to evacuate. The code word we used at American to signal the flight attendants to evacuate the plane was "Easy Victor." We would say it three times over the intercom system. If the intercom failed to work, we would switch the emergency lights on, which would also signaled the flight attendants to evacuate the aircraft. The last T stood for how much time we had left before touchdown.

Once Bob finished briefing the number one flight attendant, he turned to me and said. "Curt, you have the radios. I'm going to make a quick PA then we'll land this puppy." He reached down and picked up the interphone and said, "Ladies and gentleman we'll be landing in five minutes. I just want to inform you that on landing if you see fire trucks approaching the aircraft do not be alarmed. We have shut down our right engine due to mechanical difficulties. The aircraft is flying fine. There is no reason to worry. Once we taxi clear of the runway, they will be inspecting our right engine as a safety precaution. Would the flight attendants please be seated."

I was impressed that Bob told the folks the truth. So many captains that I had flown with wouldn't have told the passengers the truth for fear of scaring them. When I made captain, I would always tell the folks the truth when we were having problems. I might not go into great detail about the problem we were having, but I knew that people accepted the truth better than some flimsy excuse.

I was rolling the plane back on final as Bob completed his PA. He turned to me and said, "Curt, do you feel confident about landing this aircraft?"

"Yes sir."

"Okay then, the landing is yours, and I'll back you up."

He called approach, "Minneapolis Approach, American 524 is ready to land."

"Roger American 524, descend and maintain twenty five hundred and your cleared ILS approach runway 11R."

Bob read back, "Roger, cleared approach 11R, American 524."

I discovered that the actual aircraft flew much nicer than the simulators did in training and was surprised at how well the aircraft flew on one engine.

We broke out of the clouds inside the outer marker and could see the airport. As the aircraft descended towards the runway, I could feel my adrenaline flowing. With my endorphins pumping, my senses were acute to every little movement of the aircraft as I pulled back on the yoke and flared the aircraft. I gently pulled back on the throttle and pushed the yoke slightly forward to ease the aircraft onto the runway. Slowly lowering the nose, I cautiously put the left engine in reverse, slowly adding power while applying brakes to stop the aircraft. Too much reverse applied to a single engine during landing could cause the aircraft to veer off towards the edge of the runway. I knew my landing was smooth when I heard the passengers in back clapping after touchdown. Once I got the aircraft slowed down, Bob took the controls and taxied her off the runway and set the brakes.

The emergency vehicles pulled up alongside the aircraft. They inspected the right engine for fire and smoke. Thank goodness for us, there was none, and we were given taxi instructions to our gate. Bob taxied her in, shut her down then called for the parking checklist. Once the checklist was complete, he turned towards me and said, "Curt, good job."

I looked at him and said, "Thanks, also thanks for letting me land the aircraft. I wouldn't have blamed you if you had taken the landing."

"Well, you've been making such good landings all month that I figured you would do as good if not better job than I could."

I knew he was exaggerating, but it felt good to hear it anyway and thanked him again.

We could tell that the passengers were glad to be safely down. As they were deplaning, they kept popping their heads into the cockpit and congratulating us on a job well done.

When maintenance arrived, they took a look at the aircraft and found a hole twelve by eighteen inches in the fuselage inboard of the right engine. Upon further inspection they discovered that all thirteen rivets that held the stator vane to the turbine had failed allowing the stator vane to disintegrate and blow out the left side of the engine into the cabin. We were lucky that no one was hurt. If the engine had failed on liftoff at O'Hare, it might have been a different story.

Our final leg back to Chicago was cancelled, and the crew was told to deadhead back on the next flight to O'Hare. Since I lived in Minneapolis, I was released by crew tracking and went home.

In January of 1991, I was awarded a captain's bid in Chicago and had to return to Dallas for captain's training on the MD-80. It was fun being captain and I was really enjoyed my job. Later that summer, I heard rumors that American was planning on opening a base in Nashville, Tennessee. Paula and I were tired of the commute plus the cold winters and snowstorms of Minnesota. The commute was costing me several additional hours a week away from my family that I wouldn't have if I lived at a local base. Paula could see the stress the commute was adding to my job, especially when I had to pull reserve. We decided to call a family meeting and discussed the idea of moving to Nashville. The girls thought it would be exciting. So in the summer of 1992, we sold our house, packed up our belongings and moved to Tennessee. I placed a bid for a Nashville Captain slot and in September, I was awarded one with an October school date. Of course with the move, came a change of equipment, and I found myself back down in Dallas for training on the F100.

Paula and I drew up some house plans and built our dream home. My daughters were growing up and with my airline job we could afford to take nice family vacations. I felt fortunate to have a career that allowed us the luxury to do so.

I was having fewer and fewer nightmares about my mission and Vietnam. When I had first returned home from Cambodia, my nightmares were so terrible that I would lie in bed waiting for the first light of the new day, which brought with it the relief from the nightmares. But now, they were fewer and farther between. I now understood what the philosopher Nietzsche meant when he said, "And if you gaze long into an abyss, the abyss will gaze back into you." I had learned through the years to avoid gazing into the abyss, but deep down in my subconscious, I knew that the abyss was always there gazing back at me!

In the mid nineties, I was flying with a young copilot named Adam Hughes. Adam had a keen interest in war and combat. He was especially interested in the Vietnam Conflict and had read several books on the topic. In our discussions, he seemed well educated on the subject. One day we were sitting in the cockpit shooting the shit about Vietnam when, out of the blue, he asked, "Curt, do you think we left any American POWs behind when we pulled out of Vietnam?"

"Why do you ask?"

"Oh, I just finished reading a book called "Kiss the Boys Goodbye. In this book, the author claims that we left over three hundred POWs who were being held captive in Laos and Cambodia. She presents some pretty strong evidence to back up her claims."

I answered with a question, "Do you think we would do that to our own men?"

"I'm not sure. I would hate to think we would, but her evidence sounded pretty plausible. What do you think?"

Without much thought, I answered, "I hate to say so, but I think I would have to agree with her."

"Why's that?" he asked.

I wasn't sure what to say. Suddenly, I felt that I needed to tell my story. I started telling him how I had traveled to Cambodia back in 1984 and while there I had heard of sightings of Americans. I didn't expect him to believe me, but after a few minutes into the story, I could tell that he believed every word I was saying. I thought to myself, "Oh shit, Curt, what are you doing?" I quickly told him, "Adam, I'm just jerking your chain," and quickly changed the conversation to another topic.

I was surprised and worried by this sudden urge to want to tell someone my story and wondered why now, after all these years?

By the spring of 1998, I felt I had pretty much gotten over this entire mess. I hadn't thought of Com for a while and was living, what I perceived to be, an emotionally healthy life. I was out flying a three day trip. Our first leg of the day was to fly from Dallas to New York's LaGuardia where we would change planes then head to Toronto. It had been snowing all day in New York and after landing, due to the congestion in the ramp areas, it took us over two hours to taxi to the gate. We had to wait another hour for our outbound aircraft to arrive at the gate. By the time they cleaned and refueled our aircraft, our 2000 hrs departure was pushed back to 0100 hrs. When we finally departed, we had only eight passengers onboard. It was close to three in the morning by the time we landed in Toronto then it took another thirty minutes to get to the hotel. The whole crew was very frustrated and exhausted. When I got to my room, I took off my uniform and crawled into bed. Being so tired, I didn't even bother to brush my teeth. I had just closed my eyes and swear that I hadn't fallen asleep when I saw Com walk out to greet me. She was wearing her satin red dress. I reached out to hug her, and as quickly as she appeared, she was gone. I sat up in bed and turned on the light on the nightstand. As I looked at myself in the mirror, I could see tears running down my cheeks.

The next day when I awoke, I couldn't stop thinking about Com, wondering what had become of her. Was she okay? Did she think about me as much as I've thought about her over the years? Even though I knew it had to have been a dream, it seemed so real. During the next few days, my mind was clouded with emotion. My memory flowed with facts and details of my mission. It was as if that dream, somehow, released all my subconscious feelings and forced them to the surface. I spent hours trying to come to grips with my emotions as they kept turning to tears. I needed to talk to someone about my feelings, but whom? I couldn't tell Paula. It would destroy her trust in me and probably ruin our marriage. Then I remembered what Colonel Jim Sizemore had told me years earlier. So on Saturday, I went down to a Catholic church to a priest who I had never met and went to confession. In the confessional, I told the priest about my deep dark secrets. Father told me to not be so hard on myself, that what I had done was for the love of my country and our men. He said that God knew my true intentions, and that I needed to learn to forgive myself. Father thanked me for coming and told me that if I ever felt the need to talk, to be sure to come back. As I left the confessional, I realized that the few minutes of talking with Father really helped.

A few days later, I came up with the idea that if I wrote a book about my experiences, maybe it would help relieve the stress and guilt that I felt. I knew that I couldn't reveal what really happened. I remembered too well what I had been told could happen to me and my family if I violated the contract that I signed. I spoke to a publisher friend of mine and asked him a hypothetical question. If I wrote a manuscript about an event that actually took place, but due to circumstance beyond my control, I couldn't admit that it took place, could I write the story as it happened but have the story end as a dream? He explained that in the publishing world that wouldn't work. He said that when a publisher markets a book, they need to know how to classify it. Is it fiction or is it fact? He went on to explain that if you have a story that is factual but you cannot admit that it is factual it automatically becomes fiction. He suggested that it be written as a novel. I thanked him for his advice, and tucked the idea of writing a book away and continued flying.

As the years passed, Vietnam became to my daughters as World War II was to my generation, a thing of the past. We watched how warfare was changing during the first Gulf War. With the new technology, we would never again have soldiers like Audie Murphy. War was becoming impersonal and something that we could watch on TV from the comfort of our homes. People would now expect to win wars without sustaining casualties.

Chapter 21

Autumn

It was one of those warm, late autumn days of Indian summer. November of 2003 was drawing to a close. Tomorrow was Thanksgiving. I was out on the front porch enjoying one of the last nice days before winter would grasp its final hold for the season. The falls in Tennessee were much later than the ones up in Minnesota. I was sitting in the swing on our front porch enjoying the weather. My oldest daughter was due home from college later that night. I hadn't seen her for a while and was looking forward to catching up on her life. Paula and my younger daughter Holly had gone to the grocery store to get our Thanksgiving turkey. I felt happy to have the holiday off and was looking forward to spending it with my family.

One of the down sides of flying for a career was the holidays. To the airlines, the holidays were just another typical day, and a majority of the employees had to work them. I had been fortunate since flying for American that I had only worked one Thanksgiving. My seniority number was high enough that with selective bidding and the willingness to bid the bad trips, I was able to hold most the holidays off.

We lived at the end of a cul-de-sac and therefore, we

didn't get a lot of traffic down our street. I was sitting there swinging back and forth, daydreaming, when I notice a car turn the corner and head up the road towards the house. Expecting Paula and Holly to be coming home any minute, I had been watching for them. The car leisurely came down the road as if they were sightseeing. When the car drove into the cul-de-sac, it stopped for a moment then slowly drove up through our gates. It pulled into our circular drive and parked in front of the house. Not recognizing the car or the driver, I stood up and walked over to the front steps. I figured it was one of my daughter's friends. With two daughters, there were always friends dropping in at the house. As I stood there, a young man got out of the car. He smiled and said hello as he walked towards me. There was something that looked familiar about him. He appeared to be part Asian. Having been in the martial arts for years, I was used to being around Asians and figured he was interested in learning martial arts. He was five foot eleven with a trim build and jet black hair. As he approached I said, "Hello, can I help you?"

"Yes, I'm looking for Mr. Gray."

"You found him, what can I do for you." I said as he extended his hand for a shake.

As we shook hands he said, "Hi, I'm Curtis Lee." A sudden chill ran through my body as he spoke. He continued, "I believe you knew my mother Com."

"Yes, I do." I replied as I felt my stomach sour from emotional conflict. "Come over and have a seat."

We walked over to where the swing and two rockers were. My heart was racing as we sat down.

Curtis opened a bag he was carrying and withdrew a small wooden box and handed it to me and said, "My mom wanted me to give this to you." The top had a rose carved in it, and I could tell that it was handmade.

I thanked him as I opened the box. Placed inside was

the heart necklace that Com had given me years ago in Vietnam, which I had given back to her while in Cambodia. Underneath the necklace was a photo. I carefully picked the photo up and looked at it. It was a photo of Com and me hugging each other. It had been taken at the monastery over nineteen years ago.

I felt stunned as I looked at the photo. I had never seen it. The only photo that I had of Com was the one she had given me when I was in Vietnam. I had forgotten how young and beautiful she was. Tucked beneath the photo was a folded piece of paper. I took out the paper and unfolded it. It was written in broken English but readable. It said, *With this box your son and me. Luv, Com.* Below the note was a smaller metal box. As I stared at the metal box, I could feel Curtis intently watching me. My mind was running wild with thoughts, Could this be? Is this a dream? I had only spent one night with Com. I looked up at Curtis and he smiled. Not sure what to do next, I asked, "How is your mother?"

He looked down at the deck and softly said, "She passed away."

Hearing about Com's death was almost too much to handle. I sat there in silence. I wasn't prepared for any of this. I fought to keep the tears from my eyes as I slowly said, "I'm sorry to hear that, what happened?"

"She died in the spring of 1998." He then went on to explain, "Before mom died, she made arrangements for me and grandmother to leave Vietnam. She wanted me to go to California to live with one of her cousins. Because of mom's position, she knew several high-ranking people in the government. When she got sick, she had one of them pull some strings. He obtained the proper papers and arranged for us to leave. I was only twelve and a half at the time. A few days before mom died, she handed me the box and made me promise that when I got older, I would try to locate and deliver the box to you in person. Mom told grandmother that she wanted to be cremated and have her ashes place in the box."

I was in shock as I listened to his story. Could this be true? I was holding Com's ashes. I asked Curtis, "Did your mom ever marry?"

"No, she did not."

He told me that his mom had talked a lot about me while he was growing up and started telling me what she had told him. As I listen to him tell his story, I felt as if it was only yesterday that it happened. He said, "Mom said she watched with fear as you sprinted into the rice paddy to catch the helicopter as the soldiers shot at you. She knew that after the helicopter left, the soldiers would come and search where they thought you might have been hiding, so she snuck out of the hootch and worked her way over towards the other side of the village. She said that after you were extracted, the soldiers searched several of the hootchs including the one you had been in. They discovered the hole in the ground and knew that something had taken place. They spent forty minutes looking around, but after not finding anyone, they left. Mom remained in the deserted village for another hour then carefully uncovered her scooter and headed back to Phnom Penh. She said she felt scared as she rode down the dirt road leaving the village, but once she got back on to the main highway, she felt safer with all the other traffic. She rode home, changed clothes then walked to work as usual."

"Did she tell you what happened when she went to work that morning?"

"Yes, mom said when she arrived at work that morning there was a lot of commotion in her office. At first, she was worried that they might suspect her. They told mom that Sang had snuck into the general's office and had stolen information about the whereabouts of prisoners and tried to sneak it to an American spy. Headquarters said they were lucky they intercepted her before she was able to deliver the information. They said they felt sure after interrogating Sang that she didn't have any accomplices. During her interrogation, she said she had met an American spy on the streets. After they got to know each other, he invited her to his hotel room where they made love. After a few days, the spy promised her that he would take her to America with him if she could gather information about American POWs. Sang told her interrogators that having never had someone show her so much attention; she fell instantly in love with the spy, and within a few days was willing to do almost anything for him. Even though Sang admitted stealing the information, she denied having anything to do with the killing of the soldiers. She admitted driving by the post on the scooter but swore she didn't do it. They didn't believe her and tried to torture a confession out of her. Unfortunately, she died during the torture. Mom said she was shocked when she heard the news of Sang's death. She said it felt like she had lost a sister and wanted to cry but knew she couldn't.

"Mom said they told her that when they picked up Sang, they went into the spy's hotel room. There they found his clothes, briefcase, and suitcase but couldn't find him. They put a watch on the hotel, but he never came back. Early the next morning, a patrol reported seeing an unmarked helicopter extracting someone from a rice paddy. When General Samrin heard this report, he quickly called the work compound and ordered the commander to immediately move the prisoners. Mom asked if they shot the helicopter down and captured the spy. They told her no, that he got away. She went right back to working as usual and within a few weeks the episode was forgotten."

"Curtis, how did your mom have you without General Samrin getting suspicious?"

"Mom knew that being caught with the photos she had taken of you would be a death warrant, so she took the film out of her camera and hid it in the bottom of a vase full of dry flowers. She didn't know anyone in Cambodia that she could trust to develop the film. A month later she started getting sick in the mornings and within a couple of weeks realized she was pregnant. She understood that if she had an Asian American baby, her coworkers would put two and two together and realize that she was in cahoots with Sang, so she asked to be transferred back to Da Nang. At first, General Samrin said no, but after a few weeks, Mom went back to him and explained that her aunt was deathly ill and wanted to return to Vietnam to die. She told the general how important it was to her to be able to take care of her aunt during her final days. General Samrin, after hearing Mom's reason, changed his mind and issued orders for her to return to Vietnam. He thanked her for her loyalty and good work and wished her the best."

"Curtis, did your aunt pass away?"

"No, she's still alive and living in Vietnam. That was the only excuse mom could come up with that she thought would persuade the general to let her leave Cambodia."

Curtis went on to explain, "Upon returning to Vietnam, mom took the film and had it developed. She kept the photos, through the years, to remind her of your time spent together. After returning to Vietnam, mom got assigned to Ho Chi Minh City, the old Saigon, where we remained 'til she died. When she moved, she took her aunt and mother with her. As I was growing up, she would tell me stories about the times you spent together in Vietnam and Cambodia. Mom said she had lived her first twenty-four years in freedom before Vietnam fell to the communists and always wanted him to live in freedom. She continued to hate the communists and had been saving for years and was planning on leaving Vietnam when she got ill. One day, when she got home from work, she had a bad coughing spell accompanied by a shortness of breath. At first, she thought it was a bad cold, but the cold never got better."

"Do you know what caused her death?" I asked.

"It ended up being lung cancer. Thank God, it took her fast. You know, she always wondered what became of you and what you had done with your life. She missed you terribly. She said she could never love another man the way she loved you."

Sitting there listening to Curtis tell about his mom was tearing my heart apart, so I quickly changed the subject. "Where have you been since she died?" I asked.

"After mom's wake and cremation, my grandmother and I left Vietnam and came to live in America. We moved to Sacramento where mom's cousins were living. I instantly fell in love with America. Mom had taught me how to speak English when I was a child, so it wasn't hard to start school."

"How did you like going to American schools?"

"I like American schools and the opportunity to learn. I did real well in high school and graduated first in my class last spring."

"Wow, that's great. What are you going to do now?"

"I've been accepted to Harvard and will be starting this winter semester."

There were so many questions to be asked and answered. "How did you ever find me?"

"The only information that I had to go on was your first and last name and that you had been a helicopter pilot in Vietnam and had worked for the Red Cross. I also knew that you were within a year or two of mom's age. During high school, I started using the Internet to do research for schoolwork. One day while doing research for a class paper it occurred to me that maybe I could locate you by using the Internet. I figured that if you had flown helicopters, you must have had a pilots' license, so I went to the Federal Aviation Administration web site, got their address and sent them a letter. It took them over eight weeks to respond. They were of no help. All their letter said was they had five Curtis Grays with pilot licenses, but they couldn't legally disclose their personal information.

"Mom had told me what unit you had been in while in Vietnam, but I couldn't remember. I contacted the Red Cross, but they said they had no record of you. Everyplace I checked seemed to be a dead end. Then luckily one night, I went with a group of friends to see a movie called *We Were Soldiers.*"

We Were Soldiers was a Mel Gibson movie about the battle of Ia Drang, which was the first time they used helicopters in a major battle in Vietnam.

Curtis went on to explain that while leaving the theater, he was talking to one of his friends, telling him that his dad had been a helicopter pilot in Vietnam and wished he could find him. An older gentleman in the crowd overheard their conversation and said he didn't mean to pry into their conversation but was wondering if he had ever contacted the VHPA. Curtis said he had never heard of VHPA and asked him what it stood for. He said that the initials VHPA stood for Vietnam Helicopters Pilot Association and ex- plained that they had a detailed database on Vietnam Helicopter pilots. Curtis thanked him and told him that he would give it a try. He rushed straight home, got on the Internet and pulled up their web site. He was disappointed to find that they didn't have an address directory that he could access on the Internet, so he decided to contact them by sending an e-mail to their web-master. The next day when he got home from school, there was an e-mail waiting for him with my address.

Curtis apologized for showing up unannounced but said he was afraid that if he had called first I might think it was a prank and hang up. After all this time, he was not willing to miss the opportunity to see his father. I told him that it meant a lot to me that he had come in person. I got up and went over and gave him a hug. As I hugged him, I wondered how I would ever be able to explain him to my wife and daughters when my mission to Cambodia supposedly never took place. Just then, I noticed Paula's car coming down the street. I turned quickly to Curtis and said, "Curtis, I'm sorry that I didn't know about you, but please allow me some time to decide what to tell my wife and kids about you."

He smiled and said, "No problem, I understand. Whatever you think is best is fine with me."

We walked over to the driveway to greet my wife and daughter as they got out of the car. "Paula and Holly, I want you to meet Curtis Lee. He's the son of a good friend of mine from Vietnam. Curtis this is my wife Paula and my daughter Holly." They both said hello. I watched closely as Paula shook his hand. I could tell that she suspected something by the way she looked at him then looked at me, but what, I did not know. I knew that he was too young for Paula to expect that I had fathered him in Vietnam, but the more I looked at him the more I could see myself. I looked back at Paula and wondered if she would also notice the resemblance?

Epilogue

There never would be any American POWs returned from Southeast Asia during or after 1984. The Vietnamese started their withdrawal from Cambodia in 1989 and with the help of the United Nations, Cambodia elected a new constitutional assembly and leaders in 1993. This did not stop the different government factions from fighting amongst each other, and throughout the nineties, Cambodia continued to have domestic upheaval and unrest.

As for me telling Paula the truth about Curtis, after hours of soul searching and discussions with Curtis, we both decided that Paula and I had a good marriage, which was built on trust and it would be best, under the circumstances, to not tell her or my daughters the truth. It would be too hard to explain, plus, as Captain Donaldson told me years ago, "They would never believe you."

I continue to stay in contact with Curtis and we talk weekly. He is, literally, the son that I never had.

I thought for a long time on how to finally bring closure to my relationship with Com. Knowing how much she had wanted to live in freedom, I decided what better way to bury her than to spread her ashes over this great country of ours. It was the fall of 2004 when I got this notion. I called Curtis and told him my idea. He said he thought it was a great idea and said he would like to be with me when I did it. He mentioned that he had a fall break coming up and would have a few days off, and was wondering if we could do it then. I told him yes, that I would book him a flight and get checked out in a small plane. I hadn't flown a light aircraft in years and went out to the local airport and got checked out in a Cessna 150.

I picked Curtis up at the Nashville Airport. We ate an early supper then drove out to the local airport for our farewell flight. I did a quick walk around inspection of the aircraft then we both climbed in, and I read the checklist.

The air was as smooth as glass as we departed the airport traffic area and headed west. It was one of those gorgeous autumn evenings when you could see for miles from the air. The sun was starting to set as I gave the controls to Curtis. I reached in back and grabbed my briefcase. I open it and carefully lifted out the rose carved box. Raising its cover, I took out the photo of Com and I, along with the silver box containing her ashes. I took one final look at the photo then carefully tore the photo into small pieces and placed them on top her ashes. Curtis and I said a prayer for Com then I opened my side window and slowly dumped her ashes out over the countryside. When finished, I set the silver box back into my briefcase, closed it then placed it in back. I took the controls back from Curtis and with tears in my eyes turned the aircraft back towards the field and headed home.

www.ingramcontent.com/pod-product-compliance
Lightning Source LLC
Chambersburg PA
CBHW020620260626
47157CB00003B/1085